MADE TO love

Michelle,
Love always
deserves a
chance.
Suzanne xo

Made To Love

First Edition - April 2017

ISBN-13: 978-0-9953375-1-0

Cover Design by Najla Qamber Designs
Edited by C. Marie
Proofread by M. Ute Editing
Interior Design & Formatting by Jersey Girl Design

Manufactured in the United States of America

10 9 8 7 6 5 4 3 2 1

Other Books by S.M. West

Red (Love in Color #1)
Love Happens Anthology - Hitch

To my muse, for making fantasies a recipe for lasting love.

Made To Love Playlist

"Leather Jacket" – Arkells
"Here Comes The Night Time" – Arcade Fire
"Starving" – Hailee Steinfeld
"Roses" – The Chainsmokers
"Reflektor" – Arcade Fire
"Electric Love" – BØRNS
"Fragile" – Kygo, Labrinth
"I Wanna Be Adored" – The Stone Roses
"The One" – Kodaline
"Can't Help Falling in Love" – Haley Reinhart
"Scars to Your Beautiful" – Alessia Cara
"The Drugs Don't Work" – The Verve
"Mercy" – Shawn Mendes
"Just Say Yes" – Snow Patrol
"R U Mine?" – Arctic Monkeys
"You & Me" – Marc E. Bassy, G-Eazy
"Love Me Now" – John Legend
"The Best Day of My Life" – American Authors

"If she's amazing, she won't be easy.
If she's easy, she won't be amazing.
If she's worth it, you won't give up.
If you give up, you're not worthy."

Bob Marley, Guitar Songbook

One

OLIVIA

"I hate you," I seethe as beads of sweat trickle down my forehead, the salty fluid stinging my eyes. A few drop onto the gym mat as I push up to stand, completing what feels like my millionth burpee.

Jonah chuckles, playfully tapping the sole of my right runner with the tip of his shoe. Now in my final rep, down in plank position, I prepare to do yet another push-up. His nudge only serves to grate on my nerves, which is most definitely his intent.

In a singsong tone, he replies, "Stop being a cry baby and give 'em to me, darlin'." His apparent amusement at my distress only pisses me off more. "Keep your elbows tight to your body," he directs in his back-to-business tone.

A snarl slips from my parched lips. "Seriously, I fucking hate you," I say as I pant, collapsing into a puddle of mush. My body is a mass of overworked, inoperable muscles. With my face planted in the sticky, smelly vinyl mat—*gross*—I'm unable to move, even if I wanted to.

"My, my, you're a catty one today, swearing and all. Liv, cut the sass. We're almost done," he says light-heartedly in his southern twang. My disgruntled nature during a workout is nothing new to him. In fact, if I were anything but, he'd be surprised.

Placing my water bottle on the floor beside my lifeless body, he chuckles again as I longingly gaze at the appealing clear liquid. The thought of the cool water coating my dry lips and tongue, sliding down my scratchy throat is practically orgasmic. If only I could pick the damn thing up. Though a seemingly simple task, lifting my arms right now is like raising the Titanic—insurmountable. I can't wrap my head around the command. Nothing, body or mind, works. I'm wiped.

"I don't suppose you'd help me with the water?" I ask, my voice sickeningly sweet. "Like, say, lifting my head and pouring it down my throat?"

"Would you like me to swallow for you too?" he deadpans, one eyebrow raised, hands on his lean hips.

"No, I think I could handle that part," I sarcastically quip with a slight grin. I manage to raise my head a few inches off the floor and smile weakly at my torturer.

His blue eyes twinkle at the hilarity of my exhaustion. He's seen me at my worst, my current incapacitation is nothing. Focusing on his outstretched hand, like a mirage in the blistering desert, I find a way to thrust my aching, protesting body into a sitting position. Lifting my hand, I gesture for him to bring his to mine. I've already overdone it. His beautifully sculpted arms bunch and flex as he effortlessly pulls me into standing. I almost cave, forgetting to be mad, and praise him for the assist.

"You're a tyrant," I grumble instead, belying my gratitude. Every muscle—including many I never knew existed—screams in agony. I'm going to be sore tomorrow, and probably more so the next day. The thought has me groaning in dread. I'll be back in his torture chamber in less than forty-eight hours.

What the hell am I doing to myself? Oh, yeah, I'm getting fit and healthy, putting myself first for once in my life. I got myself into this mess, and now I'm paying for it. I'm intent on cleaning up my body, mind, and spirit.

Okay, I didn't do it all by myself, but I was certainly a participant in my downward spiral, though a reluctant and unwitting one. I did the unthinkable and equated my worth to the actions of another—a man, no less. I shudder at the thought, at my stupidity. In my defense, I was in love. I was entrenched in a long-term relationship and had a family to think about. Nevertheless, the fact of the matter is, I lost sight of *me*. I stopped caring about my appearance, my health, my life, and my dreams.

Shit, how did I end up down the rabbit hole of negative thoughts so fast? Oh yes, Jonah—I blame him. Wanting to inflict as much pain as I'm physically drowning in at this moment, I set my sights on him. What better person to direct my wrath at than the one who put me here?

"I believe you meant trainer, not tyrant. Come on, I'll give you a quick rub down. You better have a nice, long, hot-as-you-can-take-it bath with Epsom salts tonight. You were great today. You gave it your all, and you'll be feeling it," he says matter-of-factly.

"Nope, tyrant fits better. And yes, I'm well aware I'll be in hell tonight and definitely tomorrow, thanks to you." I lightly swat his rock-hard bicep and delicately walk toward the massage table. This is the best part of my daily dose of exercise.

Jonah Carson isn't cheap, but he's highly recommended as *the* go-to personal trainer to reshape your mind and body. With a waiting list as long as my arm, I was fortunate to jump to the front of the line because of a referral from one of his longest and dearest clients, my best friend Tamsin.

At first, I hemmed and hawed about hiring him. He was expensive, way more than some of the other trainers I interviewed, and I needed to be frugal with my money. I was no longer a stay-at-home mom with a husband as the sole breadwinner. I had a new life and a new business. Still, with my life upended and my whole focus on getting back on track, my health was important.

I am worth it.

Then I met Jonah and all my reservations flew out the window. Twelve years my junior, this sweet and sexy man from Nashville was mesmerizing. I was a goner, and not in a sexual way. If I was going to have a personal trainer, I wanted him. His body was a work of art. While I'm not going for perfection, I certainly wouldn't mind firm, defined muscles like his, and fewer bumps and bulges.

I fell hook, line, and sinker once we started talking. We clicked instantly. I saw in him someone who would push me to be my best, yet also understood that I was vulnerable. I had a ton of work ahead of me, and shedding forty pounds would be the easy part; I also had all my negative talk and baggage to eliminate. I was rebuilding my confidence and rediscovering me.

It was the way he spoke to me that drew me in. The way his eyes and tone softened as he asked me why I wanted to lose the weight, I could tell his meaning was deeper. He wanted to know my reasons beyond changing my physical appearance. I knew he would know when to be hard on me and when to go soft. On Jonah's part, as he's said many times since, he recognized in me the determination and sarcastic sass ingrained in him. He often comments that I'm the sister he never had.

So together with my lawyer, we worked the expense into my alimony. Truthfully, my ex-husband, Pete, didn't begrudge me anything in the divorce. In fact, he would have given me everything if I'd asked. I think he figured—or wished—if he gave me what I wanted, I'd stay.

Strong hands deftly work the backs of my thighs and calves, kneading and massaging my tight, sore muscles. My moans are slow, lingering, and uncontrollable. By now, Jonah's unfazed by my inappropriate sounds. At first, when we'd started this exciting love-hate relationship…okay, there isn't any hate; you simply *can't* hate Jonah—although there are moments almost daily where I plot his death as he tirelessly works me to the bone. Even with all of that, his intent comes from a loving place.

Where was I? Oh yeah, back to my moans. The first few times he administered his massage, he shamelessly snickered at my noises to the point of tears streaming down his rugged face. Between his fits of laughter, he stated that I was like a porno soundtrack; "one horny vixen" was how he put it. In the beginning, I was uncomfortable and embarrassed. Try as I might, it is hard to control my vocal enthusiasm for his magical hands—and yes, I know that sounds all kinds of wrong.

Yes, surprise, surprise, I'm not silent during sex either. I've tried, believe me. I've spent years trying to perfect silent sex, but I've failed miserably. Unless there's something stuffed in my mouth—*get your mind out of the gutter*—I whimper and scream as I orgasm.

I'd like to think Pete enjoyed my verbal satisfaction when we were married. Truth be told, I have no clue—he never said a word either way. In fact, when we had sex, he was mute. Don't get me wrong, I don't think you *need* to be vocal during sex or that being silent is a no-no; it's not about that. It's that I never knew if my pleasure or oral encouragement turned him on or bothered him. I never knew what he felt or what he was thinking at any given moment in time, and that was the crux of it, the downfall of our twenty years of marriage. I never knew.

Two

OLIVIA

After a scalding hot shower, a balm to my weary muscles, I feel like superwoman—strong and sexy. This is why I keep coming back. Yes, the results are motivational and I do love Jonah, but it's the inner strength and confidence I can't get anywhere else that keep me coming back for more.

It also helps that I love the reflection in the mirror. This new outfit rocks. The downside of losing weight is having to constantly buy new clothes until I get to my ideal weight. Okay, I'll shut it—there is no downside to getting closer to your goal.

Gazing in the full-length mirror, I admire my most recent purchase. As I twirl around, my lips curve up into a smile at my image. The flouncy hem of my red pencil skirt swirls in parallel with the white peplum knit top like the blooming of a flower. My ensemble is figure flattering, oozing feminine charm yet also appears professional, and my strappy black high heels make the outfit complete. Yes, this will definitely do for my meeting with a prospective client. I seriously need to land this account.

As I head out, my phone buzzes with an incoming text. Glancing at it as I descend the stairs, it's Pete, my ex. It's his third text today asking me to dinner, tonight. With the first text, I said no. He wants to rekindle our relationship—his words—but there's nothing to rekindle. The second text I ignored, and now, I intend to do the same.

Jonah is cleaning-up when I walk back into

his home gym, wiping down the last of the equipment. His house is huge with the perfect layout to keep his home separate from his fully functional gym and yoga studio.

"Whoo-eee," he drawls, ending with an appreciative whistle. "You're going to work or on a hot date?"

"Work—why? Is it too much?" I ask, now doubting my fashion sense.

"Hell no!" His emphatic response settles some of my uncertainty. "It's perfect. You look gorgeous, as usual. I've never seen you in that outfit before."

"It's new. I had to buy a few more work clothes because some of my stuff is now too big. Sin will be thrilled," I say, stating the obvious. Since hitting Tamsin's size, she's been the willing recipient of my clothes that no longer fit as I move down in weight.

Sin, her rather apt nickname, is blessed with a sinfully sexy body. She has curves that she's never had to work at—well, that's not completely true. After having each of her four children, she did have to watch her diet and exercise for some time. She is a tall, curvy blonde with the body of a pinup model.

"The struggle is real," Jonah ruefully remarks with a grin. "Lunch is ready, let's eat." My workout schedule varies daily. Once a week, we have lunch following my session and his private chef prepares a nutritious meal.

He doesn't lunch with all his clients. In fact, I'm one of only three he ever shares a meal with, and I'm fortunate to be among his close friends. Jonah's been in Toronto for five years and while hugely popular professionally, he's selective with his friends.

When he traveled north, he was following his then fiancée from Nashville to Toronto. She was accepted into the National Ballet of Canada and not long after uprooting his life, leaving his family, friends, and business for her, she cheated on him with another dancer. Though devastated, he stayed to make a go of it.

Jonah met Tamsin because of his ex. Sin was a costume designer, working with the National Ballet at the time. They met at an after party and immediately hit it off, so much so that Sin became his client, and that's saying a lot because she would rather peel off her skin than exercise.

The meal is delicious, as always. Emeline has made one of my favorites: salmon avocado maki with mango sorbet for dessert. Chewing his sushi, Jonah asks, "So who are you meeting dressed like that?"

Staring at him, I try to decipher the meaning behind his words. "A new client, hopefully. She's opening a boutique hotel and needs an interior designer. Why?"

"She? It's a woman?" he clarifies, running a hand through his stark white-blond hair.

"Yes," I answer warily, not sure what he's getting at, though I'm pretty sure I won't like it. "Why?"

He quirks an eyebrow at my tone, a grin creeps across his face, softening his chiseled jaw. "Just curious. You're hot and I'm wondering if I have to worry or not." I open my mouth to object but he barrels on. "Come out with me and a few of the guys tonight. Brad will be there, I think you'll like him. I know he'll like you." His eyes approvingly rove my body. "He's a good guy."

Shaking his silly suggestion off, I look him straight in the eye, blatantly expressing my annoyance at having this conversation *again*. "No, thanks. Brad's closer to my son's age than mine," I hiss. "And last time I checked, I'm an adult. I don't need you worrying or taking care of me. Thanks, but no thanks."

Tossing the napkin on the table, I rise, not upset, just frustrated. I don't want to go through all this again.

"Liv, don't go. You haven't had dessert yet," he protests. "Millie will have my balls if you leave without having the sorbet, she knows how much you love it."

"Well, you should've thought of that before you decided to play matchmaker for the hundredth time. J, you need to get this through your thick skull: I'm not interested. I'll never go out with a man younger than me," I declare. "And I've told you that many times, so please listen."

"All right, all right," he says, walking toward me with his hands up in surrender. "Sorry. I just think you're selling yourself short. Who cares about age? You're a beautiful woman, inside and out. Any man, no matter his age, would be a fool to not want to go out with you," he places his arms on my shoulders.

My hands wrap around his strong forearms, anchoring myself to this magnificent man who cares about me. Gazing into his loving eyes, I reply, "Thank you. I love you and appreciate you being the president of the Olivia Cassidy fan club. I'm just not ready to date, and even when I am, I'll never date a younger man."

Coming from a marriage where I always felt like I was lacking no matter what I did—so much so that I actually gave up for a while, faded away—I can't imagine dating someone younger. I could never keep up.

"I'm a forty-two-year-old divorcee with two practically grown kids and a new and risky small business." I can't help but smile despite how freaking scary it sounds. "I've got enough on my plate right now. A guy is the last thing I need. What I do need is you and I want you in my corner, but you need to let me find my way."

"Darlin', I can do that, but I won't stand by and let you discount yourself. You deserve the best. You've come so far in such a short time. You should be proud of yourself and you should celebrate," he encourages. "Many would have bailed on life. You didn't. I won't let you forget that."

I rest my forehead on his, peering into his warm eyes. Before, I never knew I needed Jonah Carson in my life; now I can't imagine my life without him.

"Oh, sorry," Millie gasps from the doorway. Turning, the petite ginger, Jonah's personal chef, is flustered and beet red from head to toe. She abruptly turns, heading back the way she came.

In three long, quick strides, Jonah's at her side. Gently placing his hand on her elbow, he halts her retreat. "Millie, it's okay. What's up?"

She averts her gaze, scanning the room, faltering when she lands on me. A brief but discernible flash of resentment—or something close to it—flits across her features before she looks away. With her big baby blues regarding Jonah, it's clear as day, and it all makes sense.

She has a crush on her boss.

"I'm so sorry. I was…um, I was…checking that everything was okay," she barely whispers, her eyes now stuck on his Adam's apple. Her hands mangle the dishcloth and I wonder what the hell it ever did to her.

"Everything was wonderful," I pipe up, attempting to break the tension. "I'd love to devour your sorbet, but I've run out of time. Besides, I don't need the extra calories," I add in my default, self-deprecating manner. "Thank you so much, Millie. It was truly divine. Jonah." He turns to me. "I'll see you Thursday."

Walking toward me, I raise my hand to stop him. "Don't worry, I'm swimming tomorrow," I reassure.

I usually see him five days a week, but there are times when a celebrity client is in town, as is the case right now, then he rearranges his schedule to squeeze them in. I forfeited my time with him tomorrow so he could exercise with some Hollywood bigwig.

Like me, most of his clients are accommodating because Jonah is just that kind of guy. Despite how much agony he puts me through, I'd reshuffle my life for him.

Restarting his walk my way, he warns, "You better."

His arms wrap around my back, pulling me in for a hug, while Millie's visible over his shoulder. Every twitch and squirm of her body confirms my suspicion. The lovely Emeline Walton is attracted to Jonah, her narrowed eyes give away her detestation at his focus on me. I wish to end her misery, but by the look of things Jonah is oblivious. She silently scurries out of the room.

Breaking our embrace, my mouth curves into a Cheshire grin as I drawl in my best Scarlet O'Hara impersonation, "Why Mr. Carson, I do declare, I think you have a secret admirer."

Furrowing his brow, he tilts his head to one side with a puzzled expression. "What?"

"Miss Emeline is smitten with her boss," I playfully deliver, fiddling with the collar of his shirt while he continues to examine me in bafflement.

"Ah, you're too transparent," he finally says with a sly grin. "You're playing with me. You're trying to get me all ruffled. This is because I suggested meeting Brad, isn't it?"

"Nope. Millie has a crush on you. You should've seen the daggers she was throwing my way while you hugged me, even though she didn't completely own it."

He laughs, batting my hand away from his shirt. "Cut it out. You've got no clue what you're talking about," he says, quickly refuting my claim. "Listen, if you change your mind about tonight, we'll be at Swig. Text me and I'll come get you," he adds like the mention of Millie's infatuation never happened.

Now it's my turn to study him and wonder. He seems uneasy with my observation, quickly dismissing the idea and changing the subject. I'm eager to push, but if I do, I need to be prepared to get the same back in spades. I'm not in the mood, nor do I have the energy for that kind of repartee right now. I enjoy trickery and games with Jonah, but I'm not up for playing with my heart.

"Ah, trust me, I won't change my mind," I fire back with a big assuring smile. "But thanks for inviting me. Besides, I have the kids this week and I'm saving my empty calories for my trip to Montreal next weekend."

"Montreal?"

"Yes. Girls weekend away. Sin, Erin, and me." I grin, unable to conceal my delight at the prospect.

"Sin? She managed to get a weekend away from the kids?"

"Yep. It was her idea," I volley another surprise at him. "In fact, Colin's taking the weekend off so he can watch the kids."

Arching his eyebrows, he does a triple shake of his head like a Looney Tunes cartoon character. Colin is a dear, but works like a fiend.

"I'll see you later." I wave, then wink at an awkward Millie, who has slipped back into the room.

Three

OLIVIA

I've got a date with chicken salad, Penny Reid, and a vodka martini. I need a drink tonight, and I deserve it—I landed the freaking account! Eliza Preston loved my ideas for her new hotel and was thrilled with my suggestions on palette and ambience for the public spaces like the lobby, bar, and spa. Landing this account is beyond my wildest dreams, and it'll put me in martinis, chicken salads, and all the Penny Reid books I want for a while.

I enter the house to pitch blackness and hear muffled sounds, like someone talking in the background. As I carefully walk through the darkness, a stream of light glows from the back of the house.

For now, I'm renting an executive townhouse in the Annex. It's literally three streets over from where I used to live—or I should say, where Pete and I used to live. He got the house. As much as I loved the place, I didn't want any part of our old life together.

When I found this spacious three-bedroom for rent, I loved it. The only thing holding me back was the price, but Pete didn't flinch at the cost. As an investment banker, he makes money hand over fist, and like I said, he hasn't withheld any.

Entering the family room, Paige is prone on the leather sofa, watching *The Walking Dead* on her tablet, her thick brown hair fanned out on the arm of the couch.

A smile graces my lips. It's been a week since I last saw her, and my heart skips with delight and trepidation. I love her like crazy, but our relationship has been a work in progress since she hit her teens. Seriously, what mother-daughter relationship isn't during the teenage years? Still, we've drifted apart more so since the separation, and things have been rough between us for months.

Our custody agreement is one week on and one week off with Mondays as our switch days. She was supposed to be here last night, but she had a volleyball tournament and asked to sleep over at her best friend's. I was torn, wanting her here with me because I miss my kids when they're with their dad. But to keep the peace, I gave in and let her stay the night.

"Hey sweetie," I whisper, my lips gently kissing her satiny, soft hair.

Paige hardly acknowledges me with a look close to, if not certainly of annoyance. At times, she barely tolerates me, and there are moments where I'm persona non-grata. When she's in the anti-mom camp, she doesn't hide her anger and frustration at my leaving her father. Despite trying to explain it to her, to make her understand that it was the hardest decision of my life, she doesn't want to hear any of it. All the blame lies with me; her father is the saint and I'm the pariah. Needless to say, our time together can be trying at best, and at worst, downright brutal.

"How was your game last night?" I ask, sitting on the coffee table and leaning over to stroke her hair.

Paige rolls her eyes with a short, harsh exhale. "Fine." Abruptly sitting up, she clicks off the lamp, banishing us into darkness.

"Hey, Paige," I call out. She's on the move as I blink, trying to adjust to the dark. Flicking on the lamp, she silently glares at me like I'm holding her hostage, waiting for me to say more. "Not nice, kiddo. Let's try this again," I say patiently. "How was your volleyball game?"

"It was fine." Her tone's softer this time. Gathering her school books and things, she wraps her arms around her belongings. "Um, so I'm going to do homework," she says, motioning toward the door—her escape route. I'm now used to this tactic and latch onto her shoulder, turning her to fully face me.

"Hey." Despite my frustration, fatigue at this routine, and hurt feelings, I remind myself that I'm the adult and try to act like one. "Have you eaten?"

"Yes."

"Will you please sit with me while I eat?" I ask nicely. "I'm just going to whip up a salad, it won't take long. I'd love to hear how your week was."

She lets out a heavy sigh like she's bearing the weight of the world and studies me. I plaster on my most sincere smile, parking my own aggravation at the situation because it'll only backfire. I only want to spend time with her, reconnect, get things back to the way they used to be, when she eagerly wanted to share her day with me. I was under no illusion that she shared everything, but still she was pretty open on most things, including boys. Now, some days I'm lucky if she can string three words together for me.

My plan of attack is to kill her with kindness. It's my last hope. We've bickered, yelled, and cried, and none of that has gotten us any closer to the way things were. I wanting things the way they used to be is selfish and likely unrealistic.

In her eyes, I took a sledgehammer to her life, her family, and her home. She blames me for all of it and what she's feeling is understandable, so how can I expect things to go back to how they were? It also doesn't help that she's a teenager and is thus convinced that she knows everything. I just need to find a way to reach her and make her understand without badmouthing her father. While I had my reasons for leaving him, for walking away from a twenty-plus-year relationship, the last thing I want to do is affect her relationship with him.

"I've got homework," she repeats.

"I know, you already said that. You could do it while I eat," I hopefully suggest.

"No talking?" she clarifies, contemplating my proposal.

"Just a little," I cautiously reply. "I promise to keep it to a minimum so you can get your work done."

"Fine." She sighs and leads the way to the kitchen.

We work in silence, Paige hunched over her laptop at the kitchen table and me throwing together my chicken Caesar salad. I forgo the martini, despite how much I deserve and want it, and I'll read after dinner, when Paige is sure to disappear to her room.

"How was your game?"

"Fine. We won." Her monotone voice hits me square in the chest. It's hard to move past her cold indifference to me, especially when we used to be close.

Being a stay-at-home mom afforded me the luxury of heavily investing in my kids. I followed Drew's hockey, soccer, and baseball days, and helped at Paige's dance recitals and volleyball tournaments. I also assisted with homework, failing relationships, and plans for college.

Fortunately, my relationship with Drew is as strong as ever. He doesn't know all the gory details about the end of my marriage with his father, nor does he want to. He hasn't picked sides. In fact, on occasion, he's hinted at understanding why I did what I did.

I sigh at thoughts of Drew. I miss him. It's been over a month since he was last home for his nineteenth birthday, but he'll be back in a few days after finishing his final exams. It's hard to believe his first year at Western University is done. While so much like his father in some ways, he's also got a lot of me in him. He's the best of both of us.

I try again, switching gears. "Honey, if you don't want to talk about volleyball, you pick what we talk about."

Paige's big, round brown eyes—so much like mine—pierce my chest like daggers. "I don't want to talk," she says with petulant scorn. "I've got to get this done."

"Paige, I'm trying here. Can't you meet me halfway?"

During the separation, things were rocky and at times, intense. Paige held out hope that I'd come to my senses, or that either Pete or she would get through to me. Once the divorce was final, we drifted further apart.

I so wish I could give her what she wants. I want to find some common ground, a compromise, but I won't give in at the expense of my needs and happiness. Some might call me selfish and a horrible mother; nevertheless, I must give to myself first if I'm going to be able to give to my kids. It's like the safety instructions on an airplane: I must put on my mask first before putting on theirs, or else I won't be able to help them.

"Why are you dressed like that?" she asks out of the blue, ignoring what I just said.

Her question throws me for a loop. *What is it with this outfit?* "Um, I was working. I met with a hotel owner and landed her as a client." I glow, deliberately sharing my elation, hoping it's contagious.

"It's nice," she says, so low that I nearly miss it. "You look really pretty."

"Thanks." My smile is uncontrollable. It's something, a tiny something, but it's huge to me. I love the moments when she likes me, wants to talk to me. A compliment? Damn, I'll take it. It has nothing to do with being vain or needing the praise and everything to do with being close to her. Those moments remind me of her childhood when I was her best friend, or at the very least someone she looked up to, loved, and trusted.

"Ouch," I wail, there's blood gushing from my thumb. In my exuberance, I sliced it with the knife.

"Mom!"

Her concern is evident as she springs out of her chair and rushes to my side. Gingerly holding my wounded finger like Florence Nightingale, she tends to my injury. Placing pressure on the cut with a towel, she's able to stem the bleeding. Then she instructs me to take over while she gets a bandage. I could do this myself—it's not a big or deep nick—but instead, I'm basking in her love and attention.

She returns with a bandage in hand, asking in a deep, gruff voice, "Moon of my life, are you hurt?" It's a poor imitation of the magnificent Khal, and a silly smile covers her face, telling me she knows it was bad. I can't help but laugh, and I do so even more once she joins in.

"Thank you," I say once my giggles subside. Cradling her cheek, I lean in to gently kiss the tip of her nose.

"There you go." She lightly kisses my thumb, resting it back down on the counter.

"I need a Drogo hit after that." I smile at my reference to our shared weakness. "You up to watching some with me?"

We've been known to watch countless episodes from season one just to get our fix. It's the actor as much as the character we love, and we know our favorite scenes word for word.

"What kind of question is that? Hells yeah," she exclaims. "I'll pop some popcorn."

She likes me again. My heart swells with joy. These are the moments that make it all worthwhile.

Four

OLIVIA

As I close my laptop, the honk of a car blares through the walls of my home—my girls are here. Grabbing my bag, I dash out the front door, almost forgetting to set the alarm. Both Erin and Tamsin are gabbing in the front seat of the car, idling at the curb. I wave to Mrs. Foster, my sweet, nosy neighbor who lives across the street. She's a major gossip who boldly watches and shares the comings and goings of everyone in the neighborhood with anyone who will listen.

"You off gallivanting?" she hollers like she's my mother and I owe her an explanation.

Quickly nodding, I duck into the car. I'm not letting the street know my business. "Hey girlies," I greet them as I slide into the back seat.

"Let's get this party started," Erin shouts as she puts the car into gear.

"Hey love, how are you?" Sin asks, turning to face me.

"I'm so ready for this getaway." I sigh. "I'm going to be super busy once we get back and this is exactly what I need to recharge before all that begins."

"Recharge?" Erin echoes, eyeing me in the rear-view mirror, her perfectly arched brow raised in question. "What are you talking about? You're single, carefree, and have Pete's money, why do you need to recharge?"

Tamsin's eyes widen and her head swivels between us, finally landing with a sharp glare at our friend. I effortlessly dismiss Erin's callous and clueless response. Having known her for more than half my life, I'm used to her careless comments that suggest everyone else's life is a picnic compared to her high-stress one.

She's a litigator for one of the top mining companies in Canada. Single and career-minded, most of her time is spent traveling, in court, or hooking up. I've known her since high school, and she's one of a small handful of friends I keep in touch with, although she is definitely the closest.

Her obsidian eyes are still zeroed in on me. "I didn't mean anything by it," she flippantly says. "I just mean, I'd love to be a divorcee living off my ex-husband's money and dabbling in starting my own business." Her comments are now defensive, practically spiteful.

She flicks her long, black, pin-straight hair over her shoulder. Her bright red manicured nails catch my eye like sharp claws having drawn blood. How fitting—that's her speciality. Despite her combative and selfish nature, she can be vulnerable and sweet—or at least she used to be able to.

She had a strict and cold upbringing. Her father is a stoic, hard man, though he was less so while her mother was alive. She died after a long battle with cancer when we were in high school. After that, her father shut down. Erin only received his attention for academic achievements and consequently, from a young age, Erin developed her 'I don't give a shit' exterior and an insatiable drive to be number one at everything. Underneath it all lies a woman who can be kind and loving.

"Whatever," I say dismissively, trying to tamper my simmering anger.

Erin doesn't understand why I ended things with Pete. She acts like my marriage was perfect. Sure, from the outside looking in, we appeared happy, and Pete's good looks certainly added to the perception that everything was roses, never mind that he could also be funny and charming. He always was when we were out with company.

But she didn't have to live with his neglect or indifference, or the countless times he stood me up simply because he forgot about me. My personal favorite—*not*—was how he'd ignore me at social gatherings while flirting with women like he was single.

I'll never forget years ago when we went to his first office Holiday party. He'd recently joined the firm, so it was my first time meeting his colleagues. Upon arrival, he disappeared, leaving the hostess to introduce me to people. I was alone the entire party, and one guy even asked across a large space, "Where's your husband?"

He was practically shouting given the distance between us, and I think he was drunk. Awkwardly, I said, "I don't know."

He then loudly responded, "What a fool. If you were my wife, I wouldn't let you out of my sight."

Everyone around us stopped talking and stared at me. I wanted to disappear. I later found Pete talking to some blonde in a corner. Of course, he apologized profusely, and I stupidly let it slide.

I wasn't going to share those moments with Erin; they were too embarrassing. Besides, something told me she'd say it was my fault. She was a huge fan of Pete's.

After the separation we argued a lot, then finally, we agreed to disagree. Now, she gets upset with anything I do. I'm hoping this trip will help us get past that.

"No," Sin strongly interjects. "You're working night and day to get Cassidy Designs off the ground. Don't downplay all the sweat and tears you're putting in to it. You deserve to recharge," she ardently states, deliberately demonstrating her displeasure at Erin.

"Thank you, Sin." I grin, reaching to squeeze her hand.

My relationship with Sin is different. While I've known Erin longer, Sin and I are closer. When necessary, we tell each other like it is, but it's not behind a wall of indifference or attitude. We met first year of university, two strangers living together in a dorm on campus.

"Yes, I've been working hard and I do deserve this trip," I respond with conviction.

"Liv, I'm sorry. You do deserve it," Erin chimes in with a sheepish grin, likely realizing she came on way too harsh.

Fiddling with the stereo, Erin taps the screen and the rumbly voice of John Kay fills the car with the classic and empowering words of Steppenwolf's "Born to be Wild".

From that point on, the ride is entertaining and goes by quickly. We arrive in Montreal at after eight in the evening, and once we're checked into the hotel, Erin insists we hit a nightclub. Sin tries to bail, claiming fatigue and wanting time to soak in the mammoth tub. Despite understanding her desire to chill, I coax her out, begging her not to leave me with the teenager locked in Erin's body.

Our night is fun and reminiscent of our university days, and we call it a night at after one AM. The next morning is spent at the spa followed by shopping at Mile End, then we head back to the hotel to get ready for dinner.

Erin made reservations at some restaurant she can't stop raving about.

Our shopping was fun and successful, and I found a chic, vintage, A-line floral swing dress to wear to dinner. Erin's wearing a quintessential little black dress, and Sin's lovely in her simple yet classic, red high-waisted pencil dress. We're all dolled up and ready to hit the town. Our hotel is close to our destination, but thanks to the three-inch heels we're all wearing, walking is easily vetoed in favor of an Uber.

Beaulieu's is nestled along a narrow cobblestone street in old Montreal. Its fieldstone exterior in browns and grays and deep red front door are eye-catching. Entering the building, the space looks to have been the living and dining room at one point in time. It's inviting and almost pastoral with its wide-planked, uneven wood floors and small, quaint tables, each adorned with a single pink camellia in a petite glass vase. Contrary to its languid atmosphere, the sound of an alternative band, Arcade Fire's "Here Comes the Night Time" fills the air, adding an upbeat vibe to the dining room.

We're seated beside a huge, beautiful fireplace that anchors the room. While not lit, there are charred white, gray, and black ashes and wood remains in the open hearth. Coupled with the faint, welcoming scent of smoke, there's a homey yet stylish charm about the place.

Seated in the middle, a counter-high wall runs along one side of the open kitchen, enabling patrons to see the culinary magic unfold. On the adjacent wall, there's a diner-style order window. Instead of aluminum, it's made of dark, burnished wood, complementing the rest of the décor.

"This place is lovely. Great choice, Erin," I praise. She's the foodie among us and is constantly inviting us to one restaurant or another to discover the latest up-and-coming chef. I love food, so it's no hardship to join her on these gastronomic adventures.

"I've been dying to come here. I've heard so much about Chef Samson Beaulieu. He's one of Canada's top chefs," she gushes. I've heard those words perhaps a dozen times already on this trip.

"It's real nice," Sin adds. "And I'm starving."

"When are you not?" Erin says jokingly.

We order champagne and a platter of oysters, and we all choose either seafood or fish for our main courses since Erin tells us that's what the restaurant's known for. I wonder if the meal will live up to the hype. We've been to restaurants where the notoriety of the chef creates so much expectation that nothing but perfection will do. Inevitably, it falls flat.

Every five seconds, Erin eagerly glances in the direction of the kitchen. Strategically seated, she faces the kitchen, desperately hoping to catch a glimpse of the chef. Sitting beside her, I also have a direct line of sight. Try as I might, I'm unable to determine who he is. Sin sits across from Erin with her back to the hustle and bustle of the culinary creations underway.

By the time our entrees arrive, we're having a great time and on our second bottle of wine. My seared scallops with Swiss chard and leeks in a garlic brown butter sauce have me salivating from looking at them. The aroma is decadent and with my first bite, an involuntary moan releases from my mouth at the explosion of rich flavors. Erin gasps beside me. Thinking my inappropriate sound shocked her, I turn to apologize, but she's frozen, mesmerized by something in her line of sight.

Straightening my spine, I take notice. The room's atmosphere has shifted. It's electrically charged with a buzz, and a different kind of babble zips through the air. It's not the usual din of dinner conversation; it's now exhilarating and gleeful. Sin and I notice the uptick in energy at about the same time, sharing an alarmed and curious look. As if synchronized, our gazes glide in the direction of the vortex, of what has Erin's undivided attention and the room in an uproar.

A tall, definitely over six feet, broad-shouldered man with short brown hair casually saunters toward the kitchen carrying a basket of vegetables. *Hello, hottie.* He is remarkable.

Like a moth to a flame, all eyes in the room follow him as he enters the kitchen, the invisible pull strong and palpable. Seemingly oblivious to being center stage, he gets to work; if he does notice, he certainly hides it well.

Even with the dim lighting, I can tell his eyes are light. Vivid and intense, they're either blue or green; I'm not sure which from this distance. His face is striking, almost as if it's carved out of stone. Flawless. Symmetrical with chiseled cheekbones and a matching strong, square jaw.

At first glance, you'd think each feature would be too angular or severe to be attractive, but somehow, they combine in an eye-catchingly perfect way. And his lips. Kissable. Full and pillowy. If even possible, what makes him more attractive is his open and relaxed manner. Without any effort, he oozes confidence.

"Fuck me sideways, he's even more gorgeous in person," Erin says in a husky tone.

"Who is he?" Sin asks.

I look to Sin briefly before I find my gaze flitting back to the formidable specimen of a man, and I gawk as he slips a chef's jacket over his tight black tee. The starched white material clings to him, encasing his defined muscles. Broad, fit and defined, but not excessively muscular. He's completely at ease being the main attraction, managing his staff without so much as a glance at the dining room.

"That's him," Erin says, transfixed on him. In fact, almost every person is looking in his direction. Scratch that, every woman is craning her neck to see him, the striking chef who is now tasting what looks to be a sauce.

All three of us silently stare as he removes the spoon from his mouth and his tongue sweeps across his luscious upper lip. Simultaneously, we all exhale a breathy sigh when his tongue darts out to lick his lip for a second time. *Phenomenal.*

Despite him being younger, I'd be a fool to not appreciate his beauty. A woman can admire no matter the age; as long as he's an adult, there's no harm in that. It's not like I'm jumping into bed with him, although the thought does send warm tingles to my nether regions.

Reining in my foolish fantasy, I notice Erin is still in her trance. "That's Samson Beaulieu?" I state the obvious. "Wow, forget the food. My appetite is quenched just by the view," I quip with a sip of my wine and another appreciative glance at his outstanding side profile.

"Oh, my God, I have to meet him," Erin declares, shifting back into woman on a mission.

"What?" Sin and I simultaneously ask.

Oblivious to our question, Erin wipes her mouth with her napkin, then reaches for her purse. "You can't go over there. That's stalkerish and gauche," I state.

Applying her lipstick and running her fingers through her hair, she acts like I'm not even there. Sin chimes in, "Erin, let the man work. We can admire him from afar."

Several women have left their tables—husbands, partners, and dates be damned. They are lining up around the kitchen counter and I grumble at the human barrier blocking our view.

The hostess approaches the mob of women, directing them to stand at the order window. *Damn.* That's why they designed it like that. It's not for table orders; it's for the gaggles of women ogling and attempting to harass the chef.

"Shit," Erin mutters, a hard glint in her eye at what I'm sure she's seeing as her competition. "Let's wait 'til it dies down."

Sin and I nod in agreement and dive back into our divine meals. No surprise, the line-up of women neither dwindles nor dies. No sooner do a few women go back to their tables than new ones join. It's amusing to observe some of them shamelessly flirting and lingering well after the chef has returned to his work.

At one point, the hostess interrupts the mob to talk to the chef. Entering the kitchen, she turns her back to the diners, and his face is front and center. Wow. The room gasps in appreciation at the sight.

During their conversation, his gaze wanders from the entrance to the far corner, then in the direction of our table. His eyes fleetingly click with mine. It's only a second, maybe two, yet the intensity has me squirming in my seat and preparing to shy away. He beats me to it and moves on.

My gaze remains stuck on him. A mere second later, his roving eyes stop and swing back to me. Our gazes lock. My breath hitches, palms clammy. All noise, movement, even the air dims and slows as he notices me. His subtle grin widens to a bright smile complete with two panty-melting dimples.

Heat rises from deep within me, spreading like wildfire, and my heart threatens to pound right out of me. Just as quickly, our connection is broken when the hostess says something, snapping him out of our moment. He abruptly reverts to her. With a curt nod, he turns his back on me.

What just happened? Forcing my gaze anywhere but at the kitchen, at him, I glance around the room. This is silly. He's a young pup. I'm now gawking at younger men. *Great.* Clearly, it's been too long since I've had sex if the good looks of a younger man kick my heart rate into overdrive and heat body parts. I need to get laid.

Erin sharply scrutinizes me; Sin does too, although hers is with a cute and amused expression on her face. It's obvious they noticed what went down. *Terrific.* Refusing to acknowledge anything, I ignore them and finish my meal.

My willpower has left the building. Without realizing, I find myself glancing in his direction and sometimes, our eyes even meet. When they do, he pulls out his sexy smirk or a full shit-eating grin, dimples and all, as if to say he caught me red-handed. In each instance, I'm inevitably the one to blink and turn away first.

Through this all, his adoring fans continue to show up, and though I'm unable to hear what he says to them, he is charming and polite, nothing else. Despite his professional manner, it's embarrassing—although not surprising— some of the women try to touch him or climb through the small opening. All the while, he remains calm and friendly, but keeps his distance.

We are finishing our dessert when Erin says, "That's it, I'm going. There's no way I'm passing on a chance to meet him. And who knows? I might just entice him to try my tasty delights," she says suggestively with a waggle of her brows.

Sin licks her fork. "You should go too." She points the silverware at me. "I saw the way he was checking you out and the looks you were giving him."

"What are you talking about?"

She laughs, her soft blonde curls bouncing. "Don't even try to deny it."

"You're delusional. I gave him no looks," I emphatically state. Standing, I place my napkin on the table, and without a second glance, I say, "I'm going to the restroom."

Five

SAM

The sexy brunette with long shapely legs strides briskly past the doorway, toward the restroom, head held high. Despite the half-dozen women crowding the kitchen window, she's the only one I've got eyes for.

I don't usually do this—actually, I've *never* done this. I've never glanced twice at a guest or even thought of one with personal or sexual interest. Since becoming a celebrity chef—something I still can't willingly admit to being—my one and only rule is to never overstep the professional boundary. Up until this moment, I've never even flirted with the idea, let alone actually wanted to approach a patron for personal reasons.

Yet this woman I only just laid eyes on makes me want to break that rule. I've never been so immediately taken with a woman before. Sure, she's lovely, and watching her is interesting and revealing, her posture's self-assured yet approachable. She's intriguing, but I don't lack for attractive women. I have beautiful women around me more often than not. Some would say I'm fortunate, but it's a nuisance.

She is not your average pretty woman, though. That's what has me staring, going back for a gander or two when I can. It's her vibrancy, her warmth. Her bright, pure smile illuminates her whole face, like the blinding colors of an unforgettable sunset or the hypnotic timbre of falling rain. She's alluring. I want to talk to her. To know her. To touch her. To taste her.

Shaking my head in hopes of knocking some sense into me or at least ridding myself of the temptation, I inhale deeply, preparing to get back to work. Maybe I'm just horny—it has been a while since I last had sex, and my dry spell is probably messing with my head. I can't stop imagining her under me, me in her, us together, wrapped in sheets. Shit, I must stop these torturous visions or else it's going to be a long night.

With a forced grin, I step to the window and greet the eager eyes and beaming smiles of the two women anxiously waiting to meet me. Talking to these women is work; yes, I'm truly grateful for the attention, but at times it's exhausting. It takes away from the reason I became a chef: to cook and share my passion for divine food and flavors.

I don't want to sound ungrateful. If anyone told me years ago that I'd be a celebrity chef with two restaurants and my own show on the Chef's Network at the age of thirty-five, I would have laughed in their faces. It truly is a dream come true. It's a tough, fickle business, and I must make the most of my high; I'm well aware that I could as easily wake up tomorrow and find myself forgotten and discarded by all these fans.

The two women who were sitting with the enthralling brunette step up to the window. The sleek Polynesian one is ballsy, brashly stepping in front of the two ladies already at the window. The blonde appears to be the opposite of her friend, demure and uncertain. It's obvious she'd much rather be back at their table—or cleaning toilets for that matter—than here.

"Excuse me," says one of the ladies, indignation apparent as they are pushed back.

Neither shy nor put off by the snide comments from the women behind her, Ballsy stares at me with what I'm guessing are her *fuck me* eyes.

Wanting to prevent the catfight that is likely mere seconds away from breaking out, I say, "Excuse me, if you'd kindly wait your turn, I'll be with you in a minute." I motion for her to step back, now looking to the redhead who has shoved her way back to the front.

Ballsy is about to clock Red when Blondie grabs her arm, whispering something inaudible in her ear. Blondie's posture and expression are terse and reproachful—thank goodness one of them has some sense. With an eye on both sets of women, still wary as to how this could go, I sign the cookbooks in front of me. With my charm at full throttle, I'm hoping to placate and eliminate any lingering animosity among the women.

Gushing profusely with thanks, Red and her friend return to their table, leaving Ballsy and Blondie staring at me expectantly. Surprisingly, they are now the only ones milling around.

My heart stutters as the captivating brunette walks by. Like a magnet, my body straightens and pivots in her direction.

"Olivia," Blondie calls as she tugs the brunette's arm, forcing her to stop, though she does so hesitantly. *Olivia.* Deep, fawn-colored eyes, wild and wide, erratically dart around the room like she's seeking an escape route. As if sensing my gaze, she regards me with an almost laser-sharp focus.

There's a subtle shift in her demeanor, the rise and fall of her chest slowing as a lively glint appears in her eyes. As she bites her bottom lip, I wonder if she's struggling with an attraction to me. My cock twitches and I can't deny that I like the idea of affecting her in such a way.

Her big eyes possess me, dark like chocolate and deep, so deep, almost bottomless. She truly is enchanting. Blondie says something to her that goes unanswered. Our connection doesn't waver. Eyes locked; it's just us, her and me. We're oblivious to anything around us.

The order window is designed to limit contact with the patrons. Until this moment, I've always been grateful for it. Now, I want to destroy the wall, knock it down into a pile of rubble at our feet so there's nothing between us. I want to see all of her.

"I'm Erin," Ballsy says seductively, extending her hand through the window. My urge is to be rude and ignore her, but reluctantly I peel my gaze from Olivia, shaking Erin's hand, giving what I'm sure is a weak and unconvincing smile.

In less than a beat I let go of Erin's hand, my gaze whirling back to the object of my desire. Taking Olivia's hand I warmly say, "I'm Sam, and you are?" Even though I know her name, I want an excuse to hear her voice.

"Olivia," she responds. Her voice is smooth, sweet, and poised. Still clasping her slender hand, my thumb lightly caresses the inside of her silky wrist. Tingles shoot from my chest straight to my groin, and my balls tighten and ache with want.

Olivia returns the gesture with a touch of her own. Her thumb grazes the top of my hand. Back and forth, several times. Tender. Neither of us pulls away.

Erin clears her throat and Olivia regards her with what looks like a question. The women share a brief and silent yet loaded exchange. What the hell it means, I have no clue, but more than likely it has something to do with me.

With Erin's shrug of indifference, Olivia gently tugs her hand out of my hold and nibbles on her plum-colored bottom lip. What I'd give to taste her. "And this is Tamsin," she says, bringing her friend forward.

"Hi Tamsin." Extending my hand, I smile. "Pleased to meet you, I'm Sam Beaulieu."

Tamsin blushes. "Hi Sam."

Erin huffs, "Can I get a selfie with you?"

"Ah sorry, no selfies." Next to autographs, selfies are the most requested. I now refuse them after my image was inserted into an uncompromising picture that went viral.

"Aw, seriously?" Olivia says with a frown. Her light tone suggests her sulky expression is exaggerated, but I'm not sure if she's working it for me or her friends.

Either way, her pouting lips are lusciously tempting, and thoughts of sucking on her delectable bottom lip continue to assault me as my cock hardens. Sucking in air, I will it down. *Focus.*

"That would be the best part, proof that we were here. Actually, the best part is the food, second best would be a photo with you," she professes with a grin. *Is she flirting?* "You sure you won't reconsider? Three beautiful women wanting to be with you?" she taunts temptingly.

She *is* flirting. My heart rate kicks up a notch and taking her lead, my cock stirs again. *Down boy.* She's bold and spirited, not brash like Erin. I like a woman with just enough spunk for me to leave me wanting more. With Olivia, I certainly want more.

Although she's a bit of a conundrum. At first, when Tamsin forced her to stop, she was skittish like an animal caught in a snare. Now, she's playful, dare I say even enjoying herself. Her eyes twinkle and a ghost of a sly grin teases her mouth.

"Are you sure you won't take a selfie with us?" Erin seductively pushes with a swift glance in Olivia's direction. Her suggestion is immediately apparent and while not necessarily wise, I'm no fool. I'm not passing up the chance to touch Olivia.

Glancing between them, two attractive but wildly different women, both waiting for my response. One is sexy and sophisticated, someone I'd like to get to know, and the other is a weird cross between sex kitten and barracuda. Erin seems willing to play any game to get her way.

"Okay, just one. With all of you." Stepping out of the kitchen, I stand beside Olivia, determined to capitalize on the opportunity to be close to her. Casting her doe eyes at me, her grin falters as she realizes the implication of this impromptu photo. I cautiously wrap my arm around Olivia's waist. "Is this okay?" My voice is low and husky.

Inhaling, she glances at Erin, who encourages her with a wide smile and a nod. "Of course." She says it casually, though the rapid thumping of her neck's pulse point indicates otherwise.

I'm one to talk—my heart's hammering against my ribcage as her soft, inviting curves meld into my embrace. Her scent is scintillating, spicy like nutmeg or cinnamon with a hint of cocoa—absolutely edible.

Tamsin sidles up to Olivia's other side and, no surprise, Erin slips in on my vacant left. Wrapping her arms around my middle, Erin tucks herself snugly into the crook of my arm. Hanging limply at my side, my arm doesn't move. I'm not interested in her. Besides, she's doing enough for the both of us.

Just another reason I refuse selfies—the proverbial copping a feel. Unfortunately, more times than not, women use the occasion to touch the merchandise. Mind you, I wouldn't complain if Olivia were taking liberties with my body.

With the click of the phone, I abruptly step out of Erin's grasp, taking Olivia with me. My fingers tighten on her hip and my cock twitches. Feeling her soft, warm flesh in my grip has me thinking of all the other places my fingers would like to stroke, explore. Gasping, her eyes and pretty pink lips widen, her mouth forming an O.

Heat rises to my cheeks at my forward behavior. Damn, this woman has me blushing. Blushing! Have I ever before? Sure, I'm a take-charge kind of guy, but still, I've never been so dominant with a woman I've only just met. Surprisingly, Olivia brings out the caveman in me. It's a new, weird, and exhilarating feeling.

She tenses in my hold, her flustered anxiousness causing shallow, rapid breaths as her cheeks pink and her pupils dilate.

Having crossed some imaginary boundary, she shifts from sassy to anxious. While I'm willing to wager she's turned on, I also get the feeling she'd take the first opportunity to bolt. I won't give her the chance.

"Is this your first time at Beaulieu's?"

"Yes," Erin rushes to answer. Both Olivia and Tamsin nod. "I've been wanting to come for months. The last time I was in Montreal, I didn't get a chance to eat here."

Looking at Erin, Olivia takes the opportunity to slip out of my grasp. With one, then two steps, she's no longer in arm's reach. Tracking her movement, I'm intent on preventing her from retreating farther. Our eyes connect. She reacts on instinct and halts. "Where are you from?" I direct the question at Olivia.

"Toronto," Tamsin and Erin say in unison. Olivia remains silent, fidgeting with her arms, folding and unfolding them before clasping her fingers in front of her. She's not nervous, more likely. . .restless.

"Ah, how long are you here for?" Again, my question is for Olivia. I wish we were alone.

Having finally found her voice, she says, "We leave Monday morning."

Her tone is smooth and strong, defying the uneasiness she just displayed. Her deep, penetrating eyes pin me to the spot like an arrow hitting its mark.

With her gaze on me, I impulsively blurt out, "Go to dinner with me." It's not a question; it's a command.

She stares, stunned. I'm as surprised as she is at my invitation. My shock is at voicing my wish, not the request itself—I was certainly thinking it, but to act on it? To actually ask a patron out? That's a first for me. This could blow up in my face, six ways from Sunday, and all the possibilities rapidly flash through my mind as I wait for her response.

"Sweet baby J," Erin spouts with a shrill, almost wicked laugh. "I can't even." She raises her hands in the air then quickly drops them, sharp smacking rings out as they hit her thighs. Straightening her spine, she crosses her arms and glowers at Olivia.

The three of us gape at Erin. I'm confused. Tamsin looks upset. Olivia appears shocked, but I'm not sure if that's because of my question or Erin's behavior. Erin strikes me as a woman who is used to the attention, but I'm not willing to give it to her. She's not my concern.

"Olivia," I strongly prod, desperate for her answer. Preparing for rejection yet hoping for acceptance, I steel my spine. Her eyes swivel in my direction.

Clearing her throat, she pushes her shoulders back, chest out, and it takes everything I have in me to keep my eyes on her face.

"Um, thank you, Sam, but I'm going to have to decline."

Before I can push the issue, we are interrupted. "Chef," Marie, my hostess, says. "Sorry to disturb you. May I have a word?"

Without acknowledging her, I eye Olivia with my most determined expression—I'm not giving up. "Ladies, excuse me."

With short nods, they leave, and Marie informs me that Monsieur Daniel Thibault is here. He's an acquaintance and a fan. When he discovered I might open another restaurant, he expressed interest in backing me. Now's my chance to show him what my vision is, and I definitely want to explore this opportunity.

"Lead the way," I respond, eyes still on Olivia as she speaks to the server. With her table in view, I don a warm smile and extend a strong handshake. "Daniel, welcome to Beaulieu's. I'm so glad you finally made it."

The older man adds a forceful yet jovial clap on my back to our handshake. "Sam, it's good to be here. It's my daughter's birthday," he says, gesturing to the petite lady sitting beside him. "She's as interested as I am in the culinary world, and I'm treating her to dinner in one of the best restaurants in town. Yasmine, this is Sam Beaulieu, the magnificent chef I was telling you all about."

The wisp of a woman smiles, her ruby lips a sharp contrast to her fair features and light blonde hair. "Mr. Beaulieu, it's a pleasure."

"Pleased to meet you." I take her hand, and she beams and invites me to join them.

"I'd love to. Unfortunately, the kitchen needs me. Please let me prepare a special meal for you," I insist. Turning on the charm, I add, "In celebration of your birthday." Knocking their socks off is my goal. They both eagerly nod. "Excellent. Any allergies or anything you don't like?"

With another deep belly laugh, Daniel says, "Surprise us, dear boy. We're adventurous when it comes to food. There's nothing we don't like or can't eat." Smiling, I consider the limitless possibilities for their meal.

Daniel mentioned he might show and he's the reason I came in tonight. I couldn't risk missing him. He's been to my other, more casual restaurant many times, but I'm looking to open a new one more in line with Beaulieu's and want him to experience the kind of place and food he could potentially invest in.

Yasmine giggles, placing her hand on top of mine on the table. Her gesture doesn't completely surprise me. I've been in similar situations before—it's an occupational hazard—but I'm more uncomfortable with her bold move in the presence of her father. Her eyes are dark and suggestive. Looking to Daniel, his eyes are glowing with joy and something like approval. *Shit.*

"Great, I'll get started."

Abruptly removing my hand, I head to the kitchen, and catch Olivia settling the bill. She's definitely another reason I'm glad I came in tonight.

For a split second, I hesitate, torn between what I want to do and what I need to do. I've been networking for months, trying to find the right investor for my new venture since my usual investors have their money tied up right now.

I've had a lot of interest, and the celebrity factor certainly helps, but I don't want just anyone to invest. I need to know who I'm getting into bed with, and while there are contracts to safeguard potential pitfalls in an agreement of this nature, I have friends who've gotten into horrible messes because of the wrong investor.

I know Daniel. He's a successful businessman and has experience investing in restaurants, but I'm having a hard time finding out how those ventures worked out. I need to pursue this with Daniel. I don't want to lose the opportunity; otherwise I'm back to square one.

Even with that sobering fact, my yearning trumps everything. At the kitchen counter, I beckon Anton, my sous-chef and good friend. There's no one else I'd pass the reins to.

"I'll be back in a few. Get started on the amuse-bouche and seafood platter for table three."

"Certainly, chef." Friend or not, in the kitchen, I'm in charge, and our friendship is left at the door.

"Bon."

Swinging to face the dining room, my gaze goes to her table. Olivia is gone.

Six

OLIVIA

Ah, shit," I screech, stumbling, almost snapping my ankle in two.

Old Montreal's beautiful cobblestoned streets feel like you're in a quaint European town, but no matter how pretty and romantic, the uneven stones are murder for women in high heels.

We tiptoe gingerly down the well-lit street, very aware of the danger should one of our heels lodge between the stones. It's as real and as dire as taking my next breath.

"Are you okay?" Sin stops, waiting for me to catch up, and I gratefully latch onto her arm with a shaky breath.

"Yes, barely." My light laugh belies my unsettled nerves and she joins me. After all, what else are we supposed to do? "How much longer 'til we reach asphalt or a cab?"

"Soon," Erin calls from ahead, closer to the upcoming intersection and what looks like smooth road. Not too much longer now, just a few more steps.

"Olivia," a deep, urgent voice calls from behind.

When I halt abruptly, my heel snags on a stone. Sin and I sway, unsteady, and gasp before turning, the magnificent beauty of Sam Beaulieu's lightly jogging toward us. His formidable form is backlit by the moon, each stride smooth and confident.

"Eek," Erin squeals, her voice sounding closer as she gently bumps into my back.

We sway back and forth before we're able to

stabilize our trio. Huddling under a vintage streetlight, we're mesmerized by the tall, lean man approaching us with a sexy smirk brightening his already handsome face.

"I seriously don't believe this," Erin mutters. She's starting to piss me off. It's not like I'm pursuing him.

"Ladies, you left without saying goodbye," he playfully admonishes, holding his hand over his heart like he's wounded by our callous departure.

"We're so sorry," Erin purrs, stepping out from behind me to plant her palm on his forearm.

Sam briefly flicks his eyes to her before shifting to pin them on me, their sea green depths shimmering with something akin to hunger.

"Olivia, can we talk for a moment?"

Fits of giggles erupt from both Sin and Erin. Yes, these are my best friends, although I'm seriously reconsidering that at this moment as the two grown-ass women act like a bunch of star-struck teenagers.

Hanging my head in sheer embarrassment, I mutter, "Would you please leave us alone?"

Sam confidently inches closer to me, then it hits me—my friends' lame outburst has diverted my attention from the real concern. *Sam.* I'm wildly turned on by this hot young man standing before me.

Stepping back, out of the circle of light, I'm plunged into darkness. Moving into the same spot I just vacated, his striking frame is illuminated by the fluorescent glow from above, like a spotlight beaming down on the main attraction. If I didn't know he was a chef, I'd swear he was a model.

"I don't usually do this," he says.

"Do what?" I'm confused, my mind reeling and heart battering.

"Chase women."

I snort. *Real attractive, Olivia.*

"Is that what you're doing?" I quirk an eyebrow in question. He nods once, his smile still in place. "Well actually, come to think of it, of course you don't. They usually fall at your feet," I sarcastically add at the memory of the evening's revolving door of women surrounding the kitchen. I bet tonight was an average turnout for him.

"Fall at my feet?" He chuckles, one side of his lips tipping up in amusement. "I must've missed that because I don't remember any women at my feet. I'm pretty sure I wouldn't have forgotten that."

"I guess we see things differently," I quip. "What do you want, Sam?"

"I want you to go out with me."

Didn't he get the hint? I shot him down in the restaurant.

Damn, he's beautiful. He could have anyone—so why me? I'm not chopped liver, but I'm past my prime—although they say forty is the new thirty, whoever the hell 'they' are. I've got two children, stretch marks, and less than perky breasts.

"I live in Toronto," I say, stupidly blurting out the first inane rebuttal that springs to mind.

"I know, you already said that, but you're still here tomorrow, right? Have dinner with me then." His voice is a rumble, low and sexy, stirring sensations deep in my core.

"Why?"

"Because I want to get to know you."

"Why?" I sound like an echo chamber.

"Because I like you, and something tells me I'm going to like you even more once I get to know you." His smile is blinding, especially those panty-wetting dimples.

"I'm forty-two," I boldly announce, trying to thwart his lunacy. I fully expect him to nod and walk away. He doesn't; instead his iridescent eyes remain fixed on me, darkening and growing hungrier by the second.

I'm wildly flattered by his attention and I'll definitely pull this moment out when I need an ego boost or some inspiration for my spank bank, but he's way too young. I'm too old. I'm not a cougar. Never will be.

"Okay," he says, drawing out the word, and I wait. Silence ensues. He's still smiling, clearly entertained. I remain silent, waiting for him to tell me his age...or maybe he needs a bit more time, then it will hit him. He'll realize this is crazy and walk away. We continue to stare at each other in awkward silence, or at least I think it's awkward. His sexy grin widens. He's mouth-watering.

"And you are...?" I ask, refocusing on my mission, losing patience with his persistence.

He cocks an eyebrow as if he has no clue what I'm getting at and tucks his hands into his pockets. "I'm what?"

"How old are you?"

"Does it matter?" he challenges.

"Yes," I state, my tone emphatic.

"I don't think so," he volleys. Instinctually, I give him the stink eye and grumble as his suggestive grin grows in contrast to my concern.

"I tell you what, go out with me, and on our date, I'll tell you how old I am."

"Seriously?" I'm now a mixture of incredibly tickled and irritated by his determination. "You know I could Google you, right? I'm pretty sure I could find out your age with a few clicks, Mr. Hot-Shot Chef."

"I'm sure you could, but where's the fun in that? Go to dinner with me tomorrow night?" he asks sweetly, his irresistible dimples teasing me. Clenching my thighs, I attempt to ease my achy core.

"Coffee," I counter, and my stomach flip-flops, surprised I didn't say no.

Now I'm bargaining? *What the?* It's not supposed to go like this. There's only one answer for me to deliver: no. Plain and simple. *No.* Clearly the fool in me has taken over.

"Lunch."

Our negotiations are now in full swing. In the glow of the streetlight, the dusting of scruff on his prominent jaw and assertive stature make him dark and even more alluring.

"Coffee," I repeat with less conviction.

What am I doing? I need to walk away. I can't go on a date with this man—or should I say *boy*, given our likely sizeable age difference? *Damn.* No, he's definitely all man. Confusion and the giddy exhilaration of riding a roller coaster attack my mind and body. Why can't I just say no?

"Dinner," he starts again.

"Fine, lunch," I relent, folding like a house of cards.

So much for my conviction—though I did change the meal on him. *Ha!* Like that's some big win. While I certainly did fold, I do feel some victory in making it lunch instead of dinner. That evening meal comes with too much pressure and expectation. I don't want him to think I'm easy, because I'm not, although he is awfully tempting.

"Excellent. Give me your phone and I'll text myself so I can contact you with the details."

As I rummage in my purse, girly squeals sound from behind me. Ignoring their childish behaviour (to be fair, I'm biting back a silly grin myself), I hand him my phone.

After a few taps, he hands the phone back, not letting go of my hand. The warmth and strength in his hold calms my nerves and excites me. "I'll talk to you tomorrow."

"Okay," I say with a shaky voice.

"This is for you," he says, pulling the pink flower from his jacket lapel.

I hadn't even noticed the camellia, the same flower used as centerpieces in his restaurant. Tucking the delicate bloom into the buttonhole of my jacket, his fingers lightly graze my collarbone, sending sparks shooting to the tips of my toes.

"Thank you." My reply is breathy, my heart racing.

"It's a camellia," he states, his stare warm and penetrating.

"I know, it's beautiful." I must be in the Twilight Zone; this is all so surreal. It's exciting and naughty, yet also a bad idea all around. "Thank you," I say with a small smile, truly moved by his sweet and romantic gesture.

"Do you know what a pink camellia means?" he asks coyly.

I shake my head. Captivated. Hanging on his every word.

"It means longing and desire," he rumbles. A startling quiver ripples through my low belly as if there's a direct connection between his deeply sexy voice and my insides. His smoldering eyes drill into mine. "Goodnight Olivia, I look forward to our lunch date."

Leaning in, he softly kisses my cheek, his warm lips lingering on my skin longer than necessary. Relishing every second of contact, I deeply inhale the intoxicating aroma of spice, freshness, and something undeniably masculine emanating from him. His mouth trails from my cheek to my ear, his lips tickling my flesh along the way. "I'll be longing for you," he whispers huskily.

Seven

SAM

Fourteen hours. It's been fourteen hours since kissing Olivia. Seeing Olivia. *Pathetic*—that's what I am. It might as well be fourteen days for how restless my night was and how my morning is dragging. Kissing her cheek last night wasn't enough; I found it difficult to leave it at that, and it also left me hard and agitated.

I have a ton of work to do before stealing away for a few hours for lunch with Olivia. I need to get this paperwork done, but my mind isn't cooperating. I can't concentrate on one simple task without being bombarded by thoughts of the sumptuous brunette who has cast her spell on me.

I'm not sure what lunch will bring and I haven't thought much further than that, though I need to figure out this distance thing. Lunch won't be enough, and I have a feeling I won't be satisfied.

Olivia is waiting in the hotel lobby at eleven thirty. It's impossible to miss her, her glossy, espresso locks tousled, softly framing her fresh face. She's a vision of sweetness in a soft, pink jersey top that perfectly drapes her torso. The curve of her breasts taunts me, and her long, lean legs are clad in faded, tight jeans, practically painted on. Her cute, black ankle boots and the Ray-Bans perched on top of her head complete her casual yet sexy look.

"Hey there." I greet her with a brush of my lips on her cheek. She smells divine and while I want to linger longer, I can't handle the temptation.

"Hi." She releases a soft sigh and looks at me with a smile.

I take her hand and as we leave the hotel, she falls into step beside me easily, comfortably strolling the streets of downtown Montreal. As we're walking, her phone rings and we stop for her to answer it. She looks down at the screen, hits a button that stops the ringing, then tucks it back into her purse.

"Everything okay?" I ask. Her pretty face is scrunched in what looks like annoyance or irritation as she nibbles on her bottom lip.

"Yes, it was nothing," she says dismissively. "Where are we going?"

"To one of my favorite restaurants. Do you like Portuguese cuisine?"

"I don't know, I've never had it."

"You're in for a treat. The food is out of this world. I thought it would be a great place to enjoy the afternoon and get to know each other."

Glancing at me as we enter the restaurant, she goes quiet and remains so as we are seated. She's contemplative. Once we've ordered sparkling wine, she breaks the silence. "You're really passionate about food, aren't you?"

I'm unable to help the big smile that spreads across my face. She mirrors me with her own lovely smile. "Yes, I love being a chef."

"It's obvious from the way your face lit up when talking about this place." I chuckle at her observation, clinking our glasses in anticipation of our meal. Our server waits expectantly to take our order.

"Do you know what you want?"

I nod, asking, "Can I order for you?"

I'm not sure how she'll react. Some women love it and others hate it, thinking I'm going all chauvinist on them. It's not that; it's that I know this menu almost as well as my own and want her to experience the best dishes.

"I don't usually let men order for me, but go ahead, I trust you," she shyly states.

"You do?" She nods with a small smile.

"Sam," the owner—a friend of mine—calls from across the restaurant. We both turn to look in his direction. Before I can say anything, he's upon us, hugging me, shaking my hand, and introducing himself to Olivia.

In his usual gregarious manner, he dominates the conversation and orders for both of us. Of course, who better than the owner to order for you, but he's cramping my style and try as I might, he doesn't get the hint. I love the man and usually enjoy his company, but right now I'd rather he be anywhere but at our table. Finally, twenty minutes in, when our appetizers arrive, he says his goodbyes. *Alone at last.*

"Sorry about that," I whisper when he's out of earshot.

"No, don't be. He's funny, and it's obvious he likes you a lot."

"Yeah, he's a good guy. We worked together years ago, before we got our own kitchens. You'll love the food."

While waiting for our meal, I take the opportunity to get to know her better, find out more about this captivating woman I know so little about but have such strong desires for.

"So, why Montreal?"

"Pardon?"

"Well, it seems like you're on a trip with your friends, so I just wondered, why Montreal?"

"Oh, it's a girls getaway. We wanted to leave the city, go somewhere fun that wasn't too far."

"And lucky me, you decided to eat at my restaurant. Montreal is fantastic for amazing restaurants, so why Beaulieu's?" I'm asking for selfish reasons.

Yes, I want to know because I want to know everything about Olivia, but I'm also a restaurateur and thus want to know what drew these out-of-town women to my spot. A part of me knows I, Samson Beaulieu, may very well have been part of the allure, regardless of the food, and while the thought brings some disappointment, I'm not destroyed—not when I'm just as interested in her.

Taking a sip of her sparkling wine, she stalls. "Um, I didn't know about Beaulieu's," she answers awkwardly, a slight tinge to her cheeks. "In my defense, I usually let Erin do all the planning and I tag along. She's the one who knew all about your restaurant."

I feign offense with a scoff and clutch my chest. She giggles, her shoulders subtly shaking as a few strands of her dark hair fall into her eyes. Resisting the urge to touch her, to brush her hair away from her face, I clasp my hands in my lap.

"I'm kidding, although you could have lied and gone easy on my ego," I jest. "In all seriousness, what did you think of it?"

Sitting straighter, all joking aside, she looks at me with her earnest coffee-colored eyes. "I loved it. The food was fantastic. You're very talented."

"Thank you." Her compliment warms me.

"Did I make up for my brutal honesty?" she quips, a grin gracing her lips.

"Ah, so it was just a ploy, telling me what I want to hear?"

We laugh and talk a bit more about what she's seen and done while in Montreal. I share a few must-sees and some of my favorite spots.

Our lunch arrives and while eating, she asks, "So how did you discover cooking was your calling?"

"Wow, that's a loaded question."

I don't usually share my entire story with many, and she has no clue what she's asking for. Never one to play games, I don't want to hold anything back, but I also sense we need more time together before I give her all the details.

"Well, it's a long story. My mother died when I was two." She gasps, putting down her fork and giving me her undivided attention. Things just got too heavy for my liking, and I'm only giving the highlights.

"My grandparents raised me. They were good people, and while we didn't have much, they gave me plenty of love. My grand-père died when I was seven and my grand-mère when I was fourteen. At that point, I had no other family, so I was put in foster care. I hated it. I constantly ran away, got into trouble. I never could stay with one family for too long and most were just in it for the measly government check. One night, I was starving. I'd been on the streets for over a week and food was scarce, so I snuck into the back of a restaurant and raided the kitchen. I was ravenous and not very smart, making a ruckus as I ransacked the fridge. The chef, who also turned out to be the owner, caught me."

"Oh no."

"It was the best thing that ever happened to me. He could have called the cops and I would have been put in juvie. Instead, he put me to work to pay for my crime and, I believe, to keep me out of trouble. We both knew he was taking a risk on me. I think we both needed it at that time. He made me go back to foster care and made sure I was put in a good home, using his connections and good name to get me in with a decent family."

"His good name? He was well known?"

"Yes. Have you heard of Bastien Villeneuve?"

"*The* Bastien Villeneuve?" she asks, astonished. I nod, and her shining eyes widen. His reputation precedes him and her reaction proves it. "Yes, I'm not a foodie, but I saw a best-of show and he was featured. He's the only chef in Canada to get a Michelin rating." She's in awe and I can't help but beam with pride.

"Yes, the one and only. He's like a father to me, the only one I ever had."

She rests her petite hand on top of mine and gently squeezes. Our eyes meet and she smiles warmly. "Tell me more," she eagerly says.

Her willingness to hear my story is heartwarming and I fall more in *like* with this woman. "He arranged it so I could work after school and on weekends at his restaurant. At first, I hated him. I was a difficult teenager with a huge chip on my shoulder. I didn't appreciate this old man stepping in and telling me what to do. He worked me to the bone, making me do many of the menial but crucial tasks of the kitchen. I'm not sure when it happened, but somewhere along the way I grew to look forward to those afternoons and weekends in his kitchen, and over time, it became my passion. I worked in Bas's kitchen throughout high school, then went to culinary school. After graduation, I went to France and worked in a few kitchens. It wasn't glamorous, but I learned a lot that year. I then worked at a few more restaurants in Montreal before opening my first restaurant five years ago, then Beaulieu's three years ago."

"I'm so impressed. You're so accomplished. And all this at your age."

I don't miss the challenge in her tone. She expectantly watches and waits for my response, reminiscent of last night. If she thinks I'm going to give away my leverage and the one thing I fear might end this all too soon, she's sadly mistaken.

"Seriously, how old are you?"

"You didn't Google me?"

She laughs. "No, I didn't. I wanted to and had the question typed in, but I didn't hit enter."

Her age doesn't bother me at all. It's her hang-up, and it rubs me the wrong way. I don't want her hesitant. I've never been one for an easy lay—perhaps that's what she thinks I want. Sure, I've had my share of one-night stands, but few and far between. While I love sex as much as the next guy, I want to know who I'm sharing a bed with. It doesn't have to be a long-term relationship, but I want some kind of connection, if only for the night.

With Olivia, I want to get to know her. Badly. The want sits as deep within me as the Marianas Trench. I haven't felt this way in a long time. Truly, I finally know what they mean by someone getting under your skin.

"Well, you'll have to wait. My age is of no importance," I reply in an aristocratic British accent. "Let's order dessert and you can tell me more about yourself. Tell me something that would surprise me."

"I have a son and a daughter," she says boldly, like she's lobbing a grenade. I'm not fazed and nod for her to continue. "Drew's nineteen and just finished his first year of university. Paige is sixteen going on thirty. She's in high school and doesn't know what she wants to do with her life except torment her mother," she quips, though it's easy to see her pride and love for her children. There is a luminosity to her eyes and her smile grows as she continues. "Drew is smart, level-headed, and my rock. Paige is my sweet girl, lots of fun and always up to something, but…" She sighs and her smile falls a bit.

I wait anxiously, hoping she'll continue. She doesn't. She picks up her coffee mug, and her pink lips pucker and blow over the hot liquid. It's a herculean effort to not lose it to thoughts of the myriad ways and places I'd like her lips on me. "Go on," I request.

"I really don't want to get into it. It would only be a downer. What I will say is, Paige and I are going through a rough patch right now. I'm not her favorite person, and it's got nothing to do with the whole mother-teenage daughter dynamic."

With a sigh, she looks at me, perhaps wanting me to change the conversation. Save her from dwelling on something that is obviously difficult and painful for her.

"Drew sounds like a good guy. What's he studying?"

"He wants to be a lawyer. He's got his whole educational path mapped out." She chuckles.

"And their father?"

"I'm divorced."

"Phew, I'm not out with a married woman." She laughs at my light-hearted tone. "Tell me about your passion. You know mine—what's yours?"

"I recently started my own business, Cassidy Designs. I'm an interior designer."

"You like it?"

"Yes, very much so. I love it."

"And you just started it? Why not sooner?"

She pauses reflectively before answering, "I guess because after I graduated, I got married and worked at a design firm, briefly. When I found out I was pregnant, starting a family became my priority."

I nod, not knowing how that would feel, but imagining the commitment and energy needed to raise children. We move on to lighter topics on the way back to her hotel. I'm tempted to hold her hand but stop myself, sensing the gesture would be too forward and too soon for Olivia. While we had a great lunch and she's dropped the age thing for now, it's still the elephant in the room.

In the lobby, she gives me an easy, open smile. "I had such a great time. Thank you." She squeezes my hand.

"I'm glad." Flipping my palm up, I capture her hand and she glances down at our entwined fingers. With my gaze on her, she raises her head, trepidation lining her lovely features. "Go to dinner with me tomorrow night."

Lightly laughing, she subtly steps back. She won't get away. I'm interested. I need more. I gently tug at her hand. Her eyes pop back to mine.

"Sam." The way she says my name hints at so many plausible meanings, some potentially negative and some hopeful. With a small smile, I'm silent. I won't provide a rebuttal until she objects.

"I live in Toronto. I leave on Monday morning," she protests without giving me anything I can work with. Raising my eyebrows, I widen my smile. "I can't do this."

"Do what? Have dinner with me? What, you don't eat? You have to eat."

Rolling her eyes, she tugs at her hand again, successfully pulling free. I deliberately let her go, not wanting to freak her out. It's plain to see she's struggling with this.

"Very funny," she drolly replies. "Besides, you never told me how old you are."

"Go to dinner with me and I will."

"Not fair." She lightly taps my bicep. "A deal's a deal. I went to lunch with you, now tell me."

"How old do you think I am?" I'm enjoying this game.

"Come on, Sam. Just tell me."

"How old do you think I am? I promise, once you tell me what you think, I'll tell you my age."

"Hmm." She taps her forefinger on her lips, contemplating. I'm not buying it; she has definitely already speculated on my age, and it obviously bothers her. There is no way she hasn't guessed. I don't call her on it, though, as I'm enjoying her performance.

"Thirty."

"Nope. I'm thirty-five. Now go to dinner with me."

Olivia's face is impassive. Tilting her head to the side, she silently examines me. I'm not wild about waiting for her response, but I like the attention of her beautiful eyes roaming my face.

"Okay," she quietly says. "Tomorrow night, dinner. Goodbye, Sam." She plants a quick, chaste kiss on my cheek before turning toward the elevators.

Eight

OLIVIA

The smooth mauve stick glides over my lips and I smack them together. Sin's perched on the tub watching my every move. "You look great, Liv. So, you like this guy?"

My phone vibrates and lights up as I'm placing the lid on my lipstick—Pete, *again*. I hit the home button and huff. He's being obnoxiously incessant. He even tried calling me when I was out with Sam yesterday.

Turning to face Sin, she's got her 'I've got your number' look on her face and I wonder if she knows Pete's hounding me. Resting my hip on the vanity, I answer her question. "Yes, he's really charming and sweet, but this can't go anywhere, so stop looking at me like that."

"How am I looking at you?" As I walk out the bathroom, she trails behind me with a teasing grin on her face. "Like I know you're looking forward to this date?"

"It's not a date. It's just two friends going out to dinner. I'm not ready to start seeing anyone and I'll never date a younger man," I firmly state.

"Seriously?" Erin pipes up. "Are you still on that kick? Who cares how old the guy is? He's obviously into you, otherwise he wouldn't have asked you out—not once, but *twice*," She's holding up two fingers. "Just throw the guy a bone and bone him tonight." Both Sin and Erin give in to fits of laughter.

My eyes widen at the same time there's a knock at our suite door. Erin beams like she knows who it is, and I have a sneaking suspicion it's Sam.

"Did you…? How'd you…?" I can't form a coherent thought other than being shocked that Sam could be on the other side of the door. I was supposed to meet him in the lobby. I didn't want him to know our room number.

Erin giggles and hustles to the door, swinging it open to reveal Samson Beaulieu in all his glory. He's dressed casually in dark blue jeans and a crisp white button-down shirt with the sleeves rolled up his deliciously taut forearms.

I've never been fascinated by forearms before, but when I saw Sam in his kitchen, the flex and definition of his arms had me weak in the knees. I could look at his arms in motion all day. Watching him chop, stir, taste—pure bliss.

The deep, warm baritone of his voice snaps me out of my reverie. "Good evening, ladies," Sam warmly greets us. "Olivia, you're stunning."

Heat blooms within me, flushing my cheeks. "Thank you." I'm wearing a light blue paisley halter maxi dress with brown gladiator sandals. The straps tie at my neck with an open back, and two thin strings tie midway across my bare back to keep the bodice from gaping and revealing too much.

We leave my friends with the promise of meeting up with them after dinner at some bar on Crescent Street. After all, it is our last night in Montreal, and Erin insists we go out with a bang—more accurately, she'll pick up some guy and get banged.

Sam hails a cab and takes me to a quaint restaurant that's known as a landmark in the city. He says it's a must when in Montreal, and he's right. The food is great and doesn't disappoint with a menu loaded with French bistro classics.

"So, I wanted to ask last night…how long have you been divorced?"

I nervously laugh at his personal question, yet it never crosses my mind to avoid answering. He shared yesterday, and I have no reservations sharing my past.

"Eight months. Before that, we were separated for about the same length of time."

"Wow, you were married for a long time."

"Yes."

"And do you mind me asking why you got divorced?"

"Something tells me you'd still ask even if I did, but I don't mind," I tease. It's a long and twisted story, and some people don't get it—even some of my closest friends, like Erin.

"It sounds like such a cliché. We met in my last year of university. He's a good guy and for the most part, it was a good marriage, but our relationship got to a point where we wanted different things. He couldn't give me what I wanted, and I was very much alone. I felt isolated, and that only intensified as my kids became more independent. He was wrapped up in his work, all the time. He's a successful investment banker working for one of the big banks. He's good at what he does, is driven by it, and I, ah…I felt neglected. When I tried to… God, I sound like a whiny woman," I groan.

"No, not at all," he strongly reassures. "Olivia, not at all." Reaching, he takes my hand. "Don't censor this. I want to hear it all, from the heart. I'm not judging you."

Looking deeply into his eyes, they are filled with genuine warmth. "I don't want to put this all on him. I told him for years what I needed, how I felt we'd veered off in two different directions, then it took something so silly to change everything. We were supposed to go away for a weekend, just the two of us, to New York City. It was a chance to be alone, and I was also going for an interior design conference. I was itching to get back to work and was starting to dip my toe into that world again. At the last minute, Pete canceled, using work as his excuse…again. I went alone, and that trip was my wake-up call. We were no longer partners. We were amicable, more like friends living together. Even at that, there were times when we felt like acquaintances."

Pete's lack of support and indifference about me wanting to go back to work, about pursuing my dream, really cut deep. While I'd made the choice to be a stay-at-home mom, he didn't acknowledge what I had put on hold, and now that I wanted a chance at that, he didn't care. He didn't stop me, but he also didn't talk about it or show any interest.

I knew if I started my own business, it would be in addition to all that I already did. My life would be like I was a single working mom, so I thought why not make that a reality rather than continue the building resentment, hurt, and disappointment by staying with him.

Sam's face is attentive, his eyebrows arched inquisitively. He opens his mouth, then closes it, a question on the tip of his tongue.

"You can ask. I did. I asked the same question too."

He hesitantly smiles. "Was he cheating?"

"No, he wasn't. I sometimes wonder if it would have been easier if he were. The twisted part is, I think I could have understood that better. There would have been something, someone to blame for the end of our marriage...someone other than ourselves."

I tried for years to get through to Pete, and that thought only saddens me. A marriage takes work, the love and passion at the beginning of any relationship changes and simmers, but our relationship got to the point where I was the only one trying, or at least that's how it felt. Pete didn't react or want to discuss any of it. Even when I threatened to leave, the first three or four times, it was an idle threat. The thought of walking away from my marriage was scary and heartbreaking. I don't know what I could have done differently. It wasn't a decision made overnight; I spent more than five years trying to reconnect with him countless times, shamelessly trying to rekindle our relationship, have time together outside of being parents, but all of it went nowhere.

"I understand," he says solemnly.

"It wasn't a decision made lightly, and I tried many times and in many ways. Some are too embarrassing to ever think about, let alone share," I jest, hoping to lighten the mood.

"Don't worry, I don't want to know," he says soberly. I raise my eyebrow, quizzical. His eyes smolder, pinning me. "Olivia, I don't want to think about you with him, or with any other man."

I swallow the lump that's formed in my throat. My stomach dips and a kaleidoscope of butterflies take off in my belly. "Oh," I say stupidly.

Sam's attentiveness is in such contrast to my recent years with Pete. I recall telling Pete how I was feeling and him being completely unresponsive. It was like I was talking to a wall. I don't say this to be malicious, but while he wasn't physically or verbally abusing me, it truly hurt, and it tore me up inside.

His silence and indifference took its toll on me in so many ways. I realize now I was depressed for a while and I gained weight. I stopped caring and withdrew. As much as I love my kids, there was a point where I could only do the bare minimum. I was just keeping my head above water and I hated it. I hated that I put so much into a relationship where I felt alone. I internalized a lot of negative crap. It was eating me up from the inside out.

The New York trip woke me up. Meeting and talking to people energized me, got me excited about something, and I wanted to, *needed* to get back into the design business. Ending my marriage was the hardest decision I ever had to make.

"Thanks for sharing," Sam says, bringing me out of my dark, sad thoughts. "I can only imagine what it must feel like. It sounds like you did the right thing."

"I know I did. It wasn't easy and there's still some pain from it, especially with Paige, but I truly believe in the long run, we'll be good."

When we arrive at the bar after nine, the place is packed. It's dimly lit with chic furniture and music in the background. With his height, Sam's able to spot Tamsin and Erin easily. He effortlessly guides me through the crowd, holding my hand as we're jostled and bumped along the way.

As we approach the table, my friends are with four young men and one woman. Most call out greetings, even those that don't know us. I share a look with Tamsin and her expression is amused as well as fatigued; I assume the latter is due to Erin. She made no secret of her plans for the night: to find a man and hook up. She's majorly flirting with her target, and the chase is over; she's moving in to conquer.

Erin readily introduces us to the men around the table, all of whom are cute and under thirty, if I had to guess. Sin is situated beside what appears to be a couple and she's deep in conversation with them.

One drink in—champagne for me and Stella for Sam—and a high-pitched squeal interrupts our conversation.

"Sam! It's so lovely to see you."

A blonde, five-foot-nothing waif drapes her petite frame over him, practically climbing into his lap. Sam's stunned as she leans in, plastering her chest against his and wrapping her hands around his neck.

She kisses him on the cheek, not once, not twice, but three times. It's a French thing, but that doesn't mean I have to like it. Sam's surprised and uncomfortable but he hides it well and recovers quickly, giving her a warm smile.

"Yasmine, it's lovely to see you. How are you?"

"I'm wonderful now that you're here," she exclaims, her words thick with her French accent.

I strain to hear her over the loud music and chatter; it doesn't help that her back is turned to me. She slips into French and I'm only able to understand about half of what she's saying. My high school French helps, though not nearly enough.

Sam looks to me apologetically. I swallow the lump in my throat and my irrational wish for him to get rid of her. As he nudges her out of his arms, she barely moves an inch, then he motions to me. Peering over her shoulder, she looks at me as he introduces us.

"Yasmine Thibault, this is Olivia Cassidy. Yasmine's father is a friend."

The blonde leech with her plastic smile and blank eyes coos, "It's a pleasure to meet you."

Before I can respond, she swivels back to Sam. Her thin, stringy hair whips past my shoulder and I want nothing more than to yank on it. *Shit, where did that come from?* I'm a grown woman and this gnat brings out the teenage mean girl in me.

"I almost forgot to tell you, Papa is here. He's leaving shortly. He'd love to talk to you before he goes," Yasmine says.

"Olivia, excuse me," he says, his expression contrite. "I'll only be gone a few minutes."

As he stands, his hand clasps my knee, gently squeezing, calming me. Yasmine watches, her eyes narrowing at our contact.

"Papa just adores Sam, as do I," she gushes once he's gone. I sit stonily, preparing for the barb or two I'd bet my life are about to come. I know her kind. "And how do you know Sam? Were you his babysitter or something?"

One for the blonde bimbo.

"No, I wasn't."

"Then who are you?" she rudely asks, like she has a right to question me.

Instead of telling her where to go, I remind myself that I don't know who she is and I don't care.

"Sam and I are friends." I say it as much for her benefit as for mine.

"Papa and I are huge fans of Sam. You know, on Friday night, it was my birthday, and do you know what he did for me?" Her eyes sparkle as she barely pauses. "He's so sweet, that man. We were at Beaulieu's and he made a dinner especially for me, in celebration of my birthday. He doesn't do that for just anyone."

Her words hang in the air between us like an archer's arrow mid-flight, aimed directly for my heart. She needs to work on her subtlety—her tactics are as blatant as thunder in a rain storm. I smile, though it's tight and short-lived.

If there was any doubt about me disliking this woman, it's gone now. Her relationship with Sam is ambiguous, deliberately so, thanks to her. I don't like her and these games that she so desperately wants to play. This girl is not down with that.

Sam and I are friends. *Just friends.* She doesn't need to know any more than that, and who he dates or makes dinner for is none of my business.

Tamsin rescues me by bringing me into a conversation with the young couple around childrearing. At some point, Yasmine leaves. Good riddance.

Nine

OLIVIA

An hour later, Sam's still not back. Every once in a while, one of my friends gives me a knowing, sympathetic glance. Shrugging off the silly feeling of rejection, I try to enjoy myself. It's my weekend. I'm not going to spend it wondering where my new friend Sam is, because that's just it—we're just friends. We had dinner. It was only dinner.

Like he can read my thoughts, my 'just dinner' friend comes into view over the shoulder of Jean François, the twenty-something accountant who is desperately trying and miserably failing to pick me up. Sam practically prowls toward me with his eyes narrowed, brow furrowed, and lips mashed in a thin line.

"What are you drinking? Let me buy you a drink," Jean François slurs inches from my face, and I blink as a whiff of rye stings my eyes.

His self-important smile and cocky stance permeate the confined space between us. He's annoying. Like Sam did earlier in the evening, the man's leaning in, close to my ear, so he can be heard. His hand is on the back of my chair, and it's not lost on me or on Sam that his thumb is grazing my exposed shoulder blade.

"Olivia." My name is harsh on Sam's lips.

My spine straightens in alarm and Jean François swivels to meet Sam's dark eyes, also alarmed, trying to steady himself, in case he needs to prepare for an altercation.

Sam ignores him, eyes pinned on me, softening as he nears. When he weaves his hand into my hair at the nape of my neck, I relax, his gesture securing and reassuring. My body tingles on contact. My heart rate spikes and warmth blooms in my chest.

"I'm so sorry. Daniel Thibault is a potential investor and I needed to speak with him. Then as soon as he left, his daughter, Yasmine, fainted." I fight to not roll my eyes. *Of course she did.* "She has no one to take her home."

I cut him off, seeing exactly where this is going. "It's fine. Take her home. Dinner was lovely. Thanks, Sam." I'm polite but dismissive.

He rears back slightly, obviously surprised, then he's inches from my face. "Come with me. We'll drop Yasmine off and then I'll take you back to the hotel."

As much as I'd like to spend more time with him, it would only prolong the inevitable goodbye. Like ripping the band aid off, I prefer to end this now and get the sting over with.

"Sam, I'd rather not." Also, while I don't say it, I don't like the woman and have no desire to spend another minute with her. "Tonight's our last night and I promised to spend it with my girls." Facing him, he comes closer, wedging himself in between Jean François and me, forcing the younger man to step back. "I enjoyed our meals and getting to know you. If I come back to Montreal any time soon, I'll let you know," I softly say.

A shrewd grin appears as his eyes sharpen, even more penetrating, like he's looking inside me.

"Olivia, you're so cute." He chuckles. "We're not done," he firmly and loudly states, loud enough for Jean François to catch it. He kisses me, full on the lips. It's tender, light, and over way too fast.

Before I can regain my composure, he's gone. His taste—a mixture of the hops and barley from the beer he had earlier and something spicy yet fresh—lingers long after he leaves.

Waking at six o'clock in the morning is pure torture, particularly because we'd only just gone to sleep. Erin insisted we stay at the bar 'til last call, then we dragged our sorry asses back to the hotel over two and a half hours ago.

"I'm too old for this," Sin croaks from across the room. She's slumped over the side of her bed, her blonde hair disheveled, head in hand.

"I need coffee," Erin whines.

"You said it, you get it," Tamsin and I groggily deliver in unison. Our directive takes me back to our school days when that was just our thing. Erin growls, tosses back her comforter, and stands. "Dammit, when am I going to learn to keep my damn mouth shut?"

Despite the achiness and fatigue, I giggle. Erin was always bad at this game. She stomps to the washroom with clothes in hand while we both flop back into bed. I'm so glad I packed yesterday—it means I have another fifteen minutes of shut-eye before I must get dressed.

By the time Erin returns with our coffees, Tamsin and I are as ready as we'll ever be in our current state. I'm in comfy clothes—leggings and a baggy off-the-shoulder sweater—and my hair is in a messy bun.

Before I can take the little green thingy that keeps the coffee warm out of my lid, there's a knock at our door. Erin's closest and flings the door wide open; Sam stands in the doorway, looking like every woman's fantasy. His brown hair is slightly wet, likely from just showering, and he's clean shaven. His black faded jeans mold to his long, sculpted legs and his white fitted t-shirt defines his firm, broad chest. The pièce de résistance is the leather jacket casually slung over his shoulder. He looks like he just walked off the runway. *Be still my heart.* If I weren't hungover, I'd think my lightheadedness was because of him.

"Sam," Erin cheers. She's obviously had her mandatory espresso shot before the coffee she has in her hand. She's way too chipper for having gotten only two hours sleep.

"Ladies." His voice is deep and smooth.

His eyes flit from Erin to Tamsin, then rest on me. Just a look from his piercing eyes has me undone. With my lack of sleep, no makeup, and grungy attire, I'm in no shape to face him.

Erin grabs her suitcase, rolling it 'til she stands directly in front of Sam. "Lover boy, you blew it last night. Good luck," she states with a pat to his pec.

Sam arches his brow and Erin matches his expression in jest as she walks out of the room. Sin is right behind her.

"Tamsin," Sam warmly says with a tip of his chin.

"Sin," I call to her. She veers back to look at me questioningly. I don't have to ask— it's in her face. "It was you."

"Me? What are you talking about?"

"I thought it was Erin who told Sam our room number the other day, but it was you, *and* you told him when we were leaving today." Her face flames and that's all the confirmation I need. "What happened to chicks before dicks?"

Sam coughs, eyes wide, shocked at my crass comment. Sin laughs and winks at me.

"Exactly," she responds, like that answers everything, before leaving us alone.

Sam enters the suite, shutting the door behind him.

"Hi." His tone is low and heavy.

I fidget with a loose strand of my hair, trying to weave it back into my haphazard bun. Covering my hand with his, he steadies then lowers it. With his other hand, his finger twines around the wayward lock, intent on wrapping my hair around his finger.

"So soft and shiny," he rasps. "I told you last night, we're not done." His voice is soft like silk against my skin, and shivers cascade down my spine.

"Sam, this was two people getting to know each other over a couple of wonderful meals. It's time for me to go home." One side of his mouth quirks upward and he shakes his head at me. "Besides, you're too young," I add, like that says it all.

Sighing, he releases my hair to rest his hands on my shoulders. "Olivia, it's only a number. It doesn't matter." He gently squeezes.

"It matters to me," I try again, more firmly, hoping he gets my point.

"Why?"

He's observing me like he'll find the answer in my eyes, in the way I hold myself. The weird thing is, I'm not able to answer. My reason is something intangible. I can't name it or put words to it; it's a feeling, gnawing at my insides.

It's my insecurities. It's not only his age, although that definitely bugs me. It's that he's young *and* beautiful. He can have whoever he wants. He could leave, and while that's true of any relationship...he's younger, and it feels like that makes it more of a possibility.

"I'm not ready for a relationship," I declare, gentle yet boldly honest.

My words contradict the growing disquiet at the actuality of my fears. Having been married for twenty years, being single and now faced with the prospect of dating is causing some serious jitters. That's natural, isn't it? Yet standing in front of Sam, this man who likes me, it seems weak and stupid. Stupid to walk away from the possibilities.

"Okay." His hands soothingly glide across my shoulders, up the sides of my neck. His thumbs caress my jaw as his nose delicately rubs against mine. A small whimper passes my lips and my eyes flutter close. I'm a fool.

"What if we just take it one day at a time? Let's not label it. We'll just enjoy it," he says.

My eyes open. His intense pale ones are so close, inches from me as his forehead comes to rest against mine. Our lips are practically touching.

"Olivia, you see, I like you. I want to explore this. I don't want to walk away, and age, distance, you name it—it doesn't matter, not to me. I want to get to know you." Each word strokes my heart, touches me and floods me with warmth.

The irony of this situation is not lost on me. Sam easily and willingly shares with me. He has no hang-ups or trepidation being honest about his feelings or showing affection. I've spent years with a man who couldn't give me that, a man who stopped showing me that I mattered, and now, here I am contemplating turning my back on Sam, a man who is giving me just that.

I swallow the lump in my throat. As I inhale deeply, his scent wafts over me. My lips touch his, feather light, as I whisper, "Okay. No labels. Let's just take this nice and slow."

As soon as my terrifyingly honest words leave my mouth, my heart rate spikes and I break out in a cold sweat. Before I can overthink it, take it back or panic, he slides his hands deeper into my hair. Weaving his fingers along my scalp, gently but insistently, he tugs me closer to him. My breath hitches and shallows at the press of my chest against his.

My nipples tingle, my nerve endings on fire. His assertive move ignites my craving, the one I'm so desperately trying to suppress. Like a match to a bonfire, his touch kindles my desire, starting small and mounting, smoldering deep within me.

My fists clench his tee, anchoring myself to his hard body as my knees weaken, sway, then buckle when his mouth seizes mine, blistering and consuming. Pulling me closer, he clutches me tightly, his tongue hard and demanding, coaxing my lips apart. Willingly, I give him entry, losing myself to his mind-blowing kiss.

He kisses me until I'm breathless, demolishing all kisses before. Virgin lips. Never been kissed. Taken. His lips mark me. Consume me. Raging want and a mighty need build within me as a deep moan escapes my lips.

Sam slows and his lips stop moving but remain on mine. Pressing his forehead against mine, his eyes open at the same time mine do. The wonderful crinkle at the corner of his eyes hint at his imminent smile before the upturn of his mouth against my lips. His look is reverent, like I am the sun, the moon, and the stars.

"Olivia, we're just getting started," he gruffly claims against my mouth, kissing me with his words.

Carefully releasing his fingers from my hair, he steps back. His release leaves a vacancy and a chill, not only at the nape of my neck, but deep in my core. The need to stay connected is strong. Sam places his hands on my shoulders, and the icy void vanishes.

His thumb rubs a small patch of skin on my neck. Unable to simply walk away, I kiss his scruffy cheek, not daring to go near his lips. As much as I want to, we will never leave this hotel room if I do.

With another light kiss to my forehead, he releases me. The distance is vast and icy. I shiver, quickly brushing it away before he grabs my suitcase and takes my hand.

As the hotel door inches closed behind us, I shriek, remembering my coffee. Diving for the narrowing crack in the door, Sam reacts quickly, wedging his foot in the opening. With my coffee in hand, I smile with gratitude.

In the elevator, we're still close, hand in hand, comfortably silent. Apart from my quickening pulse and my jittery stomach, everything is normal, though I'm still reeling from our knee-weakening kiss.

With my first sip, the dark, hot elixir hits my tongue; my taste buds rejoice and I release a low, satisfied moan. Sam snaps his head my way, want ablaze in the depths of his eyes. His gaze lands on my mouth.

"Sorry," I whisper, embarrassed. "It's my first taste of coffee for the day and I so need it."

He chuckles. "I get it. Just go easy on me. You're leaving and your sounds, first in the room, and now…" He pauses as I look on in eager anticipation. "You're killing me over here. What I'd like to do to you…"

His words linger without further explanation, like a tease and a promise. It's my turn to rake my eyes over his face, stopping at his lips. I'm pretty sure we're both thinking about the same thing: our kiss, the best kiss of my life.

Unable to resist, I latch onto his shoulders, on my toes, and pull him in for another soul-searing kiss. His mouth captures mine and for a fleeting, breath-catching moment, I worry how I'll be able to cope without this for the weeks we'll be apart. We haven't even begun and I'm already hooked.

Ten

OLIVIA

"Olivia, what do you think about changing around this area so the stools are over there and the chaise lounge is here?" Mrs. Preston calls from across the open space, which will one day be the lounge of her hotel spa.

With a deep sigh, I search for inner strength and sanity. While winning this project is the biggest coup of my infant career and has already brought in new clients and created buzz for Cassidy Designs, working with Eliza Preston is challenging on good days.

She has an opinion on everything, yet changes her mind like the wind. We only just agreed on the final layout of the spa, for the fifth time, last night, and I've already ordered a significant amount of the materials. There is no room for changes at this point.

"Well, Eliza, we could. It would certainly look fine. You do recall we spoke yesterday about having the stools over there"—I point to the original location—"because, as you pointed out, it would allow for more seating, give more open space for the guests, and separate the conversation area from those who want to relax."

I hold my breath and hope she buys my positioning. She didn't point that out, I did, but making her think it was her idea is my last-ditch effort. I'm not sure I can have this conversation for the millionth time.

"Oh yes, thank you for reminding me dear. I don't know what I was thinking. That makes perfect sense." She waves her dainty fingers in the air with a smile. "Well, I'm going to get out of your hair," she says, heading for the elevator. *Yes.*

"Bye, Eliza. Talk to you soon." My phone rings; glancing down at the screen, it's Sam. "Olivia Cassidy," I answer in my most professional voice.

We've been talking and texting since Montreal and I've been enjoying every minute of it. I haven't felt like this in years, and can't help but feel younger and more alive as my interactions with Sam take me back to when I was in college, or even high school. Our flirting and daily talks remind me of the fun of dating.

"Ms. Cassidy, just the person I was looking for." Sam's deep, sexy voice sends tingles down my spine. "I've been thinking about you all day and wanted to hear your voice."

"Sam." I sigh. "It's great to hear your voice too. I'm glad you called," I boldly admit.

Why is it always easier to be truthful over the phone or via text? I'm pretty sure if Sam were here in person, while I'd love to see him, I wouldn't be nearly as bold.

"What's new with you? Did you get the shipment in today?"

Butterflies take flight in my stomach because he remembered I was stressing about a shipment. I don't know what to do with that. I can't recall a time when Pete would have remembered, let alone cared, about any of my concerns, then to actually ask me about it? I'm blown away.

"It came on time." The relief is clear in my voice. "And better yet, everything I ordered was there. You should have seen me screaming and dancing like a crazy woman down in the docking area this morning." I laugh.

"Dancing? Hmmm, I definitely would've liked to see that. Were you alone?"

"What? Why?"

"I want to know who might have seen your gorgeous body swaying and moving. I don't like the idea of other guys getting a look at you."

"Sam." I quickly dismiss his caveman comment, although the edge to his voice spreads warmth throughout me. "Really? I was alone."

"Good. You're going to have to dance for me sometime." His smooth voice skitters across my skin.

"*Sam.*" I blush, even though I'm alone and he's nearly six hundred kilometers away. "Tell me about your day." I change the subject.

"My day was okay, but I'd much rather talk about you. What are you doing now?"

"I'm at the hotel, finishing a few things, then I'm meeting a prospective client for dinner."

"Dinner? Do you usually have dinner with potential clients?"

"No, but he's leaving for Europe tomorrow and this was the only time he could see me within the next month."

"He?" It's obvious where this is going. He asked me similar questions about a week ago when I told him I was going to the theatre with a male client. I had to explain it was strictly business and that the man was married. I was doing the couple a favour, and it was also an opportunity for me to meet new people and promote my business.

"Sam, they're an older couple who want their cottage renovated. I met the wife a few days ago, but the husband couldn't be there. She's in Europe and he's following her, he leaves tomorrow."

"How much older?"

"Sam! Stop this." I laugh. "It's a business dinner and it'll likely be over in an hour."

Sam laughs too. "Sorry, Olivia. I don't like that I haven't seen you in weeks. When I hear all these things you're doing, all these men you're meeting, it's just…" He exhales. "It's silly, I agree, and I won't do it again. I guess this long-distance thing is new to me."

"Me too." While I'm not thrilled with his questions, I must admit that I like the attention. I like that he cares. "And I get it, but you've got nothing to worry about. I'm not looking to start anything with anyone else. What we have is working out just fine."

"Just fine? That's it?"

"More than fine, amazing!" We both laugh.

The rest of the week flies by with work, family, and friends. Sam and I continue to connect at least once daily, and my business is doing well. In addition to the hotel project, I've two smaller ones in progress and half a dozen lined up for the next six months. There's always the risk that one or two might fall through, but for now, I'm basking in the glory of how well I'm doing.

Today has been non-stop and I'm exhausted. It's only as I step out of the shower that I realize I haven't looked at my phone since well before lunch. I put it in my bag after leaving Jonah's and never took it out again.

I worked out with Sin, refusing to forgo that no matter how hectic my day was going to be. Then from that point on, it was go, go, go.

Wrapping the towel around me, I find my phone and see that the battery is dead. While it charges, I get dressed for bed, throwing on my cotton nightie.

Instinctively, I know that if anything bad had happened or if my kids were trying to reach me, I have a land line. There'd be messages if anything was wrong, but I can't deny feeling like I should know better. No matter how busy my day is, my kids need to be able to reach me.

After about twenty minutes of trying to put all the possible scenarios out of my mind, I check the phone. There's enough juice to turn it on and check my messages. There's nothing from my kids, but I do have several texts from various people, including a few from Sam.

Sam: Livvy, are you having a good day?

Four hours later:

Sam: Hey, you ignoring me? :)

Another five hours later:

Sam: Olivia, I know you're busy, just let me know you're okay

My heart sinks when the unnecessary stress I've caused him washes over me. This is the first time I've taken this long to respond, and it hits me that part of my trepidation about not checking my phone was my concern with possibly missing a call or text from him. I'm a lovesick teenager.

I call him, but it goes to voicemail. It's after ten o'clock, he's likely in the kitchen at one of his restaurants.

Me: Sam, I'm okay. Sorry for not responding sooner. Had a crazy day and stupidly left my phone in my purse. It was a case of out of sight, out of mind. I just tried calling you. How's your day been?

He immediately responds.

Sam: Better now that I know you're okay. Gimme a sec

I smile at his text and hop into bed, waiting for his next text, but instead, my phone rings.

"Sam, I'm so sorry."

"It's okay, I get it. I got worried and wondered if something had happened. I miss you and need to see you, soon." The urgency is obvious in his voice.

I want to see him too, although I haven't told him so. A trip to Montreal this month isn't possible for me because of things with the hotel—there's no Monday to Friday, nine to five now that construction is nearly complete—but I'll have more breathing room once I get over the hurdle of the next few weeks.

He's said several times that he misses me, but I never reciprocate, although I feel the same way. I think it might be too much given that I want to keep things casual, but the part I can't figure out is why he hasn't made plans to come here. I would've thought he'd have come to visit me by now.

On one hand, I'm okay with that—the distance can sometimes work to my advantage at keeping things cool—but on the other hand, if he's into me, why hasn't he made the trip to Toronto? Does he expect me to visit him all the time?

"Where are you tonight?"

"I'm at Beaulieu's going over some of the orders for the week, then I'm heading home. Are you in bed?" he asks suggestively.

"Um, yes."

"And what are you wearing?"

"A nightie." The thought of where this could go heats my chest.

His voice gets low. "Describe it to me."

"It's white, cotton."

"Livvy." His tone is a deep rumble with an edge. "Give me more."

With a nervous laugh, I say, "It's short, just covering my panties, with spaghetti straps."

"Spaghetti straps?"

Forgetting that most men don't have a clue what that is, I smile and explain, "Think tank top, but the straps are a lot thinner, almost string-like, or like *spaghetti*."

"Gotcha. Hmmm, I like the sound of that. I can almost picture you," he muses. "But you know what would really help?"

"What?"

"If you sent me a picture."

My breath hitches, I love the idea that he wants a picture, but at the same time, my stomach twists because *he wants a picture!*

"Um, Sam, I don't think that's a good idea."

"Why not? I do."

"Ah, um, I don't want a picture of me in my nightgown on your phone for just anyone to see."

"My phone's password protected and I promise you, no one will see it. Would it make you feel better if I sent a picture of me?"

It's silly to have these concerns, I trust him, and it's not like I'm sending him a picture of my naked body. *No way!*

"Okay, but you go first."

"Alright, hang on a sec." He chuckles.

There's some rustling, silence, and a whoosh of air or something before I get a ding indicating I have a text. Clicking on the icon, the gorgeous Sam Beaulieu's smiling—no, *beaming* at me with his 'no-panties-required' dimples.

The sight of him tugs at my heart as I'd love to see him in person right now, to touch him, then I remind myself that this is better. We're taking it slow and the fact that we live in two different cities helps. It helps keep me from losing myself or falling heart first into something I might never recover from.

"Olivia?" Sam calls through the phone.

"I got it, love your smile." I let a rare, raw moment slip through. I do love his smile, and it's definitely the highlight of my day.

"Your turn. Where's my picture?"

"Hold your horses. One sec."

With a deep breath and a few mental words of positive encouragement, I look into my phone, making sure my nightie is in the pic, and click. Before I give myself the chance to examine the picture, I hit send.

"Look at you." His low, smooth tone hits me as I bring the phone to my ear. "Beautiful. Damn, I wish I was there. Now you've made my night—no, actually, you've made my week. I'm going to have naughty dreams tonight," he teases.

"You and me both."

"I like the sound of that. Tell me more."

Eleven

SAM

Bloody hell, would you cut out the racket," Bas hollers, shuffling slowly into his kitchen.

"What are you going on about?" I mumble, turning back to the stove so as not to reveal that I witnessed his awkward, sluggish, and likely painful gait.

The ragoût de boulette simmers, small bubbles rising to the surface of the rich, brown liquid. Stirring, I patiently and nonchalantly wait for him, fighting the urge to help him. Slowly, he sidles up beside me, resting his forearm on the counter and slumping over.

"What's got you tearing my kitchen apart? What happened?"

Hot anger roils within my stomach at how much weight he's lost. I see him every day and even at that, there's no missing he's rail thin. It's noticeable and disturbing. He's being eaten from the inside and there's not a damn thing I can do about it.

He won't talk to me about it, even when I push, and I'm lucky if I find out about his appointments or what the doctors are saying. I've had to force him to let me tag along. He won't say it, but he's given up. Even with treatment, it's only prolonging the inevitable. It's obvious, he's preparing to die.

"Nothing, and I wasn't tearing your kitchen apart. Exaggerate much?" I quip, trying my hardest to be natural, to fall into our easy banter and frank jabs, to enjoy the time I have with the man I consider a father.

"Look Samson, come clean and save both of us a lot of trouble. I'm not letting it go. You've been here nearly three hours now and from the moment you stepped foot in my house, I've known something's bothering you. Is it the new restaurant?"

"Not really. I mean, I still don't have any investors. Thibault's interested, but he wants to know the location before he'll commit, which is understandable. I'm just not sure where I want it to be yet. I've been thinking Toronto or Vancouver." I float the idea by him, preparing for his objection.

Bastien Villeneuve is as Canadian as they come, but first and foremost, he's Quebeçois. I deliberately held off on sharing my thoughts about opening a restaurant outside of the province because I didn't want to hear how much of a fool he thinks I am.

"Daniel Thibault?" Bas asks, throwing me for a loop. I nod. His ocean blue eyes darken. "Find someone else."

I pause, waiting for further explanation. When it's apparent he doesn't intend to offer any, I press, "Why?"

Bas runs his hands through his short silver hair; that too is thinner than it used to be. His formidable jaw appears less pronounced with his gray skin tone and sunken cheeks. He grimaces as he shifts from one foot to the other, the pain etched in the hard lines of his face and tight lips. He deeply inhales, pushing off the counter in the direction of the kitchen table.

Without thinking, I reach to help, but Bas bats my hand away. Two more steps and he gingerly lowers himself into the chair with a smug expression, proving he doesn't need assistance. I grin without any feeling behind it. I'm trying to hide my worry, trying to give him that triumph, and his pride. He deserves it, and I'll let him have it as long as I can.

"Daniel Thibault is a bloodsucking leech. He will invest in your restaurant, then think he owns you. And I hear his daughter—what's her name?"

"Yasmine."

"Yes, that's the one." He points, nodding. "I hear she's a chip off the old block. The price of their backing is always answering to them. They don't know the meaning of silent partner," he vehemently states.

"Hmmm, yeah, I've seen some of that." He's just described Yasmine. I'll definitely keep it in mind, although I'm not thrilled with potentially having to start from scratch in finding an investor.

Robert Simard and Sabine Boucher have backed my two existing restaurants and if only the timing was right, they'd be in again. I could wait to open my third and final restaurant, but now is the time.

I'm coming off the success of three seasons on the Chef's Network; they wanted me to sign for another season, but I wanted to get back to cooking. My brand is at an all-time high, and I need to capitalize on that. Besides, I'm itching to start a new project. There's nothing like opening a new restaurant, working to see your vision come to life. Bas knows all about that.

"Sam, walk away from them. Let me invest."

Not this again. From the day I decided to open a restaurant, Bas has wanted to invest. I want to do it on my own. As much as I love him, I needed to prove to him, and most of all to myself, that I could do this on my own. I know he understands. Still, he always tries to offer.

"Bas, no. I'll find someone. I'm not saying no to Thibault. I'll ask around some more and feel him out before I decide to walk away or not." I sigh. "Dinner's ready, let me dish it out."

"I'm not hungry," he grumbles, resting both elbows on the table and looking pensively at the grain of the wood. "So, Toronto or Vancouver, eh?"

"Yes." *Here we go.* He may be sick, but he's still as sharp as a tack and not easily derailed. "What do you think?" I want to know his opinion even though I may not like it.

"I think that's a good idea. Either location will need someone you trust to run it and a seasoned executive chef. Vancouver may be harder because of the distance." He voices all the things I've been mulling over.

"Yes, I agree. I do have someone in mind to run things—Pierre Gagnon."

"Good choice. Pierre can be trusted. The question is, will he want to leave Montreal?"

"I know. I haven't broached the subject with him yet. I want to determine the location then feel him out. I'm going to Toronto for an upcoming fund-raising competition and I've got a few locations to look at. After that, I'll book a trip to Vancouver."

"Excellent. Good approach. If you want, I have some thoughts on an executive chef, when you're ready."

"Great, thank you."

"Okay, now come sit, eat, and tell me her name."

"What?" I stop midstride. He looks my way, and his sage gaze holds so many unspoken words; there is not enough time or courage for either of us to delve into the depths fully.

"Get your food and come sit." Without another word, I do as he says.

Seated across from him, I blow on my stew, the dish I made for him. It's his favourite, but he has no appetite to enjoy it.

"Who is she? The woman that has you preoccupied, has you taking out your frustration on my kitchen."

I chuckle; of course he'd catch on without me having to say a word. He knows me well.

"Her name's Olivia. I met her two weeks ago at Beaulieu's." Bas now raises his eyebrows, both in shock and in encouragement, prompting me to continue. "She's from Toronto and I can't stop thinking about her. I miss her."

With my confession, thoughts of our kiss flash before my eyes. Her dark eyelashes sloped downward, fanning her blushing cheeks. Her lips wet and swollen after I took them, licking and savoring her taste, the gratifyingly subtle sugariness. Oh, to have her enticing flavor on my tongue, in my mouth again. I don't think I could stop at kissing. I want to taste all of her.

My chest pounds at the memory and like the phantom sensations of a lost limb, my body thrillingly hums as if her small hands are gripping my shirt. Her fingers deliciously pressing into my torso, hanging on for dear life. Her breathy whimpers, encouraging and torturous. Her big, expressive eyes - the most beautiful eyes I've ever seen, gazing longingly up at me, so innocent yet beguiling. And now, *shit,* I want to kiss her again. Taste her again.

"Ah, that is a dilemma. Was it a one-time thing? Do you have her number?"

"I do. We text daily and try to talk once a day, even if only for a few minutes. It's not enough. I knew I liked her, I didn't anticipate feeling like this."

Bas and I have always been honest with each other. Except for his cancer and what it means, we've never beaten around the bush, and I'm not going to start now. Besides, I could use his insight. He's married to the love of his life and has been for over thirty years.

"She must be something."

He takes my spoon and ladles a small portion of the thick stew. While I carefully observe him, he ineptly swallows, wincing as the liquid slides down his throat. His discomfort likely has nothing to do with the heat of the stew and everything to do with his pain. He tries to hide it, but I see it; I always do. He can't hide from me.

"Needs some garlic," he admonishes.

"It doesn't," I lightly retort, knowing it's perfect.

It's our routine. Any chance he gets, he advises me on how I could improve a dish. After all, he was my teacher, taught me all I know. Even with our shtick, he tells me all the time how proud he is of me.

"She's something. I'm out of my element here. Chantal was the last woman I dated and that was over a year ago, and even at that, we were over long before we ended it. I never felt like this, and come to think of it, other than Thérèse, no woman has tied me up in knots like this."

"Thérèse? Who was she?"

I chuckle at the absurdity of what I'm about to say. "Remember grade ten?" He nods. "Thérèse became my girlfriend about a month before school ended. Her family had a place in Canton-de-L'est and she was gone the whole summer. I begged for us to go to your place, but the restaurant was too busy to leave. I was heartbroken, counting down the days 'til her return, only to discover that Marc Picard had a house across the lake and they hooked up. They were together that school year and it wasn't until I started dating Martine—or was it Sandrine? Anyway, whoever it was, it wasn't until her that my heart could mend and I could finally move on," I say dramatically.

Bas howls with amusement, his frail body shaking and tears glistening in his eyes. My smile widens at the sight. I embellished the story for his benefit, even though the basics of the tale were true. I made him smile—mission accomplished. I knew he'd remember once I started to recount the time because I was an unbearable grump that summer.

In retrospect, I chalk it up to teenage angst; I've never felt anything remotely similar with another woman since. Sure, I've had girlfriends, some serious relationships, and breaking up was never pleasant or easy. But still, I don't recall this ache at separation or the deep beat of anticipation constantly and uncomfortably drumming through my chest.

Bas wipes his eyes. "I will never forget that summer. You were insufferable, even with the new neighbor's daughter, I think it was Sandrine, liking you. Well, if this Olivia is anything like that, it explains it all. Call the woman. Go see her," he's still chuckling.

"See who?" Alec asks, entering the room. The tall, striking man elegantly glides to Bas's side and leans down to kiss him on the cheek. "Mon cher, how are you?" His big, perfectly manicured hand cups Bastien's jaw and lovingly caresses him. Bas grumbles and shrugs.

"Let me get you some food." I lean over to give Alec a hug.

"How are you?" he asks, his three words pointed and laden with concern and significance.

"Good." Stepping out of our embrace, I turn my back on him before he can see the truth.

Unlike my relationship with Bas, where we are brutally honest with each other, I'm less so with Alec. I can't explain it. It has nothing to do with the man himself. I love him and trust him with my life, have known him for as long as I've known Bas. When Bas took me in, he introduced Alec to me as his husband. These two brilliant, caring, loving men adore me and raised me like a son, I've always gravitated toward Bas in a way that wasn't there with Alec.

I need to be strong for him, for Alec. Knowing the torment and anguish I battle whenever I think of Bas's fate, I can only imagine what Alec is feeling. Bas is the love of his life. To watch your partner, your lover, your best friend dying—it must be slowly killing him too.

As I dish out the stew, my phone lights up and I catch Olivia's name on the screen. Unable to wait until later, I read her text.

Olivia: Hey handsome, how are you?

I quickly respond.

Me: Missing you. What are you doing?

The little dots immediately light up and I smile. I didn't miss the opportunity to speak with her.

Olivia: Just dropped my kids off at their dad's. All alone. I'll most likely take a bath and then bed. And you?

Me: You all alone is a missed opportunity. Wish I was there to wash your back, and I could keep you company. I really like sleepovers.

Olivia: LOL. Sounds very tempting. What are you up to?

Me: Having dinner with Bas and Alec.

Olivia: Oh, sorry, I'm interrupting. Get back to them. Talk to you tomorrow.

Me: You are never interrupting. Think of me in your dreams and the tub. ;)

Olivia: Night, Sam

Me: Night, Olivia. Sweet dreams

"Hey, how long do I have to wait for my meal?" Alec jests. "This restaurant has shoddy service."

Chuckling, I put my phone down and pick up the bowl. My chest feels a little less hollow now that I've heard from Olivia.

"Gee, maybe the service would be better if I knew there was a generous tip at the end of it all."

The three of us talk while Alec and I finish our meal. It feels like old times, when I lived with them, but it also doesn't. There's this undercurrent of urgency and tension that coats each glance, word, and moment. We're living on borrowed time, and I fucking hate it. It fills me with such hopelessness and rage. I'd do anything to take Bas's cancer away.

As I sit with the two men I love like the parents I never had, a melancholy and worry descends. If I had met Olivia two years ago, I'd have already been to Toronto to see her by now. I wouldn't have let these two weeks go by with us apart. Now, I want to be with her, to visit, but I don't want to be far from Bas. I don't want to miss a minute with him because I don't know how many we have left.

Twelve

OLIVIA

"No, I don't want the chartreuse. My first choice is slate; my second is aubergine," I implore as I fondle the square patch of suede material.

Seriously, I'm loving these colors. I'm like a junkie with fabric swatches and paint chips, I could spend hours discovering shades and textures. I listen as Alfonso, one of my best furniture suppliers, tells me he'll see what he can do.

"Al, I really need you to come through. It's a huge order. I need this," I plea, stilling my voice at the sound of footsteps stomping up the stairs. I'm holed up in my office and don't have a line of sight to my stairs. *Who the hell is in my house?*

Gripping the phone like my life depends on it—and it just might—I hiss, "Shhh, Al, listen, someone's in my house." Tiptoeing toward the open door, I whisper, "If I scream, hang up and call 911."

I peer around the corner and a head of light brown hair comes into view, followed by the handsome face of Drew. A nervous laugh escapes my lips as relief floods my body.

"Mom," he calls at the top of the stairs, quizzically looking at my upper body curled around the door frame.

Another sharp laugh leaves my mouth and I relax. "Al, it's Drew. Can I call you back?" Al also chuckles and agrees to speak with me tomorrow.

Drew has a large suitcase in one hand and his hockey bag in the other. "Hi honey," I reply, stepping fully into the hallway. "What's up? What's with the bags?"

Drew drops his things, walks over to me, and wraps his arms around me in a hug. "I'm staying here for the summer, if that's okay?"

"What? Of course, this is your home, but why? I thought you were going to stick to the schedule for the summer, staying with your dad when Paige was there, then with me."

He shrugs, lugging his bags into his room. Following, I wait patiently for further explanation. Drew plops onto his bed, gazing contemplatively at me. On an exhale, he runs his hands through his already ruffled hair.

"Here's closer to work."

Placing my hands on my hips, I challenge, "Drew, I'm literally three streets down from your dad. We're practically the same distance from the site. Tell me what's going on."

He's spent all his summers during high school working for his Uncle John, Pete's brother, who owns a construction company. It's good money, plus he gets a tan and a daily workout. This will be his last summer at the site before he switches gears, putting his time in at law firms and focusing on his career.

His eyes narrow and lips purse as he looks away. "Fine, if it's a problem, I'll crash with Ken."

"Hey, it's not a problem. Never. This is your home and you don't ever have to ask to stay here, but something's up and I want to know what. Did something happen with your dad?"

If he won't tell me, I'm going to have to ask Pete. I haven't been avoiding my ex, but I have been limiting our contact given his dogged pursuit of me. He's even taken to using the kids as an excuse to contact me, and since I've ignored his texts and calls to have coffee, dinner, or anything, he's now taken to emailing my work address.

"Mom, I'd rather not get into it. Let's just say Dad knows I'm here and he's fine with it."

My son is as easygoing as they come. Nothing bothers him. Whatever this is, it's big, and if my mom-radar is still working, Pete is at the very center of it all. I'm going to have to talk to him.

"Fine, but D-man, you know I'm here and will listen whenever you want," I say. "You're always welcome here, and if you change your mind, no harm, no foul."

"Thanks Mom."

"Does Paige know?"

"Nah, I've gotta tell her. She's gonna go all diva on me, I just know it."

Chuckling, I ruffle his hair before placing a light kiss on his forehead. "Yup, she most likely will. She won't say this to you, but she's missed you. She's been looking forward to you coming home. She's been having a tough time and could use her big bro."

Drew eyes me, likely looking for signs of distress. He is aware of how bumpy the ride has been for me where Paige is concerned, and he'd like nothing better than to fix it. He's tried even though I've told him it is not for him to fix. "Mom, do you need me to talk to her?"

"No, I don't. We're getting there. This is about you. Your sister loves you and she's been dealing with a lot of change this year. She could use someone to hang out with, and also fight with." My wry smile causes Drew to laugh, nodding in understanding.

"Look, I'm heading to Jonah's right now, and then I'm grabbing dinner at the Bow. If I'd known you were going to be here, I would have done some grocery shopping. We could have had dinner here. Why don't you meet me at the Bow?"

"Sure."

"Okay, see you at seven. Aunt Sin will be there, and she'll be thrilled to see you."

"Cool." The doorbell rings.

"Can you get that? I'm going to grab my bag and I'll be down." Drew nods and heads downstairs.

As I grab a change of clothes, the rift between Pete and Drew nags at me. I have no clue what it could be about. We were all together two weeks ago when Drew came home for the summer, and everything was fine. Drew was adamant about sticking to the schedule with Paige so he could spend time with both of his parents; what changed between then and now to make him not want to spend time with his father?

"Mom," Drew calls, coming into my view as I descend the stairs.

"Coming. Who is it?"

Drew steps aside, allowing me to pass, but says nothing. His curious look has me both intrigued and anxious.

Sam. It's Sam, looking delectable with his big smile, dimples and all, directed at me. He's sex-on-a-stick, and I finally understand the meaning of that phrase. I quickly glance over at Drew where he's curiously examining me, arms crossed.

"Sam." I step closer to the foyer, but not too close. I want to hug him, kiss him, but Drew is here, so keeping my distance is my safest bet.

"Olivia, hi." Sam's gravelly voice sends shivers down my spine. "It's good to see you."

"Ah…you too." Waving my hand in Drew's direction, I say, "Drew, this is my friend Sam. Sam, this is my son, Drew."

"We've met," they say in unison. Drew uncrosses his arms and steps to stand beside me. My heart rapidly beats against my ribcage and I fear I won't be able to hear anything else, the pounding is deafening.

"Mom, I'm going to unpack. I'll see you later." Taking my hand, he gently tugs it in comfort before looking back at Sam. "Nice to meet you, man."

"You too, Drew." Sam dons another panty-melting smile, tipping his chin at Drew.

Silently staring at each other, we both wait for Drew to leave, waiting a few extra seconds to make sure he's fully up the stairs.

"Hi." My voice is breathy and small, my throat dry.

"Hey, how are you?" he asks, moving so his hand can cup my jaw before he leans down to kiss me.

The moment his mouth touches mine, the thrashing of my heart drowns out all other sound, like waves crashing on the shore. My toes curl and my belly flutters.

"Damn, I've been dreaming about that since the hotel," he whispers. "The real thing is so much better than my imagination."

"S-Sam, what are you doing here?" As soon as the words leave my mouth, my appalling tone hits me and likely him. "That wasn't how I meant it," I rush to say.

Sam shakes, chuckling at my blunder. "I missed you. I wanted to see you."

"You should have called," I add, again realizing how horrible my words and frantic tone sound.

"I wanted to surprise you."

"You can't stay here," I blurt out, heaping on another faux pas. I wince and Sam grins before his finger sweeps a stray hair behind my ear.

"As much as I want to, I wasn't expecting to stay over. I have a hotel room."

His response lessens my anxiety for a millisecond, then I'm sucked back into my chaotic thoughts.

"I'm sorry. I'm messing this up. Drew's here." Great, I'm now an incoherent idiot.

"You don't need to explain. I get it. I thought I'd surprise you. It seemed like a good idea at the time. I now see I was wrong, won't happen again. It's all good."

Inhaling deeply, my nerves somewhat settle. His pale eyes are tender and his sweet smile draws me in. We're gazing into each other's eyes when the thundering of Drew's feet descending the stairs breaks our trance. As we both step back, we're close. "I'm on my way to work out. If I skip it, Jonah will hunt me down and torture me with double the workout."

"Can I come? I could use a workout."

Drew's now surveying both of us with curiosity and something close to enjoyment. "Sam, you want anything to drink?" he asks, turning toward the kitchen.

"Ah, no thanks, Drew. I'm going to work out with your mom," he replies, talking like they're old buddies. Stupidly gazing at him, I remain mute as Sam opens his bag and fishes out running shoes, shorts, and a tank top. "Where can I change?"

I'm still dumbfounded, not registering a word he's saying. Drew answers from behind me, "The bathroom's right here."

Sam tips his chin in understanding, rises to his full height, and strides in the direction Drew indicated.

With him gone, I manage to snap out of my ridiculous dreamlike stupor, finally coming to my senses. Without taking his eyes off me, Drew gives me a lopsided grin, making his face even more adorable. Glowering for him to keep quiet, I grab my purse.

The thought of taking Sam to Jonah's feels like a stone sitting heavy in my gut. I have no clue what I'm going to say to him. One look at Sam and it'll be the Spanish Inquisition. It's obvious Drew already expects more details as to who Sam is, but the only thing I know is that I'm not ready to put words to this, to what I'm doing with Sam. Truth be told, I have no clue what we're doing.

Our drive to Jonah's is comfortable and easy, despite my nerves. I just know my personal trainer and friend—a label he makes me question all the time—is going to do something. As we walk to the door, trepidation floods my body. Jonah's eager to set me up with someone and now, I'm bringing a man here.

Jonah is as giddy as a child at Disney World when I introduce him to Sam. I provide no explanation, but by the look he gives us, Jonah clearly thinks he knows it all.

"So, Sam, what kind of workout do you normally do when you're not slaving away in the kitchen?"

How'd he know Sam was a chef? Sin must have told him. *Traitor.*

"I do a bit of everything—cycling, swimming, running," Sam responds. Of course he'd be the next Iron Man. Biting my lip to prevent myself from saying something sassy, I lace up my shoes, head down, focused on calming my nerves. I wonder if pretending to be somewhere else will get me through this; this is going to be a whole new level of torture.

Jonah claps his hands twice to get our attention and plasters on his devilish grin. "Great, I know just the routine for today." Leading us over to the treadmill, he states, "To maximize our time, we'll do some high-intensity interval training with short, intense bursts of exercise and active recovery."

Without even thinking, I groan loudly and protest, "Jonah, we did that two days ago."

I hate this routine and he knows it; something tells me that's why we're doing it. Why not let Sam see me at my worst? Jonah is going to die a painful, horrible death—if I make it out of here alive. High-intensity interval training is brutal and wipes me out every time.

Sam chuckles, but quickly schools his features once he sees my scowl. "It's not that bad, honey," Jonah quips, readying the treadmill. "You'll thank me later."

Very unlikely.

Jonah deliberately pushes me on the parts of my routine I hate and suck at. He leaves me wanting to inflict pain and wipe off his playful smile. Sam is the complete opposite, nothing if not supportive and encouraging. At times, I find myself resenting him too, feeling weak among these two strong, capable men even though I know I'm strong.

One agonizing hour and two outbursts later, I'm a sweaty, wet noodle and Sam looks like a drink of water in the desert. Even with perspiration beading on his brow and his dark hair matted against his scalp, he's magnificent.

At some point during our workout, Sam whips off his shirt. I almost fall flat on my face, my steps faltering on the treadmill at the vision of hotness before me. Jonah emits a deep belly laugh while helping me right myself on the death contraption. I don't know why I ever thought he was my friend. He's the devil incarnate.

From that point on, I've lost my game. I stumble through the rest of our workout, unable to successfully tear my eyes away from Sam's sculpted back, defined arms, and rock-hard six-pack—and *damn,* I nearly choke on my own saliva at his *tattoos.*

They're eye-catching. One on his left pec looks like a cabbage, although it could also be a heart, and a few lines of black script run across the side of his ribcage. Try as I might, I can't make out the words. Short of wrestling him to the ground and straddling him, I'll have to wait to find out what the words are.

As beautiful as they are, an uneasiness settles in the pit of my stomach. His tattoos remind me of our age difference more than ever. We are seven years apart. His body art screams young and carefree, while I am older, responsible. I'm a mother. I have two teenage children, one legally an adult. What the hell am I doing?

The easy banter and laughter between Jonah and Sam snaps me out of my troublesome thoughts. There's nothing I can do about it. They're getting along well, both downing Gatorade and joking about something. Not only do they both make working out look like sun-tanning—effortless, nonchalant—they also share similar tastes. With our session finally over, I shower and change, leaving Sam and Jonah to yuk it up and bond some more.

When I return, Jonah is alone, and his small smile grows at the sight of me. "So, you and Sam are dating?" he asks, always one to get straight to the point.

"I wouldn't call it dating. We're just enjoying each other's company. It's casual," I reply disinterestedly.

"Casual?" He snorts. "So casual that the guy flies out here to see you just because."

"He said he was coming anyway," I say, rushing to squash whatever it is he's implying.

"Really?" he volleys sarcastically. "Sam's thirty-five." His monotone voice contradicts the twinkling mischief in his eyes and his smug smirk that I want to wipe off his handsome face.

Grrr, he riles me like a sibling, although I don't know if this is how a brother would piss me off because I'm an only child. Now I'm aggravated at the possibilities of what Jonah grilled Sam about. What the hell did he ask him while I was gone? How the hell did he find out his age? And more importantly, what the hell did he tell Sam about me?

"Jonah, shut it."

"I'm only asking because I seem to recall that was your reasoning for not meeting Brad."

He leaves that hanging in the air as I battle to keep my face from flaming red. I'm not at all thrilled by him calling me out on this. I wish I had something witty to say or something sharp to throw at him, but I'm all out. I'm a fool because he's right, and I am doing exactly what I thought I'd never do. I fold my arms, staring him down, and we remain silent.

Sensing I'm not going to respond, or maybe feeling uncomfortable in the deafening quiet, Jonah says, "Sam tells me you're going to the Bow for dinner. I'm going to join you."

I smile. "Sure." Jonah raises his brow, clearly expecting a fight. "Let me text Sin and Drew to let them know we're on our way."

"Great. I'm just waiting on Millie so I can let her know she can go home."

"How is Millie?" I ask pointedly. Jonah squints, his features harsh, as both Millie and Sam join us.

Jonah does the introductions and before we know it, Millie is talking animatedly with Sam about cooking and restaurants. No surprise, like most women upon meeting Sam, she slips into admirer mode before Jonah can get a word in edgewise. I'm amused as Jonah sulks because his personal chef fawns all over Sam.

"Millie, we're going out, so I won't need dinner tonight, thank you," Jonah interjects the first chance he gets.

Millie whirls to face him, blushing like a young school girl caught ogling her teacher. "Oh, okay." Her voice is almost a whisper with a hint of disappointment.

"Why don't you join us?" I pipe up, not sure where that came from other than the fact that it will make Jonah uncomfortable. *What goes around comes around, bro.* Sure enough, Jonah glares at me, his lips tight.

"Ah, are you sure?" Millie asks, uncertain.

"Absolutely," I reply as Sam says, "Of course." Jonah's none too happy and stays silent as we pile into my car.

On the drive, Sam and Millie continue their love fest while Jonah sits in the front next to me. He mumbles something about me being careful what I ask for and at first, I have no clue what he means, but it soon becomes apparent as Sam and Millie are in their own world. They're sharing tales about culinary school and recipes, and Sam regales her with stories of chefs he's met, neither engaging Jonah or I in conversation. While I wouldn't say I'm jealous, I certainly don't like it. Not one bit.

Thirteen

SAM

The Bow is your typical Irish pub with dark furniture and lighting, booths, TV screens, and great beer on tap. We're ushered through the busy dining room to a booth in the back where Sin and Drew are already seated, their eyes tracking the movement of our small group as we near their table. Olivia's leading the pack and I'm at the rear, behind Millie.

I'm not sure how I'm going to work it, but I must sit beside Olivia. While our workout was good and I enjoyed getting to know Jonah, I've hardly spent any time alone with her. I'd hoped we would drive together, alone, to the restaurant, but unfortunately that was not meant to be.

Millie guided me into the back seat and monopolized my time. She's a nice woman and I was more than happy to talk shop with her. Still, Olivia is the reason I'm here. She's the one I want to spend time with. Now we're going to be seated with her friends and son. I don't see much alone time in our near future.

"Hey darlin'," Jonah greets Sin, along with a kiss and hug.

Sin laughs mischievously and hugs me as she says, "Sam, it's so good to see you."

She looks from Olivia to me and waggles her eyebrows, Jonah joining in on the fun. The both of them clearly want to bug Olivia about my presence. Olivia rolls her eyes and huffs in what I think is mock frustration.

Jonah pats me on the back, then fist-bumps Drew before slipping in beside Sin. Patting the empty spot beside him, he motions for Millie to join him. *Good man.* I knew I liked him. Olivia slides in beside Drew with me sitting on the end of the banquette, beside her.

After our drinks and food are ordered, I sit silently and observe Olivia with her friends. Joining in occasionally, I'm content to mostly listen and learn. I like seeing Olivia in her element. I want to learn as much as I can about this complex, interesting woman and something tells me she'll try to hide from me.

"Drew, how's school?" Jonah asks. "Still headed for law school?"

"Good, just glad exams are over, and yup, that's the plan."

"Honey, the plan can change if you want, you know that right?" Olivia adds.

"Yeah, I know that Mom. This is what I want."

"What does Erin say?" Sin asks. "I think she said she wishes she'd taken a year before going to law school."

"Yeah, we talked. I'm going to do what I want to do," he responds defensively. Unable to see Drew since I'm on the same side of the table, with Olivia in between us, I sense from his tone a strong distaste for the topic, or perhaps it's the mention of Erin that has him annoyed?

"Honey." A tall, dark-haired man saunters toward our booth with his hand wrapped around the bicep of a pretty, blonde teenager. She's chewing her lip as she scans our table and stalls when her gaze lands on Sin.

"Pippa, what are you doing here?" Sin shrieks, nearly pushing both Jonah and Millie out of the booth.

"I found her in the kitchen talking to Lou," the man states with a grim expression. "Hey," he says to the table.

"Hi Colin," Olivia says, and both Jonah and Drew chime in with greetings of their own. Olivia quickly introduces us; Colin is Sin's husband.

"What on earth are you doing here?" Sin's distress is evident in her voice, and I'm guessing the girl is her daughter. "And who is taking care of Tom and Claire?"

"Mom, Claire is taking care of Tommy. I just came to ask Uncle Lou if he'd take me out driving this weekend," states the blonde girl—Pippa, apparently.

"Have you ever heard of a phone?" Sin retorts, anger now strong in her tone. "You should have *called* Uncle Lou. Young lady, you're supposed to be watching your brother and sister. Claire cannot be alone with Tom. Seriously, Pippa, what am I going to do with you?" Without waiting a beat for her daughter to respond, Sin continues, "And you can forget about driving with Lou this weekend. You're grounded for pulling this move, and we're no longer paying you for babysitting your brother and sister since you've no clue what that means."

"Mom, seriously," Pippa wails with an eye roll. "Claire is twelve, she's legally old enough to babysit. Besides, I was only going to be gone for thirty minutes, tops. I'm heading home now."

Colin turns her to face him. "Pippa, you know better. Claire may be legally of age, but there's a reason we asked *you* to babysit Tommy and not her. One of us will take you home."

"I don't need either of you to take me home. I'm seventeen and fully capable of getting home by myself," Pippa gripes.

"Excuse me." Sin motions for Jonah and Millie to move so she can exit the booth. "Well, you could've fooled us with this stunt. It's late and dark out there, you're not walking back by yourself."

Pippa huffs, crossing her arms over her chest and glares at her parents. They share an exasperated look and Colin shakes his head, leading the way.

"Hey, Aunt Sin, Uncle Colin, I can take her home," Drew calls out.

Turning, Pippa's features soften once her eyes land on Drew. Her cheeks heat a dark pink and she immediately shifts from spunky to demure with her head slightly down. "Drew, hi. I didn't see you there."

"Hey, Pip. Uncle Colin, you're working, and Aunt Sin, stay and enjoy your night out. I was going home soon anyway. I'll take Pippa home."

"Yeah, that's a great idea," Olivia adds. "Thanks honey." She nudges my thigh and we scoot out for Drew.

Gone is her sassy teenager attitude; Pippa is now all smiles and compliant, eagerly nodding as her parents thank Drew and agree to his offer.

As Sin and Colin escort Drew and Pippa out, Jonah chuckles, "In case you missed it, Pippa is gaga for our man, Drew."

Olivia smiles, nodding. "Yes. It's been that way for a couple years now. It's just an innocent crush. They've known each other since they were babies, and I can't blame Pip for crushing on my boy," she says like the proud mama bear she is.

"I'd watch that if I were you. Miss Pip is no wallflower—she's the type to go after what she wants, and Drew seems to be in her sights," Jonah adds.

"Nah, leave her alone. You make her sound like a man-eater. She's just a girl," Olivia says dismissively.

Shortly after our meal, Jonah announces they're leaving. Millie appears flustered and excited all at the same time, adoration plastered on her face as she watches Jonah. "You came with us, how are you getting home?" Olivia asks.

"I've got an Uber on its way." I smile appreciatively at the guy.

Jonah may not know it, but that means I'm finally getting my alone time—that is, unless Sin returns, which is a distinct possibility as she's been gone a while now and hasn't eaten. Olivia says Sin's with her husband doing who knows what in the manager's office. Good for her.

Once they leave, I take Olivia's hand, turning to her. "Alone at last. I finally have you all to myself."

Leaning into her, oblivious of our surroundings, my lips are on hers, kissing, licking, and drinking her in. Her taste is as I remember, as I fantasized. Addictive. Sweet, fresh, and something indescribable yet tantalizing. Something entirely Olivia.

She fists my shirt, pulling my solid chest against her soft, inviting curves. Closer. Her breasts press into me, and she shudders at the contact. Our shallow breaths mirrored. Wanting. My hand sinks into her thick waves, gripping the nape of her neck. My other hand latches onto her trim hip, steadying, holding her in place.

Feasting on her mouth like a starving man, I've never felt more full of life, brimming and vibrating. Her eyelids close and long dark lashes fan her cheeks as I swallow her whispery moans. Her slender hands roam my body, exploring.

With each sweep of my tongue, each touch of my hand, my already thundering heart rate accelerates. I'm crazy with need, wanting nothing more than to have her, take her, here and now. She breaks our kiss and her retreat elicits a deep, feral growl from me. The loss is so frustrating.

"Sam, stop," Olivia admonishes.

Pulling back, she wipes at her mouth, eradicating our passion like it never happened. Straightening her clothes and hair, she misses the downcast of my eyes, echoing the pang of offense within my chest.

When she finally looks my way, her lips are puffy, red, and damp. Despite her rebuff, she's like a neon sign advertising our hot-blooded necking, her desire alive in her shimmering eyes, tousled hair, and rouge cheeks.

I gently squeeze her hand, which she quickly removes, picking up her glass and taking a sip. It's not lost on me that her move is a mediocre attempt at occupying her hand. *Like that's going to stop me.*

Choosing to not push it right now, I change the subject. "Speaking of crushes, does Jonah realize Millie has googly eyes for him?"

"Googly eyes?" She laughs and I nod, smiling. "I've noticed and have mentioned it to him, but he's in denial."

"Is he? Are you sure that's what it is? Or perhaps he doesn't care because he's got eyes for someone else."

Her eyebrows draw together. "Who?"

"You."

"What?"

"In case you missed it, Jonah is in love with you. Even a blind man can see that he adores you. Has he ever made a move?" I bravely ask, doubt clouding my mind before the final word leaves my mouth.

What if he has and she's welcomed it? What if she has no clue but would want something with him, and now I've stupidly enlightened her to the potential of it?

My hesitation is so unlike me, yet it's not surprising as Olivia has me experiencing many firsts. My first dogged pursuit of a woman. My first blush. My first case of indecision about my moves.

"What? You're off your rocker. Jonah and I are friends. He's like a brother to me."

"Are you sure?"

It's not jealousy prompting me to ask the question. Rather, I want to be aware of my competition. I'm not wild about the long distance between us; it's one of many things Olivia uses to put obstacles in our way. I need to understand the playing field, know where other barriers lie so I can prepare to annihilate them. Make no mistake, I intend to obliterate all her excuses, one by one.

"Yes, I'm sure. Besides, he's tried to set me up on a date with one of his friends, so stop. That's just...eww. He's twelve years younger than me."

"Not that again. Like that would stop him, or any other guy, for that matter. When are you going to get that out of your head? Olivia, you're a beautiful woman and men don't care about your age." Shaking her head at me, she finishes her drink. "What are you doing tomorrow?"

"Working. I've got an appointment first thing in the morning with a supplier, then I'm in my office for the day. Why?"

"I'm thinking about opening another restaurant and have a few potential locations to view tomorrow. I'd love for you to come with me. They're all in the afternoon. We could grab some lunch, then meet my agent. What d'ya say?" The hope in my tone is undeniably clear.

"I…I suppose, sure," she replies, though not with as much conviction as I'd hoped for.

Grabbing her slender hand again, I lightly kiss the top of it and squeeze. She smiles, her cheeks lightly tinged. The joy of her agreeing to join me outweighs the trepidation coming off her in waves as her eyes dart around the room at anything and everything but me. I wonder if I'm reading her correctly—it feels like she's gearing up to let me down rather than getting ready to build on this, on us.

Fourteen

OLIVIA

"Wow, this is beautiful." I scan the large open space, visualizing it as a restaurant.

Sam's ahead of me, his broad shoulders and well-defined back taking up a significant amount of my view—but I'm not complaining. Taking a moment, I give in to my desire to admire him. He's not only gorgeous on the outside, he's also a wonderful person. I still can't believe he came to Toronto to see me. I wanted to talk to him last night about us, about whatever it is we are doing, but Drew was there when we got back, then later, I lost my nerve.

The remainder of the evening was one big blur after our kiss. I couldn't think straight, let alone recall what we talked about. I had to put some distance between us or else we would have been going at it in the middle of the Bow. I can still feel Sam's strong arms, his hot lips devouring me, owning me. My knees buckled the moment his soft, firm lips covered my mouth—thank goodness I was seated or I would have ended up on the floor.

"Olivia?" Sam quizzically studies me. "What do you think?"

"Sorry?"

"Patti was saying the electrical and the floors need work, so we could most likely knock the price down, get a better deal. What do you think?"

"Yeah, you could. I'd want to get someone to look at the electrical, make sure it's not worse than they say before making a bid, if you want to. It's a great location and you'd get both weeknight and weekend traffic," I add.

We are a stone's throw away from my house in the Annex. This is the final location we're seeing today and it's in the best neighborhood. The Annex is in the heart of Toronto, an affluent, vibrant, and diverse community—a great spot for a restaurant.

Patti Darvin, Sam's real estate agent, leads us to the kitchen, which needs a lot of work. In fact, all the locations we've seen today need work, some more so than others. I, for one, get excited about projects like this. As an interior designer, these locations are like a blank canvas to a painter, so many possibilities. I love taking a space and making it functional and reflective of the people and its purpose, creating an energy and ambience that capture the essence of the inhabitants.

"Bonjour," a woman's voice calls from the front. With clicking heels, Yasmine Thibault steps into the doorway. My heart sinks and I bite my lip to prevent the sneer from forming. What the hell is she doing here? Did Sam ask her to come?

"Yasmine," Patti and Sam say at the same time, both going to do their French thing of three kisses on alternating cheeks.

Yasmine's eyes lock with mine, the diabolical glint in her eye unmistakable. With her hand on Sam's forearm, she plasters on a phony smile. "Olive, lovely to see you." She gives me a weak wave.

I return the gesture, pursing my lips into a thin line. I don't think I'm capable of hiding my disdain, nor do I care to. Sam corrects her, politely saying, "It's Olivia." He steps away from her, coming to my side, and places his hand at the small of my back. His presence is reassuring, though I'm still not certain if she was invited or not.

As if he's reading my mind, Sam clears up the ambiguity. "Yasmine, what are you doing here? How did you know we'd be here?" His tone is neutral although it's lined with a slight suspicion.

"Oh, she called..." Patti starts, but Yasmine rushes to cut her off. "Patti called me and mentioned what she was doing and since I was in the city, I thought I'd stop by. Papa will be thrilled to hear you're looking, although I know he's partial to Montreal."

It's clear she's lying. She likely called Patti and grilled her on Sam's whereabouts or something like that. I'm pretty sure Sam sees through it too, if the crease in his brow and tight lips are any indication.

With Yasmine's arrival, Sam cuts the visit short. Out of the blue, he thanks Patti and barely says goodbye to Yasmine, making it my turn to do the sad wave toward the plastic blonde. I can't resist donning my satisfied smirk as Sam ushers us out rather abruptly.

I'm not sure what it is about Yasmine that irks me the most. I'm not particularly threatened by her, although maybe I should be because Sam is definitely her target. I'm used to her kind of woman—just look at my BFF, Erin. As I give it more thought, it's her damn age. She's younger than Sam—I'd guess mid-twenties, at most—and I simply can't compete with that.

Back at my place, we're sitting around the kitchen table when I ask Sam, "So, which one was your favorite?"

"I think the last one. You?"

"Me too. I think it has a lot of potential. For the front space, you could shorten the foyer and extend the area just before the dining room into a funky waiting space with tables for drinks. It could have a vintage French vibe. You could also knock down the wall behind the serving area and make it an open kitchen like Beaulieu's, or you could just cut out a space at the bar to make it like a sneak peek into the kitchen so all your adoring fans could get their Samson Beaulieu fix."

Sam grabs me around the waist and pulls me into his lap. "You think you're funny, don't you?" he taunts.

His lips skim my collarbone with small pecks as he moves up the column of my neck. A tingling sensation shoots from where his mouth is worshipping throughout my body.

"I told you there's only one woman I want adoring me. And." A kiss just under my jaw. "That's." A kiss behind my ear. "You." A kiss on the corner of my mouth.

With his hands secure around my waist, he twirls me so I'm forced to straddle him. My fingers sink into the soft strands of hair behind his neck as his hand latches onto the back of my head, guiding me toward his mouth.

I should stop this. We're moving too fast. I need to keep this casual, no strings, but what he's doing to my body is making it hard for me to think. Cupping my neck, he kisses me full on the mouth. Our lips glide, skim, and mold together, each of us willingly exploring the other like this is our first, last, and only kiss.

His lips are warm, firm, and alluring. As his hands travel down my lower back and cup my bottom, butterflies take flight, low in my stomach. God, this feels so good.

Still feeding on my lips, he stands and I circle my arms tighter around his neck and my legs around his waist. He effortlessly carries me, heading for the stairs.

"Bedroom?" he mumbles against my lips, making sure I'm okay with this.

Am I? I'm not sure about us long-term, but I'm sure about this right now. I haven't felt this sexy, this *wanted* in eons. I'm alive, on fire. As much as my mind is warning me, telling me to slow down, my body's taken over. My body wants this—now.

"Yes," I pant into his mouth.

For a fleeting moment, Drew and Paige flash in my mind. Drew's not home from work yet, and Paige is supposed to come over later. With Sam's first step up the stairs, his hard abdomen pleasingly rubbing against my core, I groan into his mouth and all reservations evaporate like smoke.

His lips wander my neck, peppering my tender flesh with wet, hot kisses that curl my toes. I tilt my head to the side to give him better access.

"Mom," Paige hollers from what sounds like the front door. We freeze at the top of the stairs. There are two voices speaking, and one sounds like Pete.

Carefully putting me down, Sam rests his forehead on mine. With his eyes closed, he raggedly inhales. Without missing a beat, he gives me an understanding smile and gently kisses my forehead.

"Paige?" he whispers. I nod, taking a deep breath of my own.

"Coming," I call out and quickly descend, hastily straightening my hair and double-checking that my clothes aren't askew.

I round the corner, and both Paige and Pete stand close to the doorway, talking. They stop and look to me, then at Sam as he comes down behind me. Great, this doesn't look fishy at all.

Taking a step toward them and deliberately away from Sam, I rack my brain for a plausible reason for why we would have been upstairs that doesn't involve what we were actually doing. A transient and stupid thought runs through my mind—I could introduce him as a client. My office is upstairs, it would make sense, but just as quickly I dismiss the absurdity of the lie because they both know I don't have clients to my home. That's why I rent office space on Bloor Street, so my clients can meet me there.

"Hey," I say, hoping I sound natural and relaxed, rather than as freaked out as I feel.

With a quick smile, I prepare to introduce Sam, but Paige beats me to the punch. "You're that chef," she claims excitedly.

Pete and I glance at Sam, confused. How does my teenage daughter know who Sam is? Sam nods, smiling sheepishly.

"What?" I ask, hands on my hips, looking expectantly at Sam, then Paige, impatient for someone to tell me what the hell they're talking about.

"He's on the Chef's Network, the show about the restaurant he owns, something to do with cabbage—what's it called again?" Paige asks. Before Sam can speak, she answers her own question. "Mon Petit Chou, that's it. My little cabbage, right?"

"Yup, that's it," Sam offers no further explanation.

Cabbage? I should know what that means, but I'm too focused on not knowing something so big about him. "You have a TV show?"

"Had. I decided not to renew for a fourth season."

"You *had* a TV show? Why didn't I know that?"

Pete's eyes on us are hot and uncomfortable as he watches our odd and enlightening exchange.

"I thought you knew." He shrugs like it's no big deal. "You mentioned Googling me so I figured you knew about the show."

"Well, I didn't. I was joking about your flock of women. I figured there'd be a page or three thousand dedicated to Chef Beaulieu."

Sam emits a hearty laugh and Paige snickers like she knows what's going on when she has no clue. Pete still stares, his face impassive but interested.

"My flock of women?"

"Have you looked in the mirror?" I lob at him, my tone clipped, now feeling irritated more than anything else.

I'm not sure if it's the knowledge that he *is* a celebrity that bothers me or the fact that my daughter knew and I didn't—or maybe it's none of that and it's because I'm not only old and out of it, but also stupid, and now I have my ex-husband and temperamental daughter watching us like we're the hottest show on HBO.

Sam's grin disappears, his face still mellow and now tender as he stands taller. With two short strides, he's at my side. His arm slips around my waist, drawing me into his side.

Leaning down, he whispers so low that I'm the only one able to hear, "I'll tell you all about it when we're alone. You're the only woman I want flocking to me." His lips kiss behind my ear, feather light, fleeting.

Cabbage.

His tattoo.

I so want to know what it all means.

"Ewww," Paige squawks, stomping past us into the house. Pete growls.

Sam instantly steps back, muttering an apology as both Pete and I call to Paige, but she's gone, thumping up the stairs. Damn teenage daughters—everything is drama.

"Liv." Pete's tone is stern. "May I have a word with you?" He flicks his hand over his shoulder toward the front yard. It's not a question, even though he phrases it as one.

Shit, I am so not in the mood for this, for Pete and his lecture—not now. Nodding, I briefly peer at Sam, who looks gravely contrite as he mouths *sorry*.

Outside on my walkway, Pete unexpectedly pivots to face me. His hands clamp down on my shoulders, halting my potential crash into him.

"Liv, what the hell?"

"Excuse me?" I rear back, shaking off his embrace.

"Who is that kid?" he spits out, obviously having already come to his own conclusion.

"Pete, it's none of your business. I don't owe you an explanation, but Sam is a friend."

"A friend? Since when do your friends make inappropriate PDA in front of your husband and daughter?" His anger is evident in his furious eyes, clenched hands, and impenetrable posture.

"*Ex*-husband. You keep forgetting that part. Pete, I need you to leave. Now."

With one step toward me, his eyes narrow and drop to my lips. Familiar lust clouds his gaze and his breath quickens. So help me, if he tries to kiss me, he'll lose his balls. What the hell is it with men feeling the need to go all Neanderthal and stake a claim on a woman even if she is no longer theirs? Fisting my hands, I widen my stance.

"Liv, don't do this. Forget this nonsense, I don't fucking care what a piece of paper says, you'll always be my wife. I love you. I want to spend the rest of my life with you. I don't care what's happened or who've you've been with, I want you back." His tone is heavy and exacting.

"Pete, stop. We've been through this before. We're over," I declare harshly.

"I'm not giving up. I will get you back," he vows.

Twirling on my heels, I hurry to the front door, wanting to get as far away as possible. We've done this dance way too many times for my liking.

No movement of retreat sounds from behind me, but I'm not scared of Pete. He won't hurt me—at least not physically. I only wish he'd leave.

If I weren't focused on getting back to Paige, I'd laugh at Pete being ticked about Sam, like he has a right to give a damn. He never gave a rat's ass when we were married. He never spent time with me, just us. When the kids were young, during the rare moments when we had time to ourselves, he'd be elsewhere. I never felt considered or important then, so it's hilarious the way he's going on now.

"Liv," he calls. I halt in my tracks, but refuse to turn around. "What about Paige?" At the mention of her name, I do twist to face him. Pete is a caring and loving parent, his concern for his children genuine.

"I'll talk to her." It's all I have, all I can do, but it's not much. Pete knows what Paige and I have been going through and he's been nothing but supportive. Other men may have used this rough patch with Paige to drive a bigger wedge between us or to tear me down, but he's been my biggest advocate.

With a jagged exhale, he nods in understanding. His lips stretch into a weak, strained smile and he thrusts his hands into his pockets. With defeat clearly defined on his face, he turns his back to me and leaves.

Fifteen

SAM

"Hey, I like it." Paige laughs, popping another artichoke in her mouth. Olivia silently observes us from the kitchen doorway, pleasantly amazed, a small smile on her face.

"Hey, what are you guys doing?" She saunters in and perches beside Paige, playfully hip-checking her in the process. Paige smiles, continuing to chop the black olives.

"We're preparing the toppings for the pizza," I say, handing her a small cutting board and a bulb of garlic. "Would you please chop this? Or we could pop them in the oven whole and add them after."

"Pizza?" she asks. "I don't have any pizza crust."

"Mom," Paige whines, rolling her eyes. "We have Sam—he made it," she says with exasperation, stating the no-brainer her mother clearly missed.

Olivia's eyes widen, searching my face for confirmation. Nodding, I point to the bowl with the dough in it and the damp tea towel over it. Paige kindly took out the flour and other ingredients for me to make the dough.

While Olivia was outside with her ex, I ventured to Paige's room and coaxed her out of seclusion and her indignant mood. I was prepared to explain and answer her questions if she asked, but she didn't. Instead, she openly talked to me about my show and how she likes to cook with her mom, then we headed down to start dinner.

The front door slams with a loud bang that vibrates right through to the kitchen. It's followed by a murmured curse. "Drew?" Olivia calls.

Drew steps into the kitchen, scanning the domestic scene before him. Even barely knowing him, I can tell he's pissed—his knitted brow, tight lips, and one hand gripping his hair are dead giveaways.

"Hey Drew, is everything okay?" Olivia asks.

"Why didn't you tell me Dad was going to be here?" His tone is sharp, each word released like he's spitting nails.

"He dropped Paige off. She wanted to see you," Olivia responds in a pointed yet calm tone.

"Next time tell me so I can be sure to not be here."

"He's your father." It's all she says, her gaze holding disappointment at his manner.

They silently observe each other. Paige stops grating the cheese, now keenly interested in the deadly silence brewing between her mother and brother. After a few beats, Drew's shoulder's sag.

"Sorry," he says on a resigned breath. Striding to his mom, he hugs and kisses her, then ruffles his sister's hair. "Paiges." He smiles with a chin tip to me before going to wash his hands in the kitchen sink. "So what are we having and how can I help?"

"We're making pizzas, although I'm asking Sam to choose my toppings," Paige informs him, handing him an onion and a knife.

Quirking his eyebrow, Drew studies his sister. "And why can't you pick your own?"

"Yes, why can't you choose your own?" Olivia echoes. They're both curiously assessing Paige.

With a flip of her hair and an eye roll—which I've quickly learned, in all of two hours, is quintessential Paige—she answers like they're developmentally challenged, "Because he's a chef. His choices are killin' it. I just tried an artichoke and I loved it."

My smile grows at her praise. Coming from the youngest in the crowd and the toughest critic, I'm going to take the compliment and bask in it. Olivia also smiles and chuckles, nodding in agreement with her daughter's logic.

"You're a chef?" Drew asks, wiping the tears on his cheeks, which are there thanks to the onion.

"Yeah," I reply, lifting the towel to check the dough.

"Cool." Drew scrapes the onion into a small glass bowl, then picks up the roll of goat cheese to begin his next task.

The four of us finish the prep while chatting about music, TV, and movies, each of us jokingly taking pot shots whenever someone claims a lame or just plain embarrassing song, musician, or show. Occasionally, Olivia will stop her chore to focus on the three of us, her children and me, laughing and trading stories. She's obviously in awe of the whole thing.

Once the dough's ready, we make our pizzas. It's funny when both Paige and Drew choose the exact toppings as me; Paige can't resist calling her brother out on it. Then another round of trash talk ensues.

While eating, Drew's phone, perched on the table between Paige and himself, buzzes with an incoming text. His sister glances down. "Laura's texting you? Is that a thing?" Drew snatches the phone, glaring at his sister. "I'm only asking because I thought you weren't interested."

"We're just friends. I can't help it if she wants some of this hotness. The ladies love me."

"Stop. I'm trying to eat. Hashtag get over yourself." Paige snorts with an eye roll.

Olivia and I laugh. Her kids are funny and easygoing, both willing to make fun of not only each other, but themselves. After we've cleaned up our meal, we head out to lounge in the backyard with tiki torch citronella candles burning. The night is cool and quiet.

Gathering around the small makeshift fire pit, we roast marshmallows and continue to get to know each other. Not long after, Paige bails when her best friend, Marci, arrives, then Drew begs off for bed.

Now that we are alone, I take the first opportunity I've had all night to say something. I start, "About earlier tonight, I totally goofed and I'm sorry."

"It's okay. It seems to have worked out. I have no clue what you said to Paige, but you seem to be her new BFF. We need to be careful." Across the flickering flames, Olivia gazes at me, her expression shifting from neutral to a cute grin on her pretty face.

"What's got you smiling?"

"You," she says with a smile to her voice. "You're good with them."

"Nah, they're easy to get along with." She nods with a shiver, wrapping her arms around herself. Joining her on the small sofa, I drape my arm around her, bringing her into my side, finally holding her, something I've wanted to do all night.

She visibly stiffens and her hands push lightly against my chest, preventing us from getting closer. "Sam, the kids."

Trying to not take it personally, I inhale deeply. This is a whole new side to Olivia that I've never seen before. She's a protective mama bear and I understand the need to watch what we do around her kids. But I can't fight the feeling that this is more than concern for her kids, like perhaps she's using her kids as an excuse to keep me at a distance.

"They're inside. It's fine," I assure her, deliberately pushing at my concern.

"Sam, we can't. I haven't said anything to either of them about you and I'm sure they have questions."

"Yeah, I'm sure they do, but they seem fine with us. They're cool kids and if they had any pressing questions, don't you think they'd have asked?"

Sighing, she pulls out of my embrace and stands. With her arms tucked around her middle, she peers down into the fire, silhouetting her side profile. "Maybe, but I owe it to them to say something before anything happens in their house," she says in a monotone voice. "I think you should leave."

"Okay." I abruptly stand and grab the marshmallows, needing some distance.

Without waiting for anything further from her, I head to the back door, disappointment and sadness seeping through my thoughts. I will respect her wishes; she's a mom and knows what's best for her kids. I'm not here to make things harder for her, but it also feels a lot like she's keeping me at arm's length, and I don't understand why.

Sliding the glass door open, I turn to see her still staring, mesmerized, into the glowing pit. I don't want to leave things like this. I'm here for almost the whole week and I'm not even sure if she's going to want to see me again before I leave.

In a lame attempt at making sure I see her again, I say, "Ah, I'm judging a food competition this weekend at the Metro Convention Center. It's a fundraiser and it's being televised. Would you like tickets for you and the kids?"

"Hells yeah," Paige exclaims from behind me. Standing in the doorway, her long brown curls are in a riotous topknot on her head. Her friend Marci stands beside her with a goofy grin on her face, looking at me like I hung the moon.

Chuckling, I nod. "Okay then, I'll leave the tickets with your mom."

"Thanks Sam." Paige beams, swinging one arm loosely around my shoulder in a sort of hug. "Mom, is it okay if I sleep at Marci's tonight? Her dad will come get us in about an hour."

"Sure sweetie."

The two girls disappear into the house, gabbing and giggling. A light laughter sounds at my back as Olivia says, "Thank you."

Peering over my shoulder, she's coming up the stairs with the corners of her mouth turned up. "It was nothing. Are you going to come too?"

I gaze into the dark depths of her eyes. At her nod, I release my pent-up breath and respond with a small smile of my own.

Leading the way inside, I place the food on the counter and twirl to pull her into my arms. I want her close and am willing to risk it for one more quick embrace. "Sam," she says, articulating my name like it's a bad word. A frown mars her pretty face.

Stepping back, she puts herself out of my reach. Her sudden shuttered move jars me. I made it worse. Gritting my teeth in frustration, I curtly nod. My cell phone rings and I pull it out of my pocket; it's Alec.

"Hello. What's wrong?" I ask, forgetting all pleasantries, the awkward moment with Olivia no longer my primary concern. My heart beats a mile a minute as my chest tightens, thinking the worst.

"Sam, I'm really sorry to ask this, but I'm in a bind. Bas, the dumb fool, didn't tell me his chemo appointment got rescheduled. It's tomorrow. I just found out and I can't take him. Tomorrow is the completion of the Mount Royal project. If it were anything else I'd drop it, but if I don't do this, they could screw me. I'd ask Marie-Claire, but she's not back 'til Monday."

"Of course, I'll be there. I want to be there. What time?" My voice is stronger, more reassuring now that it's not bad news. It's not great, but it's better than what I first thought. My heart rate slows and my mind clears.

"At noon."

"Okay, I'll catch the first flight out."

"Thank you, Sam. If he'd only told me, I could have moved things around. I'm so angry with him right now. He wants to be brave and do this on his own, thinks he's sparing us the heartache, but he's not. I wish he wouldn't fight me on this. If I hadn't heard the hospital's reminder message, I wouldn't have even known. I asked him how he thought he'd be able to leave on his own, against hospital policy. He said he was going to take a cab, and would like to see them stop him. Ha! I would have liked to have seen that." His voice is angry, but also small and dejected.

I know how he feels. It's one thing to fight alongside Bas, to say fuck cancer, and even that's hell because there's only so much you can do. It's another kind of hell entirely, a kind that's a whole lot deeper and darker when the one you love and so desperately want to be there for won't let you in. Try as you might, you don't want to make this about you, but you've never felt more helpless in your life.

I think he's being stubborn and shutting us out because of his own fear of dying and showing weakness. He's a strong, proud man, and while he's never been one to shy away from admitting his faults and showing his feelings, I think he wants to be remembered for who he was, not how he died. I respect that, but also wish he'd let us be there for him.

"I know. We need to talk to him. We can't go on like this."

"Yeah, I agree. Hopefully, together, we can get through to him. Okay, have a safe flight, and thank you, again. Love you Sam."

"Love you too."

Caught up in thoughts of Bas and the worry and stress Alec is going through, I head out the door.

"Sam?" Olivia calls to me. In a moment of clarity, I realize I almost forgot to say goodbye.

"Olivia." I spin around to face her. "Olivia, thanks for today. I really loved you being there with me to look at those places, and your ideas—wow. I want to hear more, soon."

Her smile is small and thin, eyes concerned. I'm uncertain if it's my abrupt departure that has further darkened her demeanor or solely our conversation in her backyard.

"Sure." She shrugs, wrapping her arm around her middle like she's protecting herself from me.

My heart pangs. As much as I want to talk it out with her, I'm not in the frame of mind to do so right now.

"Ah, I've got to go back to Montreal for a few days, but I'll be back for Saturday. I'll leave the tickets at the front desk and text you the details. I hope you come." I lean in to kiss her and at the last minute, she turns, giving me her cheek.

"Night, Sam," she says quietly.

Standing to my full height, I carefully examine this woman that has me tied up in knots. This woman who excites me with just the thought of her. This woman I *want* to know better. Thick tension and unspoken words hang heavy in the air between us. So much promise. So much longing. So much I want to say.

I want to tell her about Bas and give her an explanation about my sudden need to leave. I want to talk about us, about her children, and reassure her that we'll take this slow. I want to tell her everything will be okay, but now is not the time. My mind is muddled with worry and exasperation at Bas, and I fear I'd just mess up even further and make matters worse. My instinct is to leave things as they are, for now.

Sixteen

OLIVIA

"You're a jackhole."

"Drew," I reprimand, channeling my mother, the most proper person I know. She'd wash his mouth out with soap if she heard her grandson utter such trash. Paige snickers as she pours cereal into a bowl.

"Mom, seriously?" Drew challenges. "It's just a game." He excitedly focuses on the TV screen where lifelike soldiers in full battle gear shoot the shit out of each other—at least that's what it looks like to me. He's playing a video game and I know better than to interrupt, but he gets so immersed in it and forgets where he is.

"Exactly, that's my point," I answer, not knowing if I have a point, but feeling like I should. I'm straddling a line between being his mother—and thus having the right to question his vocabulary or behavior—and recognizing him as the adult he is now. Drew shakes his head and ignores me. Choosing to not take him on any further, I continue packing up my things.

"So, what time is your flight tomorrow?" Paige asks.

"Seven thirty." Rummaging through my bag, I double-check that I have everything. "Your dad's picking you up tomorrow, right?"

"Yes." She shovels a spoonful of Froot Loops (her dinner) into her mouth. Mouth full, crunching around her words, she adds, "We're leaving at noon."

"Paige," I chide, rolling my eyes at her disgusting eating habits. "Drew, you sure you don't want to go?"

"Really? We've been over this—I've got work. Besides, I'll see Nans and Gramps when they visit me in September."

"Fine." I'm resigned to the fact that whatever is going on between Pete and Drew hasn't been settled.

Pete's parents are snowbirds who spend winters in Florida, and we used to vacation with them. We'd fly down just before it was time for them to come home, spend a week or so, then drive their car back. This year, Pete asked me to come, his millionth attempt at reconciling.

He's been incessant with texts inviting me to dinner, drinks, and movies. At first, I responded, declining each time. Now, I ignore him. He needs to move on. As much as I believe he thinks he wants to repair our relationship—and perhaps some part of him truly does—I also believe he's mostly afraid of moving on. I get it. What we had was far from perfect and at times, downright painful, but it was comfortable and safe.

So, he's going to Florida with the kids—well, *kid,* since Drew backed out around the same time he came to live with me. Pete's tight-lipped about what's going on; like his son, he refuses to discuss it with me.

I'm headed to Montreal. I miss Sam. It's been almost two weeks since I last saw him at the food competition, and it wasn't all I hoped for. As promised, he came back the night before his judging gig. No call or visit. Instead, I got a text saying the tickets were at the front desk and that he'd see us the next day.

I saw him all right—mostly from afar. Sam was very generous, giving us six tickets. Paige brought Marci and her other friend Jessica, and to my surprise, Drew came with his 'friend' Laura.

The seats were great, front row center, and the cooking competition was entertaining with big celebrity chefs in attendance. It was fascinating to see the big production of filming a live show, and we even got a chance to taste the food. We had fun.

What fascinated me the most was Sam. I couldn't take my eyes off him. Seeing him in his element was hot. He is a friendly and easygoing man, but in front of the cameras, he was larger than life. Charismatic. Magnetic. If I weren't already taken with him, I'd have fallen for him then and there. It was easy to see why so many women are infatuated.

Speaking of women, the fans were obsessed. The amount of attention he received at Beaulieu's the night I met him was nothing in comparison to this. The competition brought the word fangirl to a whole new level—an overwhelming and scary one. No surprise, Sam had the biggest following. He was, hands down, the hottest chef there.

After the show, the crowd was insane, so much so that we couldn't get backstage. We floundered for over an hour in a sea of crazed fans. Eventually, security came and escorted us to the after party. Sam had arranged it, but once we got there, we saw him for maybe ten minutes before he was ushered out to complete his obligations for the event.

Our brief encounter left me sad and frustrated. While he was his usual kind and social self for the short time we had alone, he was also unusually cool and distant. I think back over our brief and somewhat disturbing conversation.

"So, what did you think?" he asks, hands tucked into his pockets.

While he keeps his distance, his eyes trail my body, lingering on my lips before moving on. Again, his fiery gaze ends its perusal on my mouth, He wickedly licks his lips like he's ready to eat me. A delightful thrum courses through me, my cheeks heat at his appreciative stare.

"Amazing. Thank you so much for inviting us. I can see why thousands of women go gaga over you," I jest, although every word is true.

A lazy, sexy smile covers his face and laughter laces his voice. "I'm really glad you liked it, and I'm glad you came."

"Listen, about what happened at my place. . ." I start, daring to broach the topic and end this awkwardness, even if it only exists in my head.

A lanky, mocha-skinned man with long dreadlocks interrupts. "Sam, let's roll, man." He completely ignores me.

Sam says something short and quick in French. With hands on his hips, the man shakes his head and responds, "Allons-y maintenant."

"Sorry, I gotta go. There's a photo shoot and then dinner. It's all part of the agreement. I'm really happy to see you. I leave for Montreal first thing tomorrow, but I'll text you. We'll figure something out." Leaning in, his lips delicately graze my cheek. All too soon, the kiss is over. "Say goodbye to Drew, Paige, and their friends for me."

Since then, there's only been one text from him, three words: *How are you?* My stomach lurches every time I think about it. I answered immediately, leaving no guesswork as to how anxious I'd been to hear from him. He never responded. That was four days ago.

I suppose I could have texted him again, but given I'm already struggling with this, with us, I didn't want to. I'm not on board with the age thing or living in two different cities. Even still, I think about him—a lot—and I've missed him. I *miss* him. He said we wouldn't label things, then I freaked at my house. I'm ready for some good times; I can do fun and casual, and I'm pretty sure he'd be all for it. Besides, did I mention I can't stop thinking about him?

By nine-thirty in the morning, I'm in Montreal, outside Beaulieu's. No one is here, and I'm realizing I'm not sure I thought this through well enough. My attempt at surprising him, reciprocating his sweet gesture with one I think he'd like, is failing miserably. I might have to call him after all and tell him I'm here.

Just as I pull up my Uber app, a delivery van parks. A young man, barely twenty if I had to guess, hops out with a large basket of baguettes and other breads. Sauntering to the back door, he watches me as he deposits the basket and returns to the van.

"Êtes-vous perdue?"

"Ah, um." Flustered, I scan my rolodex of grade thirteen French and come up empty, so I default to asking if he speaks English. "Pardon, je ne parle pas français. Parlez-vous anglais?"

"Oui. Are you lost?"

"No. I'm looking for Sam. I'm a friend and thought he might be here."

"He's at Mon Petit on Fridays," he states in his attractive French accent. "You want a lift? I'm headed there now." Slapping the side of the van door, he smiles. I foolishly jump, the sound jolting me out of my stupor.

Quickly, I contemplate the foolishness of getting into a vehicle with a total stranger. He's a young guy and not particularly big or muscular, so I figure I could likely take him if necessary, sending thanks to Jonah for my self-defense lessons.

"Sure, thanks."

As I enter Sam's other restaurant, Mon Petit Chou, behind the bread guy, laughter fills the air. Mon Petit Chou? Chou means cabbage in French. Sam has a cabbage tattoo. I don't get it—what's his deal with cabbage? I must ask him what it means.

Two young women and a man with dreads, the same one who was with Sam when he was in Toronto, are laughing. He stands behind the bar and his French banter is light and jovial, though indiscernible to me. That immediately changes once he spies me. Abruptly stopping the fun times, his expression sobers.

"What the hell are you doing here?" His words are deep and almost menacing.

"Ah, I'm looking for Sam," I quietly reply, nervous.

"He's not here," the women respond in unison. As if telepathic, they cross their arms over their ample chests. The tall guy strides toward me like he's on a mission and I'm his target.

"Get out," he orders, pointing his long finger at the door. "No groupies allowed." Groupie? Do I look like a groupie? I certainly don't think so. Turning his wrath on the bread guy, he snarls, "Zee, why did you bring her here?"

What is it with this guy? I have no clue who the hell he is, but he certainly has a hate on for me. What on earth did I ever do to him?

"Désolé," the bread guy mumbles, giving me the evil eye before hightailing it out of there.

Thinking he's onto something, I'm about to follow suit and get the hell out of there when I hear Sam's deep, rumbly voice. My heart jerks.

"Olivia." Sam stands at the mouth of a hallway and warmth blooms in my stomach at the sight of his sexy, friendly smile. In less than five steps, he picks me up, twirling me around.

A shrill squeak crosses my lips as I grip his broad shoulders for fear of falling. My fear quickly dissipates, knowing he wouldn't let me fall. He's got me. His big hands tightly encase my waist. Closing my eyes, everything swirls and my stomach plummets to my toes. Quickly reopening them, I inhale deeply. The merry-go-round sensation is not working for me. I'm going to toss my cookies.

"Put me down," I command, digging my nails into his shoulders.

Laughing, he stops, tightening his arms around me in a hug. Burying his face into the crook of my neck, his warm breath tickles my skin and his spicy masculine scent surrounds us.

"I missed you," he huskily whispers. His lips sprinkle feather-light kisses along my neck before putting me down.

Sliding the length of his chest and abs, his hard ridges send tingles to every sensitive, girly part in my body and heat pools in my core. Nibbling on my bottom lip, I move out of his embrace, internally battling with myself for control.

Confusion and arousal invade my senses. He hasn't spoken to me in over a week, complete radio silence, and now he acts like everything is okay? As much as my mind wants to talk and figure out where we stand, my body doesn't give a fuck. It likes what it sees and wants to get to the fun part.

The tall, dark man is not amused with our display of familiarity and affection, a scowl firmly entrenched on his face. Neither of the women are that much better, their pretty faces scrunched up at me.

"Sam, what the hell?" the man inquires accusingly.

Sam chuckles, pulling me in front of him, hands on my hips. His front is nestled closely to my back. "Jerome, Anne, Tal, this is Olivia." Gently squeezing my side, he continues, "Livvy, these are my friends, and they also work here. Jerome's my manager and sometime bartender when I need one, and Anne and Tal are hostesses."

"Hi," I flatly reply, not expecting much of a welcome even with Sam's endorsement. I still don't know what I did to deserve their disdain, but at this point, I don't care.

"Olivia?" Jerome asks. "*The* Olivia? The chick from Beaulieu's?"

I uncomfortably clear my throat at the designation of 'chick', giving him one of my own scowls. Jerome smiles at me in what I think is his attempt at flirting, unfazed by my ire. Both women offer quick hellos before resuming their task of setting the tables.

"Yes, *the* Olivia," Sam responds with a smile in his voice. Not interested in providing more of an explanation to Jerome, he says to me, "Never mind him. He thinks he's my mother and my security detail on top of everything else."

Jerome starts to protest, but Sam ignores him, leading me down the hallway into a room marked *Office*.

"You're a sight for sore eyes," he says in a low, gravelly tone that puts a quiver in my belly. When he attempts to pull me into another hug, I place my hands firmly on his chest. Despite wanting nothing more than to roam his rock-hard pecs and abs, I need to focus.

"Sam, we need to talk." He nods, looking at me encouragingly. Not wasting any time, I dive right in. "I didn't mean to brush you off that night when I said we needed to talk to the kids. I wasn't prepared to do it, and because of that I backed away. It was stupid of me and not what I meant to do."

"I know." His eyes are soft and understanding.

"Okay, so if you know, why didn't you text or call after the competition? And why didn't you respond to my text earlier this week?" I fight to keep my voice calm and hope to God I don't sound pathetic and needy.

He scrubs a hand down his face and sighs. "I'm sorry." Taking both my hands in his, he tugs me closer and gently squeezes. "I agree, we need to talk, and I want to, but it's not something I wanted to do over the phone or via text. I really wanted to see you, talk to you before I left, but there was no time. I had to get home. There are things I want to tell you, but not here. Let me finish up these orders—my bartender's out today—and then we can go."

Eager to talk but willing to give him a bit more time, I nod.

"I'm so glad you're here. Best surprise ever," he says with a smile, his voice husky as he pecks my cheek before sitting down behind his desk.

Sinking into the oversized, weathered leather couch, I note his office is jam-packed. Next to the couch, which takes up almost half the room, his large, retro desk dominates the other half. A bookshelf sits up against a wall, crammed with cookbooks, some vinyl records, and a few novels. Amidst all the chaos, the surface of his desk is surprisingly neat, sporting only a laptop and lamp.

Sam types on his laptop and studies the screen like it's the Holy Grail, small lines forming on his forehead as he concentrates. Occasionally, he lifts his head with a small, sweet smile just for me before returning to his task. My phone buzzes with an incoming text—Tamsin.

Tamsin: Where r u?

Me: Montreal

Tamsin: What?? Yay! Say hi to Sam

Me: Lol stop. What's up?

Tamsin: Jonah is cursing you. Run, girl, run. U r supposed to run with him today

Me: I canceled. Tell him to check his voicemail.

Jonah hardly ever checks his phone messages, and I know that; I should have texted him. He prides himself on being Mr. Technology, all digital age, but he's not one to actually talk on the phone or to even think about any potential voicemails. Not a good way to run a business.

Tamsin: He says not cool.

Me: You're with him?

Tamsin: Yup. He suckered me into running. You OWE ME!!

Me: Pace yourself. ILY xx

I sit quietly and patiently, trying not to dwell on what Sam might have to say. Is it good or bad? Why am I stressing? We're casual—as proven by his recent aloof behavior. This is what I want. He's not pushing like I feared in my backyard. I feared he wanted more and I couldn't give it to him, and now I'm afraid I'll never be able to give him that.

Seventeen

OLIVIA

"You didn't answer me," I say, finally breaking our comfortable silence. Sam's puzzled. "You never explained why you didn't text back this week."

With a ghost of a smile, he says, "I lost my phone. It's likely somewhere in the Vancouver airport."

"What?" I shudder at the thought—losing my phone would be like losing my life. "Are you serious?"

"Yup. I was in Vancouver this past week looking at potential restaurant locations. Last time I had my phone, I was in the airport."

For a fleeting moment, my heart sinks at his news—he might open his restaurant in Vancouver? I loved the idea of his new restaurant being in Toronto. It would be a reason to be in my city. To see me. If he opens on the west coast, this—whatever this is between us—will fizzle out real quick.

"What are you going to do?" My voice is anxious at the idea of both his missing phone and his new venture being across the country. "I mean, I'd be freaking. I texted you four days ago. You've been without a phone that long?"

"I'm using Bas's right now. I was hoping to find it, but now I'm thinking I'll have to break down and buy a new one."

"Oh." I don't like knowing he did in fact have a phone; it means he could have contacted me, but didn't. Confusion and sadness set in.

"Hey, let's get out of here." Shutting his laptop, he strides over and takes my hand. As we walk out, he adds, as if reading my mind, "I don't have your number memorized, because it was programmed in my phone. I should've made the effort to get your number, but…" He pauses, hesitant.

"But what?" My stomach churns with unease.

"Let's get to my place and then we'll talk, I promise," he reassures.

Not fully calm or comforted, I force myself to not dwell on whatever it is he has to tell me. Whatever it is, even if it's something I don't want to hear, I'll deal.

His place is a few blocks from Mon Petit Chou, a refurbished loft on the waterfront. For me, it's a design mecca with its wood floors, exposed field-stone brick, fifteen-plus-foot ceilings, and windows galore. It's beautifully sparse, the furniture minimal, making the architecture the centerpiece.

"Wow, this is amazing," I gush, unable to rest my eyes on any one feature.

"Thanks."

"Don't you have people over?" My random question stops his movement, his steady gaze now on me. "What I mean is, your bed's just out in plain view, don't you…?" I trail off, weak-kneed at the dawning of his sexy smile.

"You worried about who sees my bed, Olivia?" he teases, seeming like the Sam I'm used to.

Blushing, I look away and chuckle. "Hardly.Never mind."

"Um, let's talk."

Okay, the moment is here. Linking his arm in mine, he seats us side by side on the sofa. "I'm sorry about this week. Really. I did want to call you, we need to talk, but what I have to say shouldn't be said on the phone."

I'm not liking the sound of this. Maybe it is what I feared it would be—is he ending things? Coming here might have been a bad idea.

What am I thinking? If I'm honest with myself, I don't want to end this. I'm having fun and I like Sam, a lot, but maybe it's better this way, better to get out before I get my heart broken.

"I've been distracted. My… Bas is sick. He has cancer." Sucking in a jagged breath, he continues quickly on the exhale like he needs to say it, get it all out. "At first, it was the lungs, but it's spread and there's nothing we can do. The treatment is only buying him time."

His bitter, resigned words slice through me. I selfishly have a fleeting moment of relief that we aren't over. Despite my concerns, my fears, I'm not ready to walk away, and feeling that after hearing what Sam is dealing with only proves that I care for this man.

I want nothing more than to comfort him, make it all better, but I can only do so much. This—cancer—is so much uglier and bigger than us.

"Sam." My tone is loving and heartfelt.

Reaching out, I pull him into my arms, holding him tight, and his big, hard body relaxes into my embrace with a sigh. I don't know what to say, but I want him to know I'm here for him.

"He's just finishing up his chemo treatment. That's why I left. He's being difficult and wanting to do this alone. Alec is having none of it and has been there every step of the way, as have I. He thinks he's protecting us by trying to limit what we have to see or endure, but instead he's driving us insane with worry. I've been spending a lot of time there." Pulling back slightly, he rubs his hand down his face and hangs his head low. "You've been on my mind. A lot." Gazing up at me, hurt and worry swim in his eyes.

"Sam, I'm so sorry. I've been so caught up in me and wondering why you were being aloof. I had no clue."

Shaking his head, he sharply but warmly says, "Stop." He lightly kisses my forehead. "Have I told you how glad I am that you're here?"

His lips skate along the side of my ear, trailing down my neck then stopping at the juncture of my neck and collarbone where he laves and sucks that tender spot, doing all kinds of gooey things to my insides. To prevent my pleasurable moan from escaping, I bite my bottom lip. His tongue leisurely traces my pulse point, which quickens at his languorous care.

Out of sheer desire and a serious lack of control, I lose the battle. With my hands latched onto his solid, contoured sides, I emit a low, husky moan. His tongue keeps at its seduction with licks and sweeps up the column of my neck. With each sweep, peck, and bite, I'm loud with pleasurable abandon.

"God, Sam, yes."

Humming in appreciation, his warm lips hurriedly make their way to mine. With a nip to my bottom lip followed by a lick, his mouth covers mine, his insistent tongue teasing the seam of my lips. Our kiss is urgent and voracious, like I'm his last meal. *Whoa.* Heat flames my insides.

Strong hands cling to my hips, moving me, our connection never lost as he effortlessly places me in his lap. With one leg on either side, I straddle him. Settling into him, his incredibly solid arousal is insistent between my legs. His take-charge demeanor and his obvious desire for me dissolve my restraint as I unabashedly rock back and forth against his hard length. The thin cotton of my leggings feels like nothing against the solid ridge of his erection. With a whiny, breathy whimper, I'm unable to contain myself. I couldn't stop even if I wanted to, and I don't.

"Olivia." He releases a low, pained groan into my mouth, his fingers tightening on my bottom. Relishing every second of our contact, I inhale his intoxicating scent, all Sam.

"Sam." My drawn out, breathless moan slides into his mouth.

Subtly but almost instantly, his kiss morphs into dreamy, soft sweeps and caresses. Less adamant, but no less intense. This is more than a kiss. He's making love to my mouth.

My hands slip to his waist, moving deftly for his button and fly. I need him. Inside me. *Now.* Sam swiftly lifts me, palming my ass, our tongues still tangled as he lays us down on the bed.

"Tell me to stop," he urges, his lips still against mine. "If we don't stop now, I won't be able to control myself any longer."

"Don't stop."

I want this. *I want him.* My encouragement unleashes the animal in him—within seconds, he pulls his shirt over his head then drops his jeans and boxers.

My breath stalls at the beauty of him in his naked glory. He's beyond gorgeous, his hard, sculpted body definitely worthy of worship. While I peruse his impressive frame, he only has eyes for me. His heated stare only makes me hotter, my skin prickling to be touched, sucked, and bitten.

And his tattoos—God, they are glorious. Dark ink contrasts his bronzed skin, the soft swirls and curls of the script stand out against the hard ridges and contours of his defined body. Both the delicately detailed cabbage on his pec and the black words on his ribs are taunting me.

In one swift move, he has my leggings on the floor and is working to unbutton my blouse. The enormity of what we're doing seeps through my desire-filled haze, and self-consciousness skitters like an unwanted chill over my bare flesh. The curtains are open, bright daylight streaming into the room.

I shiver. "Ah, Sam." I clear my throat in attempt to sound more certain. "Can you shut the curtains or…somehow make it darker?"

No sooner are the words out of my mouth than I recognize the absurdity of what I've said. I am confident in who I am. I love my body, but I'd be silly to deny my hesitation. In my nakedness, I'm shy and doubtful of my appeal to him, this perfect, younger, sexy man. Yes, he's made no secret of his interest in me, but things get real, fast, when one is naked.

My body is not perfect. I have stretch marks, areas that should be firmer, and scars—all of which I'm proud of. Sure, if all things were equal, I'd want my younger body in a heartbeat, but my body is my storybook. My hardships, loves, losses, and triumphs have been lived in my bones, my skin. Even with the end of my marriage and the uncertainty that looms ahead, I wouldn't change a thing. No regrets.

"Olivia." His low, sexy voice pulls me out of my heavy thoughts, the tender look in his eyes telling me he knows what's going on. His hand threads through my hair, cupping the back of my head. "I want to see you, all of you. You're breathtaking. Let me worship you, love every inch of you," he whispers before his lips brush over mine.

Something inexplicable yet powerful cartwheels inside my chest, strange and new. I've never felt this way before. With each sweep of his tongue, like the wind scattering sheets of paper, my want wildly spreads throughout my body, and desire shreds my doubts.

Eighteen

SAM

Softly at first, then more persistently, my tongue caresses her mouth. Sweet and addictive, I could kiss her all day. How she could think anything negative about herself is mindboggling and fucking crazy. She's perfect just the way she is.

With her clothes scattered on the floor, she lies on my bed, bared to me, her dark eyes are soft and inviting. Threading my hand through her hair, I cradle her head as my lips trail down her neck. Her skin is silk and she tastes like chocolate. *Fucking delicious.* I sweep the pad of my thumb over her pert brown nipple and like a chain reaction, she releases a sigh in complete surrender.

Latching onto her breast, my teeth nibble on her distended bud while my hand pleasures her other nipple. She's wildly vocal in expressing her enjoyment with whimpers and moans that drive me crazy. I want to be inside of her.

My hands explore every inch of her body, every curve, every soft swell and every taut muscle. She's so responsive. Arching, writhing, whimpering as she gives herself to me, completely trusting.

My hands and her body converse in a language of their own. My touch expresses how divine she is, every curve, every scar, every inch of her perfect, made for me. My fingers tell her how much and how deeply I see her beauty, inside and out.

Skimming my hand down between her legs,

I graze her sex. *Fuck.* She wants this. She wants me. Lightly rubbing her clit, my fingers are coated in her slickness. She pleasurably squirms and sighs. Increasing the pace of my ministrations with the pad of my thumb, my finger dips to tease her opening.

"Sam." My name is a plea on her lips.

Gradually, I insert one finger, leisurely pumping in and out, adding another while my thumb circles her tight bundle of nerves. Olivia cries out, tensing. Her knees shake and her hands tremble, digging into my shoulders. As she climaxes, her eyes hold mine. She clenches, hot and snug around my fingers.

"I need you now, mon trésor," I whisper, crazed. "Are you ready, Livvy?"

She nods, eyes piercing and needy as I open the foil packet and roll the condom on. Licking her lips as our eyes meet, and I devilishly smile. My girl likes what she sees.

I wrap my arms around her slender body, and she fits perfectly. Made for me. My mouth devours hers once more. When she willingly opens for me, I nestle myself between her legs as she arches and bucks, sliding her hot core impatiently along my hard-as-steel dick. We both groan.

"Easy, Livvy. Wait."

"I want you, Sam. Now," she declares her eagerness with her smoldering eyes and intense pants. My tongue flicks over the bud of her nipple and she whimpers, "Yes. Sam."

With her encouragement, I push inside her, torturously slow, inch by inch. With a fervent cry, her eyes close, mouth open, back curving, breasts shoved closer to my face. *Beautiful.* The urge to impale her, hard, balls deep into her tight sex is excruciatingly overwhelming, but I want this to be as good for her as it is for me.

Giving her time to adjust to my girth, her grip loosens as I bury myself deep within her. *Fuck.* She's perfect. Wet, hot, and tight. Nirvana.

We easily find our rhythm in long, hard pushes and slow, teasing pulls as I caress, stroke and kiss every inch of her body.

"Oh, my God. Sam. Yes, oh my, yes," Olivia cries. Her incessant, pleasurable pleas are an invitation to lose control as she pulses around me, my need for her so fierce. I want to stay inside her forever.

I rub her sensitive spot to match our rocking and her eyes fly open, chocolate pools of desire nailing me.

"Mon trésor." *My treasure.*

"Sam. Oh God. Don't stop."

"You like that Livvy?"

"Oh. . .yes."

Together, we tense, eyes locked. With blinding ecstasy, our bodies soar and shatter. An eruption of bliss cascades over us.

Fucking phenomenal.

As we come down, I hurriedly get up to remove the condom and return, gently collapsing on top of her small frame. I need to touch her, feel her. Swiftly rolling until I'm on my back, I take her with me. Her head rests on my breastbone as our heavy pants slow and our breathing evens out.

We both close our eyes, burrowing into each other, and rest. What feels like seconds later, I'm awoken by the light touch of Olivia's finger tracing my tattoo, the cabbage. Glancing at the clock on the wall, I've been sleeping for over an hour.

"Sorry, did I wake you?" she asks, her voice husky.

"Nah." I kiss her forehead.

She smiles, her eyes dreamy. "Tell me about these." Her hand moves from my pec to the side of my rib cage, brushing over the ink etched on my body.

"What do you want to know?" I play coy.

"This one." Her finger points to the cabbage. "What does that mean and what's the connection to Mon Petit Chou? I'm guessing there's a connection."

Nodding, I lace my fingers with hers, kissing the top of her hand and squeezing. "My grand-mère called me mon petit chou. It means my little cabbage. It's a term of endearment in French, doesn't quite have the same ring or meaning in English." I chuckle. "I wanted to pay homage to her, the woman who raised me. She was like a mother to me. So, I got the tattoo after my eighteenth birthday, and then I named my first restaurant in honor of her too. She'd be thrilled that I'm a chef and doing something I love and am good at."

Olivia pushes up, her lips kissing my neck, the underside of my jaw, and then my chest, right over the cabbage. "I love it. Mon petit chou chou—it sounds sweet. They must have loved you a lot, and it sounds like you loved them too."

"I did."

"It must have been so hard for you to lose all those you loved at such a young age. I can't imagine. Both Paige and Drew have never lost anyone, even at their ages, and I imagine when that day comes, it'll be tough for them."

"Yeah, it was, but I got lucky with Bas. I'd be living a completely different and likely dangerous life if I'd not met him."

"I can't wait to meet him."

"Oh, didn't I mention? We're meeting them tomorrow. I'm spending the day with them and since you surprised me, you're coming along."

My hand slips down from her back to her bare bottom and I squeeze before playfully swatting. She jumps, squealing, and lightly hits my chest then giggles, her eyes glittering with joy.

"Enough of that, Monsieur Beaulieu. Tell me about this one. I want to know what it says."

She looks down at the black scrawl, outlining the words with her finger as I say, "Mais les yeux sont aveugles. Il faut chercher avec le cœur." Her chestnut eyes are expectant as she patiently waits for me to continue. "It means, 'But the eyes are blind. One must look with the heart.' It's from—"

"The Little Prince," she whispers, her expression soft and bare.

"Le Petit Prince by Antoine de Sainty-Exupéry," I finish.

"I love that book. I've read it to my kids at least a hundred times. It's one of my favorites."

"Mine too. It was our thing. My grand-père and I would read it together. At first, when I was young, he'd read it to me, but as he got older, I would read it to him."

"There are so many beautiful quotes from that book. Why this one?"

"Ah, now that is the question," I tease, lightly tapping the tip of her nose. "And it's really too deep for now. I'll tell you another time. Besides, we have to go."

"We do?" Olivia clutches the sheet to her chest as I stand and walk toward the bathroom.

p. We need to shower and go. We're having dinner with the Thibaults." Her face falls, mouth downturned and eyes narrow. In less than a second, she catches herself, replacing it with a blank expression. If I'd not been looking, I wouldn't have seen it.

She thinks I don't know, or perhaps she doesn't want me to know, but I'm fully aware that she's not a fan of Yasmine Thibault. Frankly, neither am I. I'm no fool; I know what she wants, and I'm not interested.

Maybe I'm being a dick by not cutting her off. It'd most likely make Olivia happy, but Yasmine's a necessary evil for now while I explore a potential business relationship with her father.

Until I know if the Thibaults are the way to go, I won't be out and out rude in response to Yasmine's advances. I've made it no secret that I'm with Olivia and not interested, but you'd think the woman is deaf and dumb.

"Do I have to come?" she asks.

Tossing her my shirt, I smirk. "Yes, you do. If I could cancel, I would, but I can't. They know I'm looking at Toronto and Vancouver and want to know which way I'm leaning."

She slips the shirt over her head, modestly holding the sheet to her body. Now covered, she approaches, a slight frown in place. "Which way are you leaning? Do you know?"

Shuffling from one foot to another, she pulls her bottom lip into her mouth, her top teeth sinking into the luscious pink flesh. Boy, what I'd give to trade places with her teeth right now. If only we had the time. Later—I'll definitely come back to it later.

"Yup, and I think you know my preference."

Pulling her to me, her chest against mine, my lips grab hers for a quick, deep kiss. Unable to resist, I snare her bottom lip in my teeth and lightly tug, sucking and teasing her sweet, plump flesh. She moans, melting farther into me. *Shit,* I wish we could blow them off. "Let's go shower. You'll have to behave yourself Ms. Cassidy. Keep your hands to yourself," I warn teasingly.

Light, melodic laughter fills the air as Olivia replies, "Right. *I* have to keep my hands to myself? That's rich. You're on mister. You so much as touch me and I get to order for you tonight."

Knowing it's a bad move and that there's no way I'll win this deal, I agree. Sure enough, I'm an idiot, and the loser. There's no way I can keep my hands off Olivia, naked and wet, looking like she's made to be devoured by me. Not going to happen.

So here we are, having dinner with Daniel and Yasmine, and Olivia's ordering for me. Both Daniel and Yasmine watch with keen interest as she orders me the steak frites, medium rare. She's loving every minute of it with a contented smile on her face. Yasmine is mildly annoyed at the whole thing, her eyes glancing down to where our hands are joined. Perhaps *that's* what has Olivia smugly satisfied.

After dinner, Daniel insists on showing me the restaurant's wine cellar. I suggest we all go, but it's evident he wants to speak with me alone, and Yasmine works with her father to have us separated. I dread leaving them alone. Every time Olivia's been alone with Yasmine, her mood has shifted and she has withdrawn.

We're back in under fifteen minutes. My discussion with Daniel was uneventful and it makes no sense why we all couldn't have gone—until I see my phone resting on the table. Olivia's quiet and Yasmine is all smiles as she hands me the phone.

"Sam, I'm guessing this is yours. I have no clue how your phone wound up in my luggage, but I found it when unpacking from our trip to Vancouver."

Stiffening my spine at what she's obviously implying, I look to Olivia. She's readying her purse to likely excuse herself. I need to act fast and set things straight.

"Thanks. That's strange—I had it in the airport and I was never in your room, so how could it end up in your things?" I ask pointedly, not hiding I'm aware of what she's up to and that I don't like it one bit.

Yasmine laughs, and it's obviously fake. "I've no clue. Anyway, I'm glad I was able to return it to you. Please excuse me." Cutting off any further conversation, she stands and leaves the table.

Olivia is now studying me, her face expressionless, and I can't tell if she's angry, hurt, or couldn't give a shit, though I highly doubt the latter is the case. Daniel stands awkwardly at the edge of the table and when the server comes with our bill, he mumbles something about paying at the bar.

Taking her hand, I gently stroke her knuckles. Her eyes rise to look at me, guarded and confused.

"I never went to her room and she never went to mine. She did the same shit she did in Toronto, she just showed up. I fired Patti for breaching my privacy. There's no other way she would have known I'd be there unless Patti told her, and come to think of it, Patti couldn't stop apologizing and never denied my accusation."

She nods, clearing her throat. "Okay Sam, really, you don't need to explain yourself to me."

"What?" I ask, incredulous. "Why would you say that?"

"We're casual, remember? No labels. If you had gone to Vancouver with Yasmine, that'd be fine. None of my business. And if you'd shared a room..." She can't bring herself to finish the sentence, and that's when I know every word out her mouth is a lie. She doesn't mean it. Not at all.

"Olivia, we may be casual"—*we're not,* but if that's what she needs to hear to help her sleep at night, so be it, for now— "but you have a right to know. Besides..." Both Daniel and Yasmine approach the table, causing the conversation to abruptly stop.

That night we have sex again. It's hard, primal, and raw. If Olivia thinks we are casual and words weren't enough to convince her otherwise, I need to show her. Fuck her senseless. Fuck her 'til she no longer remembers what life was like without me inside her.

I take her against the fridge, over the sofa from behind, and again on the bathroom counter as we get ready for bed. Olivia's satisfying screams ring loud and clear throughout my place. I have no clue how thick the walls are between lofts, and I don't care.

In fact, knowing I'm the one bringing her this pleasure, knowing it's my name she's screaming and I'm the one causing her to lose all her inhibitions—it does something to me. She's come undone because of me and it feeds the beast in me, gives it life. A visceral, palpable stirring within my body grows and takes over as I'm driven to dine on her, to bring her ecstasy.

Morning comes too quickly as we spent barely any time sleeping. We lazily have breakfast and coffee on my terrace, trading sections of the newspaper in easy, comforting silence. Afterward, I hop in the shower, then Olivia takes her turn while I check in with Jerome on how things are at the restaurants. I'm hoping we can spend the entire day with Bas and Alec.

Coming in from the terrace with our coffee cups, Olivia's phone is outside on the table, and it buzzes as I go back to get it, lighting up the screen with an incoming text.

Pete: Dinner tonight? You and me, 7? We could go to one of our favorites? Padano?

Why is Pete making dinner plans with her? Is this a regular thing? Fighting the temptation to swipe and read the full conversation, I shove the phone in my back pocket. I won't breach her privacy because of my insecurity.

"Ready?" Olivia calls, purse in hand. She's lovely. Every time, I have to stop and stare at her, even if only for a moment.

"Yes, let me just grab my keys." I head to the kitchen counter and then course correct, turning on my heel toward her. Like defusing a bomb, I need to get rid of her phone before I explode. "You left it outside."

I hand it to her and she glances down at the screen, swipes, and then proceeds to read. I'm not sticking around to watch this. It's bad enough that he texts her for dinner dates and who knows what else, and who knows if she goes out with him. After all, he is her ex-husband, the father of her kids. He's always going to be in her life.

Having dinner isn't a big deal; it's not, but the 'you and me' and the 'one of our favorites' are. Those words are just too personal for me, a bit too cozy.

Nineteen

OLIVIA

Rapt by the sight before me, I stand in the doorway gawking at the two equally striking men, each sporting silver hair and a bold, handsome face. Bas and Alec are in a deep, animated conversation by the stove with hand gestures and all, touching each other in adoring and tender ways. Love radiates from and around them.

I never considered myself one to watch another couple, but shit, as the heat rises to my cheeks, I seriously consider grabbing some popcorn, a glass of wine, and watching these two. I can't explain it, but they're beautiful together. Instinctually, it makes you yearn for what they have, but not in a covetous way, more because every person should be looked at and loved like that.

Alec is tall and fit, his hair wavy but neatly in place, and his gray dusting of scruff gives a slight edge to his debonair features and hazel eyes. Bas is ruggedly handsome with a strong jaw lined with trimmed stubble and spiky white hair that's short but eye-catching and a complement to his deep, bold blue eyes. Each man is different, but no less good-looking.

Scintillating aromas of whatever is simmering on the stove waft through the air. Alec turns to the source as Bas shuffles over to a kitchen chair, draping a blanket over his shoulders. It's summer, hot and humid outside, yet he's covered in layers of clothes.

Upon closer inspection, despite the added bulk, Bas looks smaller than I imagined he would. Now, watching him, even without knowing about the cancer, I'd know he wasn't well. My stomach clenches at what he must be going through, what they're all going through. We lost my father to cancer, and I sincerely wish I could spare them the pain and heartache that come with the devastating disease.

"Bas, Alec," Sam says, bringing me fully into the room. Turning toward us, their smiles widen. "This is Olivia." The tenderness and, dare I say, pride in Sam's voice is clear.

Both greet me with hugs, the French multiple-kisses thing, and with ease, we settle on the deck outside. I'm nestled beside Sam on a wooden bench, Alec sits to the side in a Muskoka chair, and Bas rests in one beside him, cocooned in his blanket in the middle of sweltering July. *Shit.* He doesn't look good.

"Olivia, tell us what you've been up to since arriving," Alec encourages, his accent thick and smooth like chocolate melting in your mouth.

"Not much." Before I can catch myself, my heated gaze looks up at Sam. Images of us—in the shower, him behind me, in me, on his furniture, in his bed—flash through my mind like a heart-searing slideshow. Heat stirs low in my belly as Sam rakes his hungry eyes over me like he's reading my mind. Exhaling a burst of air and my sudden yearning, I look away. "We went to dinner with the Thibaults," I awkwardly offer.

"Daniel and Yasmine?" Bas asks. We nod. "Sam, I told you to walk away. They're bad news, trust me," he implores. Sluggishly standing, he walks to the railing overlooking his backyard and huffs. His frail hands curl in on themselves. The Thibaults clearly piss him off. "Fine don't trust me, but talk to Sal Lyons before you do anything."

"Sal? Why?" Sam asks, puzzled.

"Daniel invested in his first restaurant, Voltaire. Ask him about it."

"Voltaire? I've never heard of it," Sam says.

"Exactly," Bas snaps.

I wish I knew more about why he has a strong dislike for Daniel. I, too, don't particularly like the Thibaults, but I'm sensing now would not be a good time to ask for further explanation. Alec goes to him, gently squeezing Bas's shoulder before moving the conversation into more amiable territory.

"Bas, Alec, perhaps you can help me out." All three pair of eyes land on me as I smirk. "I'd love some dirt on Sam. What was he like as a child? Anything I should know or could use to torture him with?"

Bas chuckles, a slight twinkle in his gray eyes. "Ah, Samson, I like this one. She'll keep you on your toes. Ma chérie, I could tell you many things," he cunningly quips.

I love that he calls me his dear, ma chérie, so sweet. His immediate fondness for me warms my heart.

"Hey, let's stop right there," Sam interjects.

"Nope, I think Bas and I need to talk." I attempt to stand, but Sam's hands firmly grip my waist, pulling me onto his lap.

With his arm holding me still, the warm breath of his sexy, low voice skitters across my neck. "Nice try. You're not going anywhere."

His fingers dance along my sides. Damn, I'm ticklish. Unable to keep this tidbit a secret, I squeal and squirm. He chuckles at my reaction, continuing his playful torment.

"Stop, please, stop," I beg, fruitlessly wriggling, powerless to escape his hold.

Alec nears and then reaches over, tickling Sam's sides, which immediately provides me relief. Sam yelps and he too squirms and laughs. *Ha! We're both ticklish—good to know.* "Arrête," he calls, raising his hands in surrender.

Our laughter fills the air. Bas clings to the railing, chuckling, deep lines of mirth etching his features, but there's also a sadness, a sobering shadow in his eyes, in his not quite full smile. My chest tightens. I can only imagine his melancholy thoughts, the idea of not being around to enjoy this, to be with those he loves the most.

"Garde cette femme," Bas says out of nowhere. I think it means something like *keep this woman.* Their eyes lock as Sam straightens, seriousness setting into his expression. Nodding once, as in a promise to Bas, his gaze turns to me, soft and open, a small smile creeping along his lips.

"Samson hated his name," Bas continues, as if he's having a conversation with himself.

"Pardon?" I ask, looking to him.

"When he was a teenager, Samson hated his name. Insisted on being called Sam. Never answering to his given name. A formidable, noble name, Samson. Alec respected his wishes, but I refused."

Sam's smile is rueful, his eyes fixed on Bas, mesmerized by this man who is a father to him.

"What happened?" I want to know more, all about Sam and his life, his loves and passions, dislikes and dreams.

"After about a year of it, I'd had enough. He was sulky and difficult. Stubborn. I sat him down and told him that his name was something to be proud of, to cherish and live up to. It was his grandmother's maiden name. His dear, poor mother." Bas pauses. The tone in his voice is reflective and haunting. A slight chill runs through me, and I don't know why. "She gave him that name, wanted him to have her family name. His name is proof that she adored him. She loved him with all of her heart and wanted him to have a part of her, if not all of her."

Silence ensues, all of us caught up in his words. I try to interpret his meaning as Alec stares pensively at his husband, seeming to fully understand the magnitude of what Bas just shared.

Bas and Sam stare at each other, gazes locked. Eyes penetrating, boring into each other. Speaking a language we can't hear or decipher. I wish I could. I wish I had the code to unlock their unspoken words. The moment is poignant.

Bas is the first to break the spell, saying we need to grab food for dinner. With that, we head out and spend the day shopping, selecting fresh produce, meat, and delights from both the Atwater and Jean Talon Markets before returning to their place for a bountiful and delicious meal.

Later that night, we return to Sam's. His loft is in total darkness except for the thin slant of moonlight casting a silvery hue on the open space. In silence, he interlaces our fingers and leads me to his bed.

On the way, his free hand removes his shirt the way guys do—with one swift pull over his head. He reluctantly releases my hand to allow the fabric to fall from his arm and then immediately claims me again. Next are his pants and boxers, gone.

When he stands gloriously naked before me, my hands instinctively reach for him, needing him. Removing my clothes, he takes time to caress my skin as it is revealed. Long, calloused fingertips glide across my collarbone and chest.

As if that wasn't enough, his lips worship, gentle and hot, with the slight zing of his stubble grazing my flesh. Each kiss erases all my past lows and insecurities, every single moment of sadness, neglect, and loneliness.

He removes my jeans, then bends, twisting his torso to kiss my lower back. Teasing a path along my hips with his tongue, he returns to kneel in front of me and wraps his arms around my middle. His face nuzzles my stomach, placing hot, wet kisses on my midriff while his tongue dips into my belly button, sending shivers up my spine and curling my toes.

After peeling off my panties, he plants a hard, possessive kiss on my pussy. His tongue then licks from my entrance up to flick my clit, and I moan at his gentle yet passionate dominance. His lips continue a blistering path up my body, only stopping his glorious mapping of me to unclasp my bra.

Both naked, our gazes lock as he lifts me to straddle him on the bed. His adoration is evident and staggering in his heavy-lidded eyes. His hard cock presses snugly against my sex, and I'm unable to stay still as a breathy sigh passes through my slightly open lips and I slide along him.

Riding out my climax against him, his molten stare only serves to spur me on as my core heats, aches for release, my breasts heavy with need. His devotion consumes me and is weakening my resolve to keep us free of labels and expectations.

I scream his name like it's the meaning of life as my orgasm rips through me. He seals my open mouth with his and our kiss lingers while his hands roam my body, one gripping my breast. With the other, he guides his cock to my entrance. Gradually and eagerly, I lower myself onto him.

The sense of finally being full, cherished, and awakened washes over me. His arms envelop me, one across my back, the other on my bottom as we leisurely move together like yin and yang, inseparable, our foreheads connected, eyes locked, mouths open, sharing the same breath as we climb to our release.

"Sam," I whisper reverently.

"Livvy," he groans, thrusting to the hilt as we come together. We've never been closer, now moving as one.

That isn't sex, it's love, much more than two naked bodies entwined. Our strong connection lives and breathes in every caress, every moan, every embrace. It's remarkable and intense, and it scares the hell out of me.

It's amazing what time and distance can do for a girl's perspective. It's a week later and my fear has faded. I came home muddled and worried; the weekend with Sam had been out of this world, but I feared it had been unwise.

All our obstacles still exist—our age difference, the distance, not to mention being in two different stages in our lives. I have my family, and he's just starting out. I have no clue if he wants children or even to marry. I never want to marry again, and even at that, I am getting ahead of myself. Marriage! Who said anything about marriage? Again, my age is showing.

But a week later, my fears are gone. We are back to texting and talking daily and somehow this invisible, protective shield is back in place now that we are separated and in our own domains.

What also helped was my conversation with Yasmine Thibault. Surprisingly, she helped put things in perspective. While I still dislike the woman, what she said did make some sense.

At the restaurant that night, she was quick to speak her mind. It had been very clear that both Daniel and Yasmine wanted each of us alone. Yasmine's reason became apparent the minute Sam left the table.

"Sam and I were in Vancouver together this week," she says unprompted. Hiding my shock at this revelation—Sam never mentioned she was there—I nod and deeply inhale. "Olivia, I'm not sure what you think is going on with Sam, but you're not cut out for his world. You don't know the first thing about being a chef, and a celebrity chef no less. Sam is wildly successful and needs someone who can support him, who can help him further his goals and dreams. Really, Olivia, you're not the one." Her tone is disparaging.

Wow, she really is unattractive, vile even, beneath the blonde hair, blue eyes, and 'pretty little thing' façade she has going on. "Yasmine, what's going on between Sam and me is not your concern."

She laughs, but there's no joy in it at all. "Olivia, stop fooling yourself. You're too old, you live in two different cities, and you don't understand what Sam needs, what's good for him. I can give him that. My father and I will give him what he needs—or maybe we won't," she taunts.

"What's that supposed to mean?" I ask, taking the bait although I shouldn't.

"Sam needs at least one investor for his new restaurant. He wants us and we want him, but you see, maybe we won't want him. Maybe his business venture would look a whole lot more attractive if a certain older mother-of-two would walk away. If you care for him and want his dreams to come true, leave him alone." We stare at each other, silent barbs flying back and forth between us, neither of us backing down. "I can set you up with a man your own age, if you're really that hard up," she sneers.

Shivering and giving my head a shake, I snap out of my thoughts. While Yasmine was nasty and I really didn't like what she had to say, she did have some valid points. At the very least she reminded me that this is casual. No labels.

The past two weeks have been busy for both of us with only texts and brief phone calls. The interior plans for Mrs. Preston's hotel are in full swing and Sam is preoccupied with Bas, managing his restaurants, and planning his new one. I want to ask him about the financial backing needed for his new restaurant, but I don't want to pry. If I could I'd invest, but I don't have the funds. I know who does, but I'd never ask Pete for the money—*gawd*, what a disaster that would be.

Sam's on his way here from the airport. Unfortunately he can only stay the night, but it's better than nothing. Even with this being casual I can't deny that I do miss him.

He joins us at Colin and Sin's where we're spending the day by their pool as it's a scorcher today. Her place is packed with neighbors and kids, and Sam fits right in, stripping down to reveal his striking tats and body.

Through the sliding glass doors, outside, every woman around the pool freezes and stares. I bet if I were outside I'd hear a few gasps and moans. Sam really is that incredible, but what makes him even more attractive is how unaffected he is by it all. He doesn't flaunt his good looks, instead is just comfortable in his own skin.

"Wow," Sin says from behind me. Glancing over my shoulder, she too is transfixed by the work of art known as Sam Beaulieu.

"I know," I say wistfully, then I drop the bomb. "I'm going on a date next week."

"What? With Sam?"

Turning to face her, I shake my head no. Gazing into her troubled stare, I avert my eyes, turning away. I don't need her approval. "I'm going on a date with Mrs. Preston's cousin. She's been hounding me, so I caved."

"Couldn't you just tell her you have a boyfriend?"

"But I don't."

"But you slept with Sam, right?" she asks, and I stupidly and uncontrollably blush. "Okay, I'll take that as a yes. I know you Liv—you're not a one-night stand, casual sex kinda girl, so how is this going to work?"

"What do you mean?" I know exactly what she means, and we're showing our age if we can't hook up, as the kids call it. Not every sexual encounter has to be serious or lead to marriage.

"If you and Sam are having sex, it's gotta be more than casual."

"It's just a fling," I rush to respond, feeling queasy at the thought despite knowing it's the right thing to want.

"Does Sam know that?" Hands on her hips, she's abandoned dishing out the snacks. All her focus is on me, which I so don't want.

"Well, we've haven't said it in so many words, but..."

"So, let me ask you this: does he think you're exclusive or not?"

I don't want to respond. We haven't discussed it, although I'm pretty sure I know what Sam would say—which is exactly why I haven't wanted to discuss it. Why is she looking at me like that, like she's my mother and I'm completely clueless?

She pushes, "Okay, how about if Sam was to date or sleep with someone else, say one Miss Yasmine Thibault—how would you feel about that?"

A growl slips from my lips and my hands wrap into fists. She smirks, knowing how I feel without me saying a word.

Contrary to my reaction, I respond, "It's casual. It can't be anything more."

"Why not?"

"Because, I'm not starting another relationship. I'm almost two years on my own, and I like it. I'm getting used to it. I want to be on my own. I don't want some man to define my life. Been there, done that, and no thank you, not going back."

"And you think Colin defines my life because I've been married to him for twenty years?" she asks defensively.

"Oh, God, no. That's not what I'm saying. I just don't want to fall into that trap again. I have no regrets about my life with Pete." Sin stops her task again, and her eyebrows rise as her eyes pin me. "It's not regret. Sure, I wish things could have been different, but I can't regret my life with him. He gave me Drew and Paige. I wouldn't trade them for the world."

"Aww, honey, of course not."

"Is it wrong of me to feel like a weakling or a failure if I've found another man? With leaving Pete, I'd resigned myself to the fact that I'd never find a man that could give me what I wanted, and I was okay with that. I was happy on my own—truly. I was so alone with Pete that actually being alone is refreshing, exciting, and hopeful. Now, with Sam. . .shit, he could be everything I've ever wanted in a man. He's not perfect—who is? —but I never had it this way with Pete, ever, even when things were good. I just don't know if I'm ready. So, we're keeping this casual."

Looking back outside, unable to take her all-seeing stare after having bared my soul, I cast my eyes on everyone around the pool. "Besides, isn't it weird or all kinds of wrong to have your daughter and her friend ogling the guy you're seeing?"

She joins me at the glass and we watch Sam as he talks with Drew, Colin, and Colin and Sin's son, Finn. He's oblivious to Marci ogling him from the pool, along with Sin's neighbors, Mrs. Sims, and Mrs. Patterson. Paige and Pippa occasionally glance at him but neither stare, although it's obvious they like what they see. Seriously, what woman wouldn't?

Sin laughs. "They're human, and they're teenage girls—well, not all of them are teenagers, but they're alive. You'd have to be without a pulse and a heterosexual male to not look at Sam twice or thrice." Her sly smile matches the twinkle in her eyes. "There's nothing wrong with that."

Not long after, we bring out the snacks and beverages and Sam catches my eye as I place the tray on the table. Leaving the guys, his smile grows wider, dimples and all, with each step toward me. Even with my niggling worries about our age difference and what my priorities need to be, I can't resist him.

I'm fully aware that there are eyes on us; I'm not certain who's watching as my gaze never strays from Sam, but I'm pretty sure it's all the women. Like Sin said, I can't blame them.

"Damn, you in that bikini has me on fire," he whispers low and throaty into my ear. His hot breath tickles my neck as his forefinger blazes a trail from my collarbone down my arm to my wrist, sending tingles spreading throughout my body. "And that's saying a hell of a lot since it's a scorcher today."

A giggle passes my lips as my knees weaken and I grab onto his biceps to keep myself standing. "Well, you're pretty hot yourself," I whisper, teasing my finger slyly along the front waistband of his swim shorts, his hard abs contracting at my touch.

With a devilish grin, Sam grips my waist and again leans in. "Uh-uh, you're the hottest thing here."

His tongue quickly licks my skin, then he nibbles on my neck. He's driving me crazy with desire, my wet heat pooling between my legs. Before I have a chance to either pull back in an attempt to regain my senses or give in to my lust and completely strip down for him, he whispers into my ear.

At first, nothing he says makes sense because I'm flying through the air, screaming. Then his words register: "You're so hot that I think you need to cool off." With a splash, I hit the water, his laughter following me to the bottom of the pool.

We end up staying for a barbecue and don't get home until well after nine. Drew heads for the staircase, looking back at us congregated at the front door as Paige flicks off her flip flops.

"Hey Sam, wanna play some ball in the morning?"

"Ah, I'd love to, but not sure if I can. By the time we play and then I schlep back to shower and check out, I doubt I'll catch my flight. Don't think it'll work out this time."

"Check out?" Drew asks.

"At the hotel."

"Mom, why does Sam stay at a hotel every time he comes to visit?" Paige asks.

"Um, I..." I stutter.

Before I'm able to formulate a coherent response, Drew adds, "It's stupid. He should stay here. It's a waste of money. And Mom"—Drew looks directly at me— "if your hang-up is us, we're cool with Sam staying here."

"Absolutely," Paige chimes in.

Damn these kids. Sam's expectant eyes twinkle, but he remains silent as both kids wait for me to say something.

"Sam can stay the night," I say, looking straight into his eyes. A smile settles in his gaze as he steps in, bag and all, and closes the door behind him.

"D-man, we're on for ball," Sam declares, still staring at me like he's ready to play with me.

The kids disperse, leaving Sam and I transfixed. His sexy shit-eating grin and the dimples are out in full force. I'm done for.

"You're loving this, aren't you?"

"Well, I could deny it, but what's the point? I love sleepovers." He winks and slaps my ass as he walks by.

No matter how much I try to keep this in the casual zone, it's like the universe is conspiring against me.

Twenty

SAM

Jogging up the walkway to Olivia's house, my stomach somersaults in anticipation. It's been a week since I last saw her, and I miss her like crazy. Again, I'm only able to stay a night; I need to get back for Bas.

Originally my visit was supposed to only be a few hours tomorrow, but I couldn't fathom that. I want, *need* to spend more time with her. Now that I'm done with staying in hotels—*thank you Drew and Paige*—I plan on taking every opportunity I have to spend time with her. She's expecting me tomorrow for a few hours, but I'm surprising her with a sleepover. I can't wait.

Drew answers the door, his eyes widening, surprised but also worried, or perhaps even troubled—not exactly what I expected. Even when we first met and he had no clue who I was, his reaction was nonchalant. Now, he's shocked and almost terrified. *What the hell?*

"Hey Sam, Mom's not here."

Looking back toward the driveway, I ask, "Okay. Isn't that her car in the driveway?" He nods but doesn't say anything. "All right. No problem. I'm surprising her. I was supposed to come tomorrow, thought I'd come a day earlier."

Heading toward the kitchen, I glance over my shoulder at him. He's anxious and glued to the spot.

"Is it okay if I get started on dinner? Have you eaten?"

"Ah, Sam, ah…" Sucking in a gulp of air, he runs his hand through his dirty blond hair.

Quirking my eyebrow, I wait. He's hesitant—something's off. "My mom's out for dinner. I'm not sure when she'll be back. It may be late," he says.

It's like he's trying to tell me something without saying it, something big, but I'm completely missing the point.

Scrubbing my hand down my face, I turn to face him, man to man. "That's all right. Is she out with the girls or Jonah?" My tone is casual, even though he's got my full attention.

"I have no clue, man," he rushes to say. Now *that* was a lie. Drew and I are still getting to know each other, but the way he wouldn't look at me as he spoke the words and swallowed hard tells me he's lying. But why?

Briskly, he strides past me, eyes fixed ahead, into the back of the house. Following closely, my gaze tracks his every move as he grabs his phone and starts furiously typing. Is he texting Olivia? Or am I just being paranoid?

"Drew." My tone is serious. Looking up from his phone, his eyes are focused and intent. "What gives, man? Do you want me to go?"

Nervously, he shoves his phone into his pocket and blurts out, "Shit, no. Sorry, just distracted. So, what are you cooking? I haven't eaten."

Shaking off Drew's strange behavior, I get to work. I can't make him come clean, and maybe it has nothing to do with me. Within minutes, Drew's laid-back nature resurfaces as he helps make dinner. We pass the time in an easy and relaxed manner, laughing and trading stories. Drew's tales from the construction site are hilariously entertaining, and in short order, we're enjoying fish tacos with beer.

During cleanup, the doorbell rings. Drew looks to me, his weird uneasy expression creeping back in. "Want me to get it?" I ask.

"Nah, I'll get it. I'll be back." Dropping the dish towel, he jogs out of the room. Puzzled, I continue putting the dishes away but stall when I hear, "Get the fuck out."

It's Drew speaking, and I've never heard him that angry before. Barreling to the front door, I skid to a halt at the sight of Pete glaring at his son, his face red, scrunched and tense. Flicking his eyes to me, it takes a moment, then his features cloud and become even tenser—if that's even possible—as recognition sets in. Eyes narrowed and fists clenched, he takes one step into the house.

Like daggers, his gaze stabs me with a dark note to his tone. "What the fuck are you doing here?"

"He's welcome. I want him here," Drew bitterly spits out. My eyes shoot to Drew, who is just as tense as his father and just as pissed off. *What the hell?* "You, leave," he orders his father.

Sensing this could devolve into something real ugly, real fast, I step closer to the two men. "Pete," I tersely acknowledge him. "Drew, everything okay?"

"It'll be fine once he leaves."

"Drew." Pete's tone softens. "I came here to talk."

Despite the thick tension in the room, his sincerity is as clear as a bell. Curling his fists, Drew exhales a long, shaky breath and clamps his mouth shut into a tight line, his jaw tight.

"I've got nothing to say to you."

Calmly, I suggest, "Pete, you should go." Inching even closer to him and the door, I try for a relaxed pose, although I'm anything but.

I have no clue as to what's going on between these two. Olivia did mention something, but said both men refuse to tell her what's going on. She said it was intense and troublesome, and she wasn't exaggerating.

Pete's stance widens, placing his hands on his hips. "Who the hell are you to tell me to leave? This is my family, *my* wife, *my* son." His voice is loud and sharp.

"She's not your wife anymore. You should know that, especially considering you don't seem to have any problem forgetting what it means to be married. Leave." Drew's face is now strained and red.

What on earth is Drew talking about? Olivia said Pete didn't cheat, but maybe he did and now Drew found out about it?

Pete stills, rock solid. His face is hard like stone as he surveys his son, neither of them willing to back down. I want to step in and kick Pete out, but I also need to give these guys space. If it gets violent or heads south, I'll do what's needed.

Pete finally acquiesces. "We will talk eventually, Drew."

"Whatever. You don't have anything to say that I'm willing to listen to," Drew says dismissively before walking away.

Pete watches his son leave, his body deflating until he remembers I'm still there. With one final glower in my direction, he stalks out the door, slamming it behind him.

"Thank fuck he's gone." Drew's voice is small and defeated. "Please don't tell my mom what happened."

"Why?" I ask, puzzled.

"She'll be upset and then it'll domino from there. I can handle it. Please don't say anything."

"I won't, but I don't like the idea of keeping things from her."

"Sorry, Sam. I shouldn't have asked you to."

"Listen, I won't keep this from her, but I'll ask her to give you space. I get the sense you don't want to have to dodge her concern."

With a small, hesitant smile, he asks, "Can I ask a question?" I nod encouragingly as we continue heading to the living room. "What if you know something you feel someone has a right to know, but you don't want to hurt them? What would you do? Would you tell them?"

Shit. Maybe that's it—Pete cheated while they were married. *Fuck.* He's asking for my advice? I'm out of my depth here. I don't want to mess this kid up, but I also don't want to give him the brushoff. That would be a heavy burden to carry, and being the one to deliver that to his mother? Dammit, that's harsh.

If I could help, I would, I'm just not sure it's my place to do so. "Maybe you should ask your mom, I'm sure she's better at this than me."

"Maybe." He shrugs, a small frown covering his face. He's likely disappointed in my non-answer.

"All right, think about it: she cares about you, and if she can help, she'll want to."

She's a loving and caring mother. She's good at this and would want to help if she could. I'm not sure how hurt she'd be knowing Pete cheated; I imagine it would hurt, but how deeply now that they're divorced? Although, he's trying to get her back. There are the texts, and she did share with me that Pete thinks there's a chance. She also reassured me that there isn't, not at all.

"That's the problem, *she'll* end up getting hurt." Drew sighs, rubbing his hand down his concerned face.

It's my turn to frown, stopping at the implication of his words. Whatever is going on between Pete and Drew is about Olivia, and I don't like the sound of that.

Before we even reach the living room, Olivia calls from the front door, "Hey Drew, was that your dad's car backing out of the driveway?"

When she rounds the corner, my gut clenches at the sight of her. I could look at her all day, all the time. Her lightly bronzed skin glows in a turquoise summer dress that falls to just above her knees. Shiny tendrils randomly fall from her messy bun, prettily framing her face.

Her eyes widen when they land on me. "Sam," she says in a high-pitched voice.

"Mom," Drew says, an undeniable warning edging his tone. I'd sensed something was up from when I first got here, but now I know something is. The way mother and son are eyeing each other, their gazes laden with meaning, says it all.

"Olivia," I say, nearing them. She briefly looks at me, a small smile tugging at her lips before she averts her eyes to the door where someone is knocking.

She apprehensively looks to Drew and one more time to me before swinging back to the door. Is she worried that it's Pete? What on earth is going on?

Drew opens the door, and a tall man in a suit with salt and pepper hair and a slight paunch beams back at him. Then he spots Olivia and his already incredibly big smile grows. I can certainly understand his reaction, but I don't like it. It's too friendly, almost like he knows her, as if they're more than friends. My back stiffens and my jaw ticks as I grate my teeth and my lips tighten. I know what this is.

"Olivia, can I see you tomorrow?" he eagerly asks. "I was thinking we could go to Niagara-on-the-Lake. I'd love to spend the day with you."

He steps inside as Drew glances back at me, pity etching his tense face. Sympathy for me? No fucking way—I don't need his pity. His heart's in the right place, but I won't take this lying down.

With a weak smile for me, Drew says to his mother, "I'm outta here. I'm staying at Ken's tonight. Sam, thanks for dinner. I'll catch ya later, man."

With a curt nod, he grabs his keys and runs down the walkway like he's being chased by zombies.

Olivia shuffles from one foot to the other, her gaze refusing to settle on me. "Ah, sorry, I…"

"She already has plans," I sharply interject, stepping between Olivia and this man. "Sorry pal, we haven't met. I'm Sam." Extending my hand, I deliver the blow with a smile. "Olivia's boyfriend."

His eyes expand and shock covers his face as he looks to Olivia, who is now scowling at me. "Damn, sorry, I didn't know," he stammers while giving me a weak handshake. Now he's the one who looks like there are zombies after him.

Pursing my lips, I fight the laughter bubbling in my throat. He thinks I'm going to hit him, which I'm not. Violence isn't my thing. Besides, I've made my point.

"Hank, this is my friend Sam," she says. The word 'friend' carries such force, it's as if she punches me in the gut.

"Sam?" He nods. "Is this the guy from Montreal?" Judgment lines his innocuous words.

Olivia's taken aback at his accusing tone, as she should be. I don't like this dick. "Listen, asshole, I'm her boyfriend. That's all you need to know. Goodnight Hank." Widening the open door, I gesture for him to leave.

"I meant nothing by it. Goodbye Olivia," he says, clearly disappointed. She continues to glower, now at both of us, refusing to acknowledge him as he leaves. I close the door loudly behind him and she folds her arms, all her ire now directed at me.

"What the hell?" My tone carries a sharp note.

"What are you doing here? You're supposed to be here tomorrow," she says, stating what we both already know.

Wanting nothing more than to call her on this shit, I grit my teeth and instead grate out, "I know. Your boyfriend. Me." I point to myself. "Your boyfriend wanted to see his girlfriend, wanted to spend more than three hours with her since he has to go back tomorrow afternoon. So, your boyfriend thought he'd surprise her and come the evening before."

I hate talking about myself in the third person. It's creepy, but it seems to keep me in check, distancing my emotions from what's going on.

"Sam." Her tone softens, arms falling to her side. "Shit, I'm sorry. It was nothing. Just a date. Mrs. Preston was pushing me to go out with her cousin, so I did, to keep her happy and get her off my back."

"A date?" My eyes narrow on the woman I want to both devour and punish. "It's actually simple, Livvy. You tell Mrs. Preston you have a boyfriend—*that's* how you get her off your back."

"Boyfriend?" she counters. "Sam, this is casual." We're not casual, not by a long shot, but I'll give her what she wants to hear—*for now.*

"It may be casual, but we both know we're exclusive." The sharp edge of my voice is not lost on her, and both her eyes and mouth open at my harsh response.

We both stand tall with our arms folded, backs straight, eyes laser focused on the other. The growing quiet is deafening. With a sigh, I break our childish staring match.

"Olivia." My voice is tender; fighting with her is the last thing I want to do.

I'm not happy and she'll know it, but fuck, all I want is her. She relaxes, rubbing her temples and shaking her head before returning her gaze to me.

"Sam, I'm sorry. I should have, at the very least, told you."

"Damn straight." I want to impress upon her how wrong she was to have even considered going on a date, but my time with her is limited. I'll drill that very important fact into her when the time is right.

Pouncing, I pin her against the door. My hands cage her torso, the pads of my thumbs lightly grazing the undersides of her perfect breasts. Gasping, her cheeks flush and her nipples harden. Unable to control myself, I bend down so I'm almost eye level with her chest. My tongue flicks, feather light against the thin fabric, over her tight nipple.

Her hand dives into my hair, holding me in place as she calls out and curses her enjoyment. Through the fabric, I lick, suck, and nip as she shimmies and squirms with small gasps and moans. Once I've whetted my hunger and teased her enough, I pull up to standing. I glance down, and the wet spot of the fabric where I marked her breast pleases me to no end. In this moment, I get the primal nature of the caveman, the insatiable drive to mark what is yours.

"Did you kiss him?" I ask. My tone is razor sharp, and I don't even recognize it as my own.

Her eyes widen, staring up at me. "No," she's quick to say. "I told him I was seeing someone else. I told him about you, which is how he knew you were from Montreal. I told him I wasn't looking for a relationship, that it wasn't a date."

My fingers skim the soft ridges of her cheeks. So soft. So sweet. "He obviously didn't get the message."

"Ah, I think you fixed that. He heard you loud and clear." She snorts with a grin.

Deciding we've already wasted too much time on that bozo, I move on to what's more important: us.

"I missed you, mon trésor," I murmur before crushing my lips to hers in an intense kiss. My tongue, lips, and teeth brand her, punishing her and teaching her that she's mine. Only mine. Making sure she never forgets what this is. What we are. We belong to each other, no one else. "Only you and me, Livvy." My tone is demanding and her appreciative sounds imply understanding, but I want to hear it. I need to hear it. "Say it. Show me that you understand."

My patience is thin. Tasting her, touching her has me wound tight, burning with need. If I don't get what I want, I'm liable to snap.

"Only you and me," she whispers into my mouth.

I devour her, taking, grazing, nibbling. She tastes like heaven, like mine. Now, with her open and pliable, at my mercy, I push the point of our relationship.

"We're not casual, Olivia."

She stiffens, eyes wide and confused. "What?"

"We're not casual. We're dating. Boyfriend sounds silly, but we are an *us*. I know you don't want labels and that's fine, but we. Are. Us. Livvy."

"Sam." She attempts to push me away but I grind into her, connecting with the apex of her thighs. She gasps and sighs.

We stumble, fumbling with our clothes up the stairs and into her room. With Drew gone and Paige at her dad's, we've got the place to ourselves. I intend to use this scarce time alone to show her there is no other. Only me. Only her. Only us.

We spend the next day in bed. At first she's concerned about Drew coming home, but after texting him and learning that he's headed to Wasaga Beach for the day, she yields. Giving in to my desire to stay in bed until I must leave, we talk, laugh, eat, and make love. We avoid all talk of Hank, her ex, or anyone else.

We do need to talk about them; I need to make sure she understands it's her and me, but not now. Not when these moments, just us, alone, are few and far between. Not when we both have busy lives and distance, obligations, and stresses constantly banging on our door. For now, all I want is her. I'll deal with all the other crap tomorrow.

Twenty-One

OLIVIA

The remainder of the summer flies by and Sam and I have fallen into a comfortable but no less exciting routine. In addition to our countless daily texts, occasional sexting, and phone calls, we try for weekly visits, each of us taking turns traveling back and forth. Sometimes it doesn't work out, but we make do.

Even though this setup is working for us, I miss him when we're apart. I miss him the minute we say goodbye. I miss him the second I hear his voice. I miss him when one of the kids says something funny and I wish he were there to share it with. I miss him late at night when I lie in bed, alone, the other pillow cold and empty.

I want more, but I'm also grateful for the distance. It helps keep this thing, this relationship we have from getting too serious, or worse, Sam pushing for something I'm not willing to give.

I can't lose myself to a man, again, and with Sam, it would be so easy to do so—even more so than it was with Pete. Sam's everything I've ever wanted in a man. If this got too serious and our relationship crashed and burned, I'm not sure what that would do to me.

It's Labor Day weekend and I'm minutes away from Sam's. Paige is with her father and Drew's up at a friend's cottage before he heads back to school. I spent last night with them, both Paige and I getting our fill of Drew before he leaves. Who knows when his next visit will be, most likely not 'til Thanksgiving.

Leaving my car at Sam's, I take an Uber to the bar on Crescent Street where he is waiting. I find him sitting with Bas and the Thibaults—yes, Yasmine too. My stomach lurches as the blonde waif clutches Sam's forearm, looking up at him longingly. *Back off bitch.* Both of them catch sight of me at the same time, and Yasmine noticeably stiffens as Sam rises to greet me.

No matter how sure I am of Sam and how much I know without uncertainty that he has no interest in Yasmine Thibault, I can't help but feel sick at the sight of her, each and every time. I haven't seen a lot of her since that fateful dinner where she cornered me and made it known that my presence may cost Sam their investment, but any time since, she drops subtle hints, echoing her warning.

I told Sam about her threat and he laughed, telling me not to listen to her and that he was still unsure about whether he wanted them as investors. I took that opportunity to point out that he may already have his answer given he's not able to come to a decision. Obviously the Thibaults haven't been able to put his reservations to rest. I wish he'd walk away from them, especially since Bas is also against it.

"Mon trésor," he whispers with light kisses to my lips and neck. "God, it's fucking fantastic to have you in my arms."

My chest rapidly rises and falls as I snuggle into his strong, inviting hold. His warm breath hits my neck, sending shivers skittering down my spine as I grow hot, my core throbbing for him.

"Sam," I moan.

All too soon, he steps back, eyeing me skeptically. "What's wrong?"

"Nothing," I quickly respond. I must have inadvertently shown my displeasure at the Thibaults being here.

He eyes my features, resting on my lips longer than necessary. His eyes darken, lids heavy as his smile grows. I'm used to his appreciative perusal of me, especially my lips, but every time my stomach flutters and my cheeks flush.

"We'll go soon. I don't want them here either," he whispers. He knows me so well.

"Samson, my turn," Bas demands, standing at my side. His friendly grin is all for me.

Turning, I hug him fully, but not too tight. He's thinner than when I last saw him, and my heart aches at what it means. Though I've only known this man for a few months, I love him. It hurts to see him like this, and I so wish I could help him more. Sam is holding it together so well but there are moments when he thinks I'm not looking, when his smile falls and sadness clouds his gaze. My man is hurting and all we can hope for is time. How much or how little, we don't know.

"Bas, how are you?"

"Ma chérie, I'm wonderful now that you're here." His gruff voice is laced with tenderness. "Help me, let's get out of here," he whispers.

Unable to contain my laughter, he matches mine as both Thibaults watch us with keen interest.

"Soon," I promise.

I give a brief and pretentious greeting to the Thibaults as I sit then ask Bas why he's there instead of at home where he'd be more comfortable. He tells me Sam took him to a doctor's appointment and on his way home, let it slip that he was meeting the Thibaults. Bas then insisted on being there.

Once I've finished my drink, Bas makes his discontent known by huffing and puffing about wanting to leave. I also think he should be getting home; he looks worn and fatigued.

"Samson, Olivia's taking me home." Sam attempts to protest, his hold on my hand tightening, but Bas stops him. "Don't be long. You know where to find her."

With that, Sam and I exchange a quick but heated goodbye. I can feel his displeasure at my departure in his heavy and bothered gaze, and as much as I want to spend time with him, I'm happy to take Bas home. I too want to leave. He knows this and promises to wrap up soon, although if Daniel has his way, it won't be nearly as soon as Sam thinks.

When we arrive at his home, we're met with surprise and joy from Alec. Blueprints are scattered across his large desk, but he leaves it all behind without a second glance to lovingly embrace Bas.

Feeling like an intruder, I excuse myself to the washroom and let them have some alone time. I flick my eyes over Alec's face; the longing, love, and loss there is heartbreaking. He's mourning for what they've already lost and likely preparing himself for the inevitable.

"Ma chérie, come here," Bas playfully bellows from the living room.

I'm futzing around in the kitchen, taking my time making drinks, giving them alone time. Alec pops his head around the doorframe and says with a smile, "Olivia, come. His majesty wants you, and we know, what he wants, he gets." He winks, taking my hand and a drink.

"Our boy was being an idiot tonight." Alec laughs at Bas's description of Sam. "Instead of leaving with his love and me, he stayed behind to listen to that blowhard, Daniel Thibault."

"Bas, ease up. I know you dislike Thibault, but Sam's got a lot riding on this restaurant. He's got to do what's needed," Alec chides.

Sitting between the two men—which I only did at their insistence—my head swivels back and forth as they chat about their son. It's sweet to see and feel their love for Sam. I'm always grateful for any chance I get to learn more about his life, and I'm also blessed to be loved and welcomed by these two men. They make me feel so special.

"Ah, you're the one, ma chérie," Bas oddly states, out of the blue.

"Pardon?"

He continues like I never said a word. "I'm glad I met you before it was too late."

His words alarm and sadden me. Alec uncomfortably squirms in his seat, tsking at Bas and his blatant comment about the day when he will no longer be here.

"What are you talking about?" I'm baffled.

"Samson has a big heart and plenty to give, even with what this world has dealt him, even with knowing he was the result of a traumatic and soul-destroying event for his mother. It's not something one easily comes to terms with."

I gulp, barely able to swallow the lump in my throat that's quickly formed at his blunt, honest words. I'm confused. "What are you talking about?"

"Did Samson tell you anything about his mother?"

"He told me she died just before his second birthday."

Bas nods. "Normally, I wouldn't share this—it's Samson's story to tell—but I'm a dying man and I don't want that boy wasting any time."

"Bas, would you cut it out already," Alec interjects, exasperated. I gently squeeze his hand in reassurance. I understand his distress, but also understand where Bas is coming from too.

"I'm not going to sugar-coat anything, Alec. Ma chérie, I'm going to tell you like it is. Samson's mother was a teenager, barely fifteen, when she was raped." My stomach plummets to my toes at that horrific news.

"The gory details don't matter, just that it was life-altering. The man was never caught and most importantly, Annick Samson was never the same.

When she found out she was pregnant, she refused an abortion. She wanted the baby, and Samson was that child. She came from a poor family and didn't have the support available to her to get help and therapy to wrestle her demons. A week before Samson's second birthday, she committed suicide."

"Oh my God." I gasp, clutching my chest and blinking back the tears. Wrapping their arms around me, they both comfort me. "How do you know all this?"

My mind reels with this sad and terrible story. I think of Sam, and it doesn't fit. He's the epitome of happy and loving. To have known you came from such a violent act would be hard for anyone. I can't reconcile this with the man I know, and how Bas knows all this when both Sam's mother and grandmother were dead when he met Sam interests me.

"I didn't know Samson's grandparents, but I knew a family friend. Once I met Samson and he came into our lives, I sought information on him and his family. Also, his mother left him a letter, a beautiful letter. I never knew Annick. I wish I had. From her letter to her baby boy, you can tell she loved him dearly. She was troubled and tormented by what had happened, but she loved her boy. She did not blame him and in fact, he was the only positive thing she had. It pained her to have his life tainted by her misery. That letter made a world of difference to Samson, and his grandparents were wonderful people. I think it was their love and openness, and of course the type of person Samson is, that prevented him from growing up to be an angry and troubled man. Even when life knocked him down farther than most people ever go, he was able to rise above it."

Tears spill onto my cheeks; I can hardly imagine what Sam's mother must have endured. My heart pangs for her, for her parents, and for Sam. Living his life without a mother and knowing why she chose to take her own life is a burden many could not bear, and his grandparents—to have lost a child, their only child, in such a sad and wretched way must have been agony.

His tattoo, the Little Prince quote: *But the eyes are blind. One must look with the heart.* It now makes sense why he chose that quote above all the other lovely phrases in that novel.

His mother's love for him was with her heart, not her eyes. Seeing Sam every day could have been a torturous reminder of her tragedy. Instead, she looked with her heart. She loved him no matter the circumstance that brought him into her life. She loved him when many would have terminated or hated the child for the fate bestowed upon her.

When I turn to face him, Bas cups my cheeks, his rough thumbs gently wiping at the wetness, his blue eyes soft and loving. "Ma chérie, I didn't tell you to make you cry."

Alec soothingly rubs my back and speaks quietly over my shoulder. "Are you sure?" he jests. "I think he wanted you to know because Sam may never say anything."

"True," Bas gruffly says. "But I also told you because I want you to understand just how rare and wonderful Samson is. It takes a special kind of person to rise above that kind of beginning. He carries no anger or hate in his heart, and if anyone has a right to, he does. Take care of him. Be there for him. He'll need you. That's all he needs. Olivia, he may not have said it yet, but he loves you with all that he is." My breath hitches and my heart skips a beat. "And you love him too," Bas states. It's not a question; it's simply a matter of fact.

Twenty-Two

SAM

I'm such an idiot. I wasted half the night on Thibault, and what for? Bas is right—there have been too many hints of his controlling nature. I don't want an investor like that, and to top it off, I wasted four hours I could have spent with Olivia.

Alec texts me to say he took her home to my place once Bas went to bed. When I get home, I find her sleeping peacefully in my bed, looking like an angel with her dark locks fanning my pillow. I slip quietly under the sheets and gently pull her into my arms. I may have goofed tonight when I didn't leave with them, but holding her in my arms for the rest of the night more than makes up for it.

I wake before Olivia and she's still snuggled into me, sleeping peacefully. I quietly slip out of the bed to go to the bathroom and upon my return, my steps falter—she's too tempting in the scrap of fabric she calls underwear.

My Vedder t-shirt—the one she wore to bed—has ridden up to reveal her firm, irresistible ass, and her legs are slightly parted, providing the perfect view of her sex, inviting me to feast on her, to taste her. Never one to pass up the invitation to have my woman, I carefully pull the lace to the side and dive in.

Olivia wakes with a gasp and a whimper, my mouth on her sex, devouring her sweet pussy. My tongue circles and twirls her clit as her hands grab my hair. Her nails lightly scrape my scalp, each tug and pull of my hair directly linked to my cock and balls, which are lengthening and tightening as I consume her.

Her loud, pleasurable cries encourage me to bring her to the brink, and at the same time her gratification pushes me closer and closer to the edge. My tongue thrusts in and out, fucking her, tasting her, so wet, sweet, and tart. With one final plunge, my lips latch onto her sensitive spot and suck the ever-living daylights out of her. Like a firecracker, she explodes with shouts of my name.

Before she can catch her breath, my hands grab her hips and whip her over onto all fours. Without wasting time to remove her panties, I suit up, move the fabric to the side, and mercilessly impale her.

She gasps out, "God, Sam," beseeching like I'm the answer to everything.

Rocking back and forth from behind, I'm at first slow and steady, then teasingly deep and hard. I want to hold on, make this last as long as I can for both of us. Her face is buried in the pillow, and yet her muffled moans are still audible. I fucking love hearing her need, her desire. Knowing what I do to her drives her crazy is like an aphrodisiac.

Pounding relentlessly into her, she's so hot and tight, and I'm so fucking close. My orgasm builds in my balls, the pressure mounting and dancing up my spine, but not yet—not until she comes again.

Bending over her, my fingers flit through her slick folds and her head snaps up, mouth open as her breath catches. She arches and bows at my torturously slow rubs on her sweet, sensitive bud. It doesn't take long before she's panting and tensing, taut and ready to explode.

Pulling her up with her back flush to my front, my hand cups and kneads her breast as my thumb and forefinger pinch her tight nipple. She spasms, clenching around my cock. *Fuck.* She likes it, and I fucking love it. Knowing she's close and that I brought her there feeds my fire.

Together, with long, hard, deep plunges, I hit the spot that drives her mad, that brings her closer to blinding bliss, over and over again. She spasms around my cock, her cries carnal and piercing as she peaks.

Seeing her come undone, shattered, at her most pure, sends me barreling toward my own release. Tensing, strung tight with a glaring intensity, I erupt on a roar of, "Olivia."

Reluctantly, I pull out and remove the condom. Tying it into a knot, I toss it in the can, holding her all the while. Flipping her onto her back and myself on top, my mouth descends on hers. My tongue fills her, tasting her completely. All my want, every second of need since the last time I saw her, every minute of longing goes into our kiss.

"Damn, that was the best *good morning* I've ever had." Her voice is breathy. "You can wake me up like that any day."

"It'd be my pleasure," I huskily whisper while trailing kisses down her neck. I could take her again. No matter how many times I have her, I can't get enough of her.

"How'd it go last night? What time did you get in?" She runs her fingers gently through my hair.

"Sorry," I murmur into her breastbone. Resting my head on her chest, the hypnotic beat of her heart settles the frustration of thinking back to yesterday. "It was a waste of time. I should have left with you. I'm sorry."

"Hey," she says, her hands holding the side of my face and lifting so our eyes meet. "No need to apologize. Why do you say it's a waste of time?"

I'm surprised at her question because she dislikes the Thibaults, and while she has reason to after Yasmine's ridiculous threat, she's never said anything negative. She's always been neutral, but I know she'd prefer that I walk away. I would think she'd be happy and not want to probe or know anything else.

"Bas is right."

"He'll want to hear that," she quips, beaming with a twinkle in her eye.

Chuckling, I explain, "Yes, I'll be sure to tell him, and he'll love saying he told me so. Daniel is controlling. There have just been a few instances where he's said things that haven't sat well with me, leading me to believe he'd want to call the shots."

Kissing me, she sits up, scooting 'til her back's against the headboard, the sheet secure around her. "What are you going to do? Don't you need him?"

I pull her close. "I don't need an investor, but I'd prefer to have one. There are other investors interested, a few actually, so it doesn't have to be Daniel. It would mean starting from scratch with the vetting process, which isn't a big deal. It just delays things a bit, and could impact a few aspects of getting started. I have options, and I know I'll figure it out."

She worries her bottom lip, her teeth nibbling her lush, pink flesh. My thumb stops her chewing as concern storms her wide eyes.

"I wish I could help."

Smiling, I kiss her forehead, breathing in her sweet scent that calms and comforts me. "You do help. Seriously, don't worry about it. It'll work out."

Capturing her lips, my tongue invades her mouth. Her soft, warm skin against me, being this close to her ignites my need to taste her, be with her again.

"Nuh-uh, Samson Beaulieu." I hear the smile in her voice as she pulls away. Beholding her warm chocolate eyes, I brush a stray curl from her forehead. "We're supposed to be spending the day with Bas and Alec. We'll never get out of here if you do that."

Pushing up, she rushes from the bed with me close behind, grabbing, then picking her up from the waist. She's not getting away that easily. She squeals but doesn't fight me. In fact, she does the opposite, wrapping her arms and legs around me as I take her to the shower.

We end up at their house for the day. Bas is not well and remains in bed the entire time we're there, in and out of sleep, and Olivia insists we stay by his side. It's then I know that I love her, although I'm pretty sure it was so before this moment. I haven't told her yet, not because I don't want to—I do, more than anything—but because I know she's not ready.

"Samson, there'll be times to be strong and times to be vulnerable. Be both. Let Olivia be there for you," Bas rasps.

He's been doing that all day. Randomly, he'll offer words of wisdom, and sometimes he's even talked about times in his past, memories from his childhood or a moment with me or Alec. I gently squeeze his now frail hand.

"And ma chérie, the same goes for you. Don't waste time because of fear or uncertainty. Life will always be uncertain and not always easy, but live it."

Olivia's lips quiver as she wipes the lone tear sliding down her cheek. "I will, Bas," she reassures him, kissing him on the forehead. He closes his tired blue eyes, a slight upturn to his mouth.

Seeing her with my family, experiencing the love, kindness, and patience she has for us all cocoons me and fortifies my soul. During our stay, there are times when I must leave the room, unable to contain my anger at the unfairness of it all. Without words, she understands. She stays, takes care of Bas and Alec so I can leave, so I can pull myself together.

We leave after dinner. Bas is asleep, his breathing is labored. Alec and I discuss taking him to the doctor tomorrow, or if it gets worse through the night, the hospital. My sleep is restless and every hour or so, I text with Alec to see how he's doing—the same.

When dawn breaks, I'm melancholy for a whole other reason. Olivia leaves today. Her time, like always, has flown by. I've been thinking of solutions to our distance dilemma, but can't do anything about it right now.

I need to be close to Bas, and as much as I love Olivia and so desperately want to be near her, see her every day, I can't leave him. Besides, she wouldn't hear of it. She'd be the first to tell me no, to tell me that my place is beside my father, mentor, and best friend.

The call finally comes, the one I've been dreading since the day Bas was diagnosed. It's three in the morning when I answer on the fourth ring. It's Alec, his voice somber, low, and broken. He's our pillar, Bas's and mine, so strong and put together, and now, his world is being taken from him. His love.

I hear the anguish and despair in his four words: "Come, Sam. It's time."

Not even two hours later, he's gone. Being with Bas when he goes is a blessing and a curse. He opens his pale blue eyes with difficulty, searching, likely seeing more than is here. Finally, his cloudy gaze lands on me. I'm not sure he knows it's me until he speaks his last word to me.

His voice is quiet and strangled as my name graces his lips for the final time. "Samson."

His eyes close. Watching his final breaths, I cling tightly to his hand, so frail and cool, his body a mere shadow of who he once was. He passes with Alec and me by his side. Both of us hold our breath as we wait, hopeful, praying for his next breath but knowing it will never come.

With a squeeze to my shoulder, Alec's chin wobbles and his face crumples. With his body half on top of Bas, he buries his face into Bas's stomach and sobs, mumbling his name and sweet nothings, hopes and dreams of years spent together, of a love that will never die.

My vision blurs as tears swell and spill down my cheeks. Everything hurts. My heart's ripped from me. I can't fathom never seeing him again, never speaking to him, arguing with him, or laughing with him. Never again.

Olivia, I need her. She answers on the third ring.

Her voice is soft and groggy. "Sam?"

"Bas." I barely get the word out, my voice unsteady, foreign even to my own ears. It's all I can manage to say.

"Oh, no. Sam." Her voice cracks. "I'm coming."

That's all I need to hear. I need her.

Twenty-Three

OLIVIA

The past few days have been a blur of numbness and planning. The funeral is tomorrow, in Bas's hometown. We leave Montreal and travel about an hour to the Eastern Townships, which are known as being a taste of New England with French flare. It's picturesque with rolling hills and old, sometimes majestic country homes nestled along several lakes bordering Vermont, New Hampshire, and Maine.

Alec and Sam try to keep a conversation going, both boasting about the culinary treasures the region is known for in a manner much like Bas would have done if he were here. With pride for his home, his heritage, and the region's fine foods like canard and the freshest organic produce in the country, Bas would have regaled me about the lavender fields, flavorful cheeses, vineyards, and top-notch hotels.

Sam tenderly holds my hand. Since arriving, he and I have been inseparable. While he's been quiet and subdued for the most part, he won't let me out of his sight, and when I'm near, he takes any chance he can to touch me like he needs me to breathe.

During the drive, he shares stories of Christmases spent in Bas's home through his teens and early twenties, a place he still visits for several weeks twice a year. The mood sobers even more and we all sink into silence as it's apparent this Christmas will be different. No doubt Bas's absence will change things. It's a sad thought that he will never return to his childhood home and make more memories with them.

Bas's home is a simple, small two-story house on a large piece of land near one of the lakes. The home is old with wood and tile floors, baseboard heating, small bathrooms, and two wood-burning fireplaces. Of course, the kitchen is state of the art, feeling like one you'd find in a Michelin-star restaurant. Alec is quick to tell me that was the first renovation Bas did to the house, his eyes lighting up as he's taken back to a younger and happier time when Bas was still here.

As the day drags on and Bas's funeral nears, Alec becomes more unresponsive, holing away in the office with a bottle of cognac and a cigar. As night falls, Sam insists on taking me out, assuring me that Alec needs the time alone.

We drive to Mont Mégantic, the world's first dark sky reserve, located in Mont Mégantic National Park. He explains that with the limited light in this part of the province, the park is one of the darkest and best places on the planet to stargaze.

As we walk through the dark, my hand in his, he eagerly shares tales of countless times the three of them ventured to the park on the spur of the moment for the most exceptional celestial display. While I'm unable to see his face, I can hear the love and laughter in his voice as he relives his wonderful memories of Bas.

Laying down the big woolen blanket he brought, we sit, him perched beside me, pulling me close into his warm and inviting embrace. He tugs us down until we're lying on our backs, and the vast, starry night sky is boundless, a lit-up canvas lain out before us. It's not only stars and planets that are visible; we can also see the Milky Way, like a cloudy path of twinkling lights traversing the night sky.

"It's beautiful, isn't it?" he asks. I nod, in awe of the beauty. "Thank you for being here."

"There's nowhere else I want to be," I whisper, low and emphatic. Taking his hand in mind, I kiss his knuckles, loving him and trying to convey the depth of feeling I have for him with my touch.

"I feel close to him here. Being in his childhood home and now here, I feel him around me. God, I hope I never lose that." His voice is low, wavering toward the end.

"No matter what, you'll never lose him. I know it sounds hard to believe, but he's with you Sam." Placing my hand over his heart, I firmly press against his chest. "He's in here. He'll never be far."

Amidst the enormity of the sky and universe, it's easy to feel alone, yet also part of something so much bigger than yourself. I hope—no, I *believe* Bas is up there, somewhere, looking down on us. On Sam and Alec. Forever loving them and watching over them.

The day of Bastien's funeral is somber. Dark gray clouds burden the sky, threatening a downpour. The wind is unusually cold and fierce for September, whipping my hair all over the place. Finally, no longer wanting to fight with it, I grab hold of my wild tresses and crudely tie them back into a low bun.

The church is crowded, overflowing with people. Many have come from far and wide, including a chef or two from France and a few from British Columbia and California. Bas is—was world-renowned in culinary circles. There's no doubt he made his mark, and in the short time I knew him, he certainly made his mark on me.

The ceremony is beautiful and sad. Sam manages to say a few words before losing it, and Alec does too. Afterward, as we begin to depart the church for the cemetery, all three of us are quiet. None of us have spoken to the others since we arrived at the church. Sam and Alec are surrounded by well-meaning people who wish to convey their condolences but it's overwhelming.

Finally, the priest ushers people along, reminding everyone that we must get to the cemetery. Outside, at the grave, the wind howls and the skies darken further. The service is quick and like many, I drop a single red rose upon the casket. Rivers of tears run down my face.

Standing silently beside Sam, our fingers interlaced, I scan the crowd of people still milling around the gravesite, all of them jockeying to speak to Sam, Alec, or both. After what feels like hours, the crowd thins and the three of us are left with only a smattering of people.

Marie-Claire, Bas's childhood friend, calls Sam over. Glancing my way, he gestures for us to go, but he's torn at leaving a stoic and dazed Alec by himself. I squeeze his hand in reassurance. "It's okay, go. Alec and I will be fine."

At hearing his name, Alec nods in agreement, mutely giving Sam the go ahead to leave. As Sam's tall form, with his head hung low, ambles across the grass, Alec breaks our silence by clearing his throat.

"You don't see it, do you?"

"Pardon?" I turn to face him.

"That boy has given you his heart."

Speechless, I examine the depths of his eyes. While his expression exudes warmth, his voice is cold, almost disappointed. I'm not sure what to say; I'm not prepared for this conversation or that truth, or even my own feelings. Like him, I'm overcome with sadness, too raw and crushed to handle any more.

"You may not know it—shit, you likely didn't even ask for it, but it's yours." Alec stares at Sam where he is speaking with Marie-Claire. His arms encase her frail, petite form as he comforts the older, sobbing woman. "You better honor Bastien's request of you. You better take good care of Sam's heart. Of him. He is *the* one and only thing Bas loved most in this world. He would have given everything up for him. He made me promise, although he knew he needn't ask, to look after and protect Samson. Olivia." He turns to look solemnly at me, his eyes are fatigued, black circles ringing them. He's aged, understandably so, in these past few days. "You have the power to destroy him. Bas will rise from the dead and haunt me if I let you hurt Sam."

"Alec…" I falter, feeling the need to say something, to defend myself and comfort him, yet not knowing what to say. I have no intention of hurting Sam.

How do I feel? I love Sam, but is it *love*, love? I like him a lot. I enjoy my time with him. In fact, I anxiously look forward to it and miss him terribly when we're apart—but is that love? Am I ready to be *in* love? I'm not prepared for this deep conversation.

Bas's words are coming back to haunt me. I pushed them aside when they were spoken, not ready to deal with it, and now it's unnerving to hear something similar again, to see the belief Alec has in the power he feels I have over Sam. I'm not sure I want that kind of influence.

"Olivia," Sam interrupts my thoughts. Alec stands silent and reserved, his gaze transfixed on me, measuring my every move—at least that's how it feels. "Let's go."

As he takes my hand, fat, cold drops of rain hit my face. Sam opens an umbrella and hands one to Alec then his arm circles my waist as he steers me toward the car. Glancing back to where Alec remains motionless, he says, "Alec, you coming?"

The rain pelts down on us, each hard splat against our umbrellas unsettling me further. Alec looks like a man moored to the gloomy, dark backdrop. "No, I'm going to stay a bit. I'll get a ride back. You go ahead." His voice is heavy, pained.

Sam drives to the house in silence. Leaving him to his thoughts, I contemplate my brief but troubling encounter with Alec. Of all things the man must be plagued with since the death of his husband, why say this to me? I'm still confused and wish we had been able to finish what he started.

Alec returns several hours later, wet and chilled to the bone but more like himself, insisting on making us a simple, comforting meal of grilled cheese and tomato soup. Conversation is sparse and the evening is subdued and quiet. We all turn in early.

Sam and I are silent as we undress for bed, slipping under the covers. Wordlessly, he reaches for me in the dark. The pale moonlight slices through the thin curtains, illuminating enough of his face for me to see the deep lines of anguish in his forehead and around his mouth. His lips crush mine in an unforgiving, frenetic kiss, expressing his deep and unyielding need for me. For us.

Unlike the tumultuous storm of emotions within both of us, we make slow, sensual, silent love. For the first time ever, my moans and whimpers are soft undertones for his ears only. No effort or interference is needed to keep me quiet, and my faint murmurs are no less indicative of my pleasure than my usual loud sounds and sighs. Somehow, I know this is what he needs, and unexpectedly, I'm capable of silence during passionate sex.

Sam gives me his sorrow, his suffering with his body, and I in turn give him solace and love. Our union is no less intense or passionate than it has been previously. We move as one, our breaths hot and heavy, our kisses deep, long, and powerful. Our joining is deeply devastating in its significance and exhilarating all at the same time, reminding us that we're alive.

Once we are both spent, we cling to each other, our damp, heavy chests moving in tandem as we come down from our climax. My mouth travels his face, his neck, his upper chest, tasting and revering, adoring him. He holds me tight, wrapping his arms around me and draping one leg over mine. We both lie still, listening to the rain fall. Sam eventually finds sleep and I listen to his even, deep breaths as I'm eventually lulled into slumber.

The bed dips and rises with Sam's departure from the bed. It's just after six o'clock in the morning. I lie still, listening as he pulls on his pants and closes the door behind him. After a few footfalls, I hear the muffled voices of Sam and Alec through the paper-thin walls. Giving the two of them this much-needed time to talk, I burrow farther into the soft down covers and close my eyes.

Not long after, the strong, alluring aroma of coffee permeates the bedroom, followed by the familiar kitchen clatter of breakfast coming together. It's time for me to go home. I've been here nearly a week and I need to leave today. I'm taking the train to the airport in a few short hours. I don't want to leave Sam, I want to be here for him, but I also know that Alec and Sam need some time together. They have things to discuss and decisions to make.

Breakfast is solemn. There isn't much talking, but the tension has lifted, perhaps from knowing Bas is at rest. After a delicious and hearty breakfast, Sam loads the car with my bags and I linger in the foyer, waiting for Alec, hoping to get a moment alone.

"Olivia." Alec's deep rumble comes from behind me.

"Alec." I sigh with relief at his usual tone and warm expression. I open my arms and he envelopes me in a big, long hug, his rich, masculine cologne a welcoming scent.

"I wanted to talk to you before I left."

"Olivia." He pushes back half a step, and we're only inches apart as he peers down at me. "Me first. I'm sorry about yesterday. I realize I came on strong, and I was reacting out of fear—my fear of fucking this up, of being alone and not being enough for Sam. I'm sorry." His voice wavers and his fingers lightly squeeze my shoulders.

Blinking back tears, I force a small, reassuring smile. Seeing him this vulnerable, appreciating his honesty, and understanding where he's coming from, I want nothing more than to cry. Loving someone is a precious gift, and one that's often taken for granted. In Alec's eyes, he understands the magnitude of the gift he had and its loss.

I wish I could ease his grief, and I'm also grateful that Alec and Sam have each other. Their unconditional love for each other will carry them through. They will need each other more than ever now in their shared loss, and it's their unending love of one man, Bastien, that will bond them even stronger than they are today and pull them through this dark and miserable time.

"No apologies needed. I understand and I want to tell you that I have no intention of hurting Sam. I love him. I'll take care of him," I assure him.

"My sweet girl, I know you believe that from the bottom of your heart. It's clear as day in your eyes, in the way you look at him and talk to him, but how does that work?" My eyebrow quirks in confusion. "You live in Toronto and he's in Montreal. How do you build a life together when he has no intention of ever leaving this place? Are you prepared to uproot your life for him?"

Twenty-Four

SAM

"Sam?" Olivia calls from the front door. The muffled voices of Drew and Paige filter throughout my loft.

Splashing cold water on my tired face, I peer into the bathroom mirror. On a long, shaky breath, I steel myself, digging deep for my reserves. They're here. I can do this…I think.

It's been five weeks, over a month since his death. Olivia's been here every weekend. She's come to me, every time. I haven't asked; she just knows. Truth be told, I haven't been in the frame of mind to even think about what I need, what I want. I'm just going through the motions.

While the thought of them all being here is comforting, I'm not sure if I'm up for the company. It's been low-key and quiet when she has been here, just us, and I wonder if I can keep two teenagers entertained.

"Hey," I respond, my voice tight.

The three of them turn, each with their own warm, caring smile aimed at me. Paige and Drew coming to see me is a big deal; it means something that both of them gave up a weekend with their friends for me.

Olivia slips into my embrace, gathering me—a man almost twice her size—in her strong, inviting arms.

She perches up on her tiptoes and her lips delicately brush mine. "Hey," she whispers, her smile small and knowing, her gaze soft.

"Sam." Paige's voice cracks as she launches herself at us; it's rather dramatic, but no less sweet.

Her slender arms wrap around her mother and me. Breathing in her girly scent, it brings a small but true smile to my face. I've missed her too, this feisty, sweet girl who has bit by bit become my friend. I lean down and my lips lightly kiss the top of her head.

"Hey Paige, I'm glad you're here."

"I'm so sorry about your father. Mom's told us about him and I wish we'd met…" Her voice trails off when she thinks she's said something wrong.

"Hey." My voice is soft, understanding as I cup her cheek. She steers her gaze back to me. "He would have loved meeting you, and you." I look over at Drew, who is standing awkwardly to the side. He smiles weakly. "And thanks for coming. I'm glad you're here."

As I say the words, I realize it's true. I am glad they're here, and also grateful that we're staying with Alec for the weekend. This is exactly what we both need—young people to snap us out of our blues.

Like a hurricane, the four of us descend on Alec with chaos and upheaval, but in a good way. At first, Alec is clearly bewildered and flustered, not knowing if he's coming or going, but as the day goes on he begins to unwind, settling into his old self, the man I knew before the loss of Bas.

With a deep, hearty chuckle, Alec snags Paige around the waist and ruffles her hair. She shrieks, her fingers frantically combing through her dishevelled locks in a poor attempt at fixing the mess.

"Young lady, I think you cheated," Alec accuses.

"I didn't! You're just a sore loser," she retorts, raking all the poker chips to her side of the table.

"Sorry, Alec, but Paige is a card shark. She comes by it honestly—my father was good at poker and taught her everything she knows," Olivia explains.

Drew hands me a beer before sitting back down at the kitchen table. "Although, she *has* been known to cheat." He sends a knowing glance at his sister.

Paige's cheeks redden as she abruptly stands, hands on her hips. "Drew, shut it. That was one time. *One time.* And I said sorry and promised never to do it again, and I haven't," she protests vehemently.

Olivia and Drew laugh, obviously knowing exactly what she's talking about. "Well, now you have to tell us," I insist. "You can't leave us hanging. What gives, Paige?"

Huffing, she crosses her arms. "Sam, it was one time, I swear. I was playing with Popzie and I was losing. So, I just, um…"

"She was counting cards," Drew cuts in.

"Was not! I don't even know what that is," Paige fumes.

Alec's laughing so hard, his eyes water. "Come here," he calls to Paige.

Tugging her wrist, he pulls her into a hug, his arms banding around her middle. She willingly embraces him, resting her cheek on the top of his head as he softens in her hold. The sight of the two of them tugs at my heart. I wish he were here. I wish he could meet them. Why didn't I have Paige and Drew meet him? Damn, I hate regrets. I hate wishing for something that's futile, something that's never going to happen.

"You've got to teach me," Alec jests. Paige giggles.

Our weekend is amazing; I can hardly believe it. We have fun and truly enjoy ourselves, so much so that the time flies by. The kids surprise us by cooking dinner one night, and it is actually pretty good. Alec has a good time, a really good time, laughing for the first time in a while and smiling—boy did he smile.

They'll leave bright and early in the morning; Drew has a long day of driving ahead of him as he heads straight back to school once he drops off his mom and sister.

It's four in the morning and they're all asleep. I'm up, can't sleep.

As I drizzle olive oil in the hot pan, it sizzles and pops as I twirl on my heel to scoop the mirepoix into my hand and drop it into the skillet. Instantly, the alluring aroma of the simple but delicious base—the secret ingredient in many dishes—hits my nose. Stirring the onion, celery, and carrot by habit, I'm lost in the haze of the calming task, one I've completed too many times to count.

Her sweeping, soft, almost invisible touch along my bare back ignites a soothing and exciting sensation within me, pulling me back.

"That smells so good." Olivia's sultry voice warms me. "What are you making at this hour?"

She doesn't ask if I can't sleep; she knows. She's found me before, up in the middle of the night doing one thing or another. She doesn't need to ask— her being *her* is enough.

Placing the wooden spoon on the rest, I turn off the burner and bring her to me. My arms encircle her slender waist as I crush her chest to mine, my feverish skin tingling with want. Heat flares in her eyes and her hair is wild, cheeks tinged.

"I was making soup, but now I've lost interest and would rather make something else."

"Oh? What are you in the mood for?" she asks in a seductive tone.

"You. I want to make love to you." I nibble along the column of her neck. *Delectable.* "Although, I think I'd rather devour you. You don't need any seasoning. You taste perfect the way you are." As I suck and lick behind her ear, my fingers burrow into the tender flesh of her backside.

I move her body fully against mine and my delicate hold grows greedy. Our lips mash against each other and a landslide of emotion crashes over me, threatening to consume, drown, strangle me. I never want to stop, never want to let her go. She's made for me. I'm made to love her.

She quivers in my arms as her breathy moan slides down my throat, reverberating through my chest. Dragging her up my body, her torturous curves set fire to all my nerve endings along the way. I'm a whirlwind of frenzy and her legs wrap snugly around my waist as I carry her to the kitchen chair.

Straddling my lap, her slender hands cling to my shoulders, pulling me closer as she kisses me, hard and hungry. Going for the hem of her shirt, she prepares to lift it over her head, but I stop her.

My trembling hands still hers. Her eyes widen, cloud with uncertainty. Without thought, only instinct, I'm driven to confess.

Say it.

Words that have been on my lips many times before, but that I've held back, waited to voice, knowing she may not be ready to hear them. Now is the time to tell her.

Say it.

My entire body trembles, teeming with emotion. No doubts. I need to tell her.

Say it.

"Olivia." My voice is low, gravelly with affection. "I love you."

My fingers caress her cheek, my breath suspended as I wait. Hesitancy veils her gaze and her breath hitches as her fingers dig into my flesh.

"Sam." Her voice wavers, gulping on my name. "I…um…I…"

Grabbing me, her fingers thread through my hair at the nape of my neck as she harshly brings me to her mouth, covering mine. Her tongue invades the space, hard and demanding as she kisses me. I cup her ass and she rocks into me. My cock painfully throbs and as much as I'm caught up in my desire for her, it's not lost on me that she's not said a word in response to my raw declaration.

Working her tongue against mine, her hard nipples rub and tease my chest through the thin fabric. Her body tremors as I run my hand under her shirt, the pads of my fingers dancing across her abdomen, up to her breasts.

Palming their heaviness, then I lightly pinch her peaks, rolling them between my finger and thumb. Her head tips back, her breathing ragged as she bites her lip to stifle her whimpers of satisfaction. I love watching her lose all inhibition.

Amidst my soft, delicate kisses to her jaw and lips, she peeks at me through the fan of her dark lashes. Lifting her, I carry her to the bedroom where I show her how much I love her, how important she is to me.

She may not have said it, but the love is in her eyes. I feel the love in the way her body responds to me, in the way she gives herself to me, welcomes me into not only her body but also her heart and soul. She's stolen my heart and every time she leaves, she takes it with her. I need her to stop leaving.

I need her to stay.

Twenty-Five

OLIVIA

Looking around the yard of my old home, things have slipped since my departure. Some small part of me laments that. The place isn't as bright or cheery as it used to be. I love this home and even with the end of my marriage, this house holds a lot of wonderful memories. It's hard to completely detach from all that.

I pick up my pace toward the front door. I'm really looking forward to seeing Sam. It's been over two months since Bas's funeral and each day is getting easier for him. Since telling me he loved me, I feared things would be different, harder since I didn't say it back, but it's been good. We see each other almost every week.

I love him and I'm certain Sam knows it too; I'm just not ready to say it, to put it out there and share it with him. It's silly, but it's me being hung up on all the ways it's wrong—or more importantly, should be wrong but isn't. It feels so right. So good. So perfect.

Sam's flying in this morning and spending the weekend. He says he has good news. We're meeting for breakfast and I'm anxious to hear what it is. Maybe today will be the day I grow some balls and say it. Perhaps, but I won't dwell on it or force it; it will come.

Stopping here at Pete's house for Paige's uniform is completely out of my way and could make me late for our breakfast, another con of living with a teenager. Things have been so much better between the two of us. Paige has loosened up on her digs about the divorce, my cruelty toward her father, and destroying her life—although, when it suits her, she still plays on my guilt, using it to her advantage, like this morning.

She knows I'm eager to repair our relationship, and getting me to be her bitch is a test of how much I truly love her—or at least, I'm sure that's how she sees it. Also, I'm sure she also did it for the pure joy of it, because she can. I guess I'm the fool because here I am, at my old home, picking up her uniform for her rather than making her get up earlier this morning and come get it herself.

When I'm mere feet from the front door, Erin, steps out, donning her suit jacket. You know, the one who, although bitchy to most people is still my friend. I gasp, stopping dead in my tracks. Erin's also caught off guard, her eyes wide and shocked like she's been caught with her hand in the cookie jar. I know what this looks like, and so does she.

Despite the obvious, she's my friend, and in the moment, I dismiss what's right in front of me. "Erin, what are you doing here?" I foolishly lean in for a quick hug.

My mind runs a million miles a minute. As we separate, I regret hugging her. In my bones, I know why she's here, and yet, like someone facing a firing squad, spending their last few seconds conjuring an escape route, I dismiss the absurdity of my question.

"Um, I…" she stutters, unable to look me in the eye.

"Did you spend the night here?" As I stare at her, time slows, and she grows paler by the second. Her eyes dart all over the place, refusing to look at me. "Erin," I say firmly. If she didn't before, she must know now that I'm serious.

"Shit. Yes, I did. Let me explain," she says quickly in a flustered manner, so unlike the calm, cool, and collected lawyer she is. It's in that moment that I allow myself to take in exactly what it looks like.

"How long has this been going on?"

"Liv, let me explain."

"How long?"

"Almost six months," she whispers, shame staining her cheeks.

"How did this happen and why didn't you tell me?" I demand.

"It happened by accident. Remember you asked me to speak with Drew about law school? Well I came over because you'd asked me to, and…" She pauses, sighing, then keeps repeating the fact that it was my request, like this is somehow my doing. If she says it one more time, I fear what I might do.

Fiddling with the strap of her Michael Kors purse, she finally says, "Pete asked me to stay for dinner and then one thing led to another..."

Erin raises her head to look at me, her transformation takes place before my eyes, from the guilty, so-called friend to the confident, high-priced litigator. It's subtle, but it's definitely there in the straightening of her spine and the squaring of her shoulders. On goes her game face. I know what her stern, no-nonsense expression means—she's ready for battle.

"I remember the night. Drew had dinner with me before heading back to school. Paige was at Marci's."

It wasn't like she was invited to a family dinner. She's a smart woman and likely knew what the dinner invitation could lead to. I want her to know that I know that too, as well as my suspicion that she likely wanted it, maybe even went to my ex-husband's home with that purpose. I remember that night; I suggested she speak with Drew at my house or come to dinner with us.

Erin's shrewd. I know what she's capable of. We've been friends since high school, and I've been party to many of her schemes to get things her way, especially where a man is concerned. It's why she's an excellent lawyer—she can be ruthless and single-mindedly focused on her goal.

"You've been sleeping with Pete since then," I state rather than ask. She folds her arms over her chest and curtly nods in affirmation. "Why didn't you tell me?" My voice is hard and tight; I barely recognize it's me. I've never felt as betrayed as I do right now. She is my friend—at least I thought she was.

"Seriously? How was I supposed to tell you?" she snaps, rolling her eyes like I'm clueless, which clearly, I have been.

"We're friends. Let's park the girl code because surely you can't be so oblivious as to not know you broke it. Pete wasn't some boyfriend—he was my *husband* for *twenty years*, and your friend for that long, too. Did you always want to sleep with him?" I accuse, not liking my tone or the fact that I'm shaking. Showing her any emotion or weakness is not wise.

"He was supposed to be mine!" Her outcry is like a plea in one of her closing arguments.

"What?" I'm completely lost, shocked even.

"The night you met Pete, I was supposed to meet him but I was sick."

"What the hell are you talking about?"

"It was Rob's party and he invited Pete for me. He said he thought we'd hit it off. You met him instead and when I did finally meet him, you two were dating." She states all this like her explanation is completely sane.

"Have you been harboring that doozy for twenty years?" I ask rhetorically and continue. "You never said *anything*, and seriously, I married the man for crying out loud! You mean to tell me you potentially wrecked our thirty-plus-year friendship over a hypothetical relationship?"

"I don't know what your problem is. You left him. You don't want him. You've moved on. Everything comes easy to you. You had it all with Pete—a great husband, amazing kids, you could stay at home and do whatever you wanted, but no, you had to cry because you weren't getting the attention you thought you deserved. Then when you told me you were leaving him and your reasons." Her laugh is harsh. "I figured it was my turn," she spits out, her disdain no longer hidden.

Each word is a blow to my chest, sucking the air out of me, crushing my love for her and shattering our friendship as all her ugliness spews out over our lifelong friendship.

"But fuck no. *Now* you've got some thirty-something hottie drooling all over you. Seriously, Liv, what is your problem? Do you think you're the only one who can be loved or admired?"

"Erin, that's enough," Pete roars from behind her. She startles, shuddering at the boom of his voice as she blanches, her eyes feral and lips tight. It's written all over her face, the sick fear of knowing he heard her vindictive words.

"Pete." Her voice is husky as she pivots to face him.

Before she has a chance to spew more garbage, I barrel ahead. "I'm here to pick up Paige's uniform." My voice is neutral, in stark opposition to the maelstrom of emotions tearing up my insides.

"Liv," Pete murmurs, his hand strong and steady on my elbow. "Sorry, I wanted to tell you. Are you okay?"

I'm not letting him off the hook. He's been pursuing me for months now while fucking my friend. As much as I think he owes me an explanation and the truth, he's free to sleep with whomever he wants. We're divorced and I don't care who he sleeps with. It's Erin I'm furious with—I thought our friendship meant more than this. Instead, she's resented me all these years.

"I'm fine. Can we talk about this later? I just want the uniform."

He visibly relaxes on a sigh, thinking he's dodged a bullet. He steps into the house and returns a few seconds later with Paige's uniform, and in that fleeting moment, it hits me like a Mack truck.

Glaring, I choke out, "Drew."

I need not say any more. An immediate frown fixes on his face as he casts his eyes downward on a long and harsh exhale. Looking up, he averts his eyes, looking anywhere but at me. Clearing my throat, I prepare to tear into him as this is what has come between father and son. Drew must know.

God, what if he walked in on them? I'm beyond pissed at that thought. My heart squeezes at how torn and burdened Drew must feel to be carrying this secret, to be caught in the middle and want to tell me, but also protect me.

"Liv, please come in and let's talk." He is conciliatory.

"Pete, I think we should talk, but I'm already late for court," Erin chimes in, oblivious to the added tension between us.

He looks over my shoulder at Erin. I refuse to acknowledge her. If they think I'm talking to them, together, they are sorely mistaken.

"I wasn't talking to you," he snaps.

Erin inhales a sharp breath and gasps. "Fine," she spits back, the retreating clip of her heels sounding out.

I'm shocked at his tone. He's mad. I didn't see him this way often while we were married, but it's unmistakable. His anger only shows when he's been pushed to his limit. One thing about Pete is that it takes a *lot* to get him riled. Drew is much like him in that way, and thinking about our son brings me back to my anger and the burning desire to protect him.

"You better fix this with him, *now*. I don't care what you have to do, but you fess up to your douchebag move. Own it and let him off the hook. This has been eating him up. I've seen it but didn't know what it was about. Fix. It."

"Liv, I will. I promise." On another sharp sigh, he runs his fingers through his hair. "God dammit, I'm so sorry. I was lonely and she came on to me. I'm not putting it all on Erin, but..."

I cut him off before he can further add to the sick tightening in the pit of my stomach. Erin's betrayal hurts, and it's not even about Pete. Not once while confronting Erin were my thoughts on him, on the fact that he slept with my friend. It's the loss and disappointment of what she did, most likely deliberately, to destroy our relationship.

"Pete, stop. I don't want to hear this right now. Make things right with Drew. I've got to go. "

Taking Paige's bag, I turn my back on him. He calls my name, adding a few more lame excuses about Erin being the seductress, which I'm sure she was. I can't get to my car fast enough.

I can certainly appreciate that Erin likely did make him her target, but his dick didn't just fall into her. No matter what he says, he was willing at some point, and most of all, I hate that I even care.

In a fog, I drop Paige's uniform at the school. Then I drive aimlessly for over two hours, no thought as to where I'm supposed to be or what obligations or appointments I'm shirking. My mind reels with what happened. It takes me a while to finally realize that Erin's got me in a tailspin. I'm not wild about her sleeping with my ex, but I have no intentions of ever getting back together with him. I'm not jealous or bothered by the thought of him having sex with another woman.

It's Erin's actions and disregard for me that have shredded my heart. It's the envy and disdain in her words. It's tainted everything we've ever done. Every secret, every memory, every conversation is now ruined.

As I pull into my driveway, my heart sinks to the pit of my stomach at the sight of Sam sitting on my front steps. *Shit.* I forgot I was meeting him. His head is hung low, resting on his hands, his fingers gripping his short strands so tightly his knuckles are white.

At the sound of my car, he springs into action, and before I can cut the engine, he's opening my car door and unbuckling my seat belt.

"Jesus Christ," he rasps, pulling me into a warm embrace. "Thank fuck you're okay."

Regret and self-loathing jerk at my heart; I was supposed to meet him for breakfast hours ago. Wrapping my arms around his solid, inviting frame, I hug him tightly. For the first time in hours, I'm calm, strong, and good.

"I'm okay. I'm so sorry," I whisper into his neck.

I tenderly kiss his neck, welcoming his clean, salty taste. Warmth blooms in my chest and my shoulders relax as I finally breathe easy. Pulling back a step, he gently grips my chin and his eyes flick across my face, holding steady on my gaze for a few beats before flitting over my features again. His hair is disheveled with strands sticking up in different directions, and concern etches his handsome face.

"Where the hell were you? I called you a dozen times and also texted." His tone is a mixture of relief and frustration.

"I..." I stall, realizing how bad my reason will sound.

Starting from the beginning, I tell him about Paige's obnoxious last-minute request this morning and how she deliberately played on my guilt. I tell him about running into Erin and our exchange, although I omit some of her nasty words—it's too soon to relive it all. I explain Pete's reaction, then mine.

His arms drop from my shoulders as I continue. Taking a step back, then another away from me, his expression shutters as I end with telling him that I was driving around to clear my head.

Arms crossed and lips squashed into a thin, tight line, his voice is expressionless as he says, "You were driving around for the past few hours."

Before I can offer further explanation—and I definitely get the sense that I need to do more to make him understand—his phone rings.

"Beaulieu." His voice is low and heavy. He listens, watching me intently as he responds, "Oui..." Ending the call, he turns to me once more. "I have to go. I blew up my morning worried sick about you." His words are edged with irritation and something else—disappointment, perhaps.

Brow furrowed and jaw tense, he walks to his car without waiting for my response. "Sam," I call out, desperation lacing his name.

He doesn't stop until he's at his door. Raising a brow, he peers at me over the hood of his car but offers no response, his look cold and expectant. I've never seen this side of him, and even though I understand his frustration, I'm taken aback. Completely baffled, I'm not sure how to fix this.

"I'm sorry. Can we talk about this over dinner?"

"What are you sorry for?" he asks in a tone that suggests he doesn't want to hear my answer. My thoughts are confirmed when he continues with, "You know what? Don't bother answering. I've gotta go, and no, I can't do dinner."

I flinch at his words, his quick dismissal without explanation. I guess I deserve it since I never thought to even call him. I wonder if he'll come to my place tonight...if not, where is he going to go? He's leaving tomorrow, going back to Montreal—where does this leave us?

"Are you coming home tonight?" I ask, biting my lip and tightening my jaw to stop my chin from wobbling.

I don't want him to see that I'm going to cry. It's in this moment my stupidity at thinking this was ever a fling hits me. It never was. It's always been more than that. Seeing him hurt, seeing him leave because of my insensitive actions hurts. Real badly. I deserve this. I'm hurt because I hurt him, albeit unintentionally. My actions make it seem like he wasn't a concern to me, which is the furthest thing from the truth. I was angry, lost, and wasn't thinking of anyone.

He doesn't answer, instead saying, "You know what the funniest and most fucked up thing about all this is? I thought you were hung up on my age. I thought it was our age difference and the distance that kept you holding off, never entirely giving yourself to me, but that wasn't it. Stupid me. I was never worried or concerned. I told myself I'd wait no matter how long it took because I knew you'd come around. I knew it'd all work out, but no, I was wrong. It was Pete. You're still hung up on your ex."

With trembling lips, I begin to deny it, but Sam doesn't wait. He gets in the car, not wanting to hear what I have to say. A tight knot forms in my chest where my heart is and I blink rapidly, trying to keep the tears from spilling onto my cheeks.

There's a wide chasm between us that I caused, and I have no clue how to close it, how to get to him. Standing silently, my arms wrap tightly around my middle as he drives away.

Twenty-Six

OLIVIA

At the sound of knocking, I bound down the stairs to open the door. *Shit.* It's the last person that I want to see, and she's decked out in her full suit of armor—a high-priced designer suit. Erin stands tall, almost regal. I haven't had time to process this, her, what happened between her and Pete. Sam left two days ago and I've only heard from him once.

He texted the night he left me on the driveway to say he was going back to Montreal and needed time and space. He said he'd contact me when he's ready. Wanting to respect his wishes, I told him I understood and would wait, but I don't want to wait.

When we met I didn't want to start anything, I didn't want a relationship, and now I'm right back where I was with Pete—tied up in knots over some man. Yes, Sam is nothing like Pete and the situation is completely different, but I've found myself here again.

Disappointed and afraid this relationship will fail, I fear the longer we're apart, the longer it takes for us to talk about this, the easier it'll be for him to walk away. I seriously messed things up, and now, *Erin*.

"What do you want?"

"Liv, can I come in?"

"I don't have anything to say to you." I really don't. Pete's been trying to talk to me too, but I'm not ready for him either—although speaking with him will be easier. I don't care that he slept with Erin. Sure, it hurts knowing he lied and it was with my friend, but I'm glad that he might be moving on.

"Please. I'll keep it short, but I really want to talk."

I turn my back and she follows me into the foyer. I go no farther—she's not welcome in my home.

"Talk," I command, folding my arms and puffing out a frustrated breath.

"I'm sorry," she sounds almost contrite, but it's impossible to miss that her tone's laced with belligerence. "To make things clear, I won't apologize for pursuing things with Pete, but I am sorry for not being open with you."

Barking out a laugh, my eyes widen in astonishment at her nerve. I really shouldn't be surprised. This is Erin, always has been—I just always put up with her shit because she was my friend. Now, I'm tired of making excuses for her selfish behavior. Everyone has issues and hard times, but she's used her father's callous attitude as an excuse to be a bitch for way too long.

At my reaction, she has a dumb look on her face like she has no clue why I'd react that way. Why? Because I've been a pushover for so long and never called her out on her façade. I saw it, I just never thought she'd aim it at me. That was my mistake. That's on me.

"Pete and I are…"

Cutting her off, I hold my hand up. "Stop right there. Not now, not ever will I talk to you about my ex-husband. I don't care if you're fucking him or not. If that's all you have to say, you can leave."

The doorbell rings, and we both turn to see Sin walking in. "Hey Liv," she calls, trepidation creeping into her sunny features at the sight of Erin and me.

"Was this planned?" I snap. "You two tag-teaming me?"

"No," Sin balks.

She knows about Sam, and of course, Erin and Pete. She's been my shoulder to cry on. She hasn't said much about Erin, but she's disgusted with her stunt, though not surprised. She's been more vocal about Sam, and quick to point out that I need to fix it.

"Come in." I usher her in but leave the door open. Erin gives her a weak smile, shrinking in on herself a bit. Sin's cold reception is not lost on her. "Erin was just leaving," I offer.

"Liv, we haven't talked."

"We're done. I'll call you when I'm ready to talk, if that time ever comes."

"Liv, please hear me out."

"Erin," both Sin and I say at the same time. There's an edge, a finality to my tone, and Sin's is similar, like we telepathically agreed on this.

Solemnly nodding, she mutters goodbye and leaves. With the door closed, my shoulders sag and I exhale a sweet sigh of relief. The knot in my chest loosens but still remains. I hurt. If I think too much about it, the pain is tight, like someone's clutching my heart.

There's no future for Erin and me, but she's been my friend for almost thirty years so as much as cutting her out of my life is the right thing to do, the smart thing to do, it still hurts. I'll never trust her again. She's obviously harbored deep resentment toward me and I don't understand it. I don't know how to fix it, or if I really even care to.

"Sorry, Sin. I thought with Erin showing up here, then you, it was planned." With an arm around her shoulder, I lead her into the kitchen.

"Never. I haven't spoken to her since her first phone call after what happened, and like I told you, I told her we had nothing to talk about. I don't need friends like that. Anyway, enough about her. Are you okay?"

"Yes, I'm fine."

"Seriously?" she pushes. "This is me. You don't look fine. You've got dark circles under your eyes—have you not been sleeping?"

"I'm a mess." My chin wobbles and my voice cracks. My vision turns to liquid, tears pooling in my eyes as she envelops me in her arms. "I'm such an idiot. I love him. God, I love him."

"I know, honey." Her soothing tone and gentle embrace are calming, grounding. Her support is keeping me together. "You need to talk to him. Tell him."

"I know. I'm such an idiot. Why didn't I say it when he did? I felt it. I knew I did. I was scared." I sob, my chest heaving.

My cries are muted. I try to keep it together, contain my anguish, make no sound as I feel undeserving of her comfort. I brought this on myself. She hugs me tighter, sensing my stubbornness and reluctance to be absolved of my foolishness.

"Hon, it'll be okay. I know it will. Sam loves you. He's probably just frustrated," she soothes, rubbing my back. "Give him time, but not too much. If he takes too long, you make the move."

Pulling away, I wipe at my tears. "And what's too long?"

Her eyes are tender, filled with compassion. Her fingers tuck a stray lock of hair behind my ear, then she places a light kiss on my forehead and smiles warmly, reassuringly. "You'll know—" Sin's interrupted by my mobile ringing.

Shaking off my pity party, I nab my phone, not recognizing the number, and hit talk.

"Hello?"

As I listen to the stranger on the other end, my world stops.

Paige has been in a car accident.

Twenty-Seven

SAM

Standing on Olivia's porch, the chilly November wind whips through us like a blade slicing through butter. *Fuck,* it's cold. Alec rests his hand on my shoulder with a heavy, supportive squeeze.

The door opens and my chest spasms at the vision of her, aching with my longing for her. It's only been days since I last saw her, but they've been the longest and most agonizing of my life.

I fucking love her and only want to be with her, but with the Pete and Erin crap, she needs to figure out what she wants. Maybe—though I dare not give in to my fear—it's not me.

As patient as I'm willing to be, I can't make her feel, act, or be anything she isn't ready for. That's where my decision to leave and to have radio silence came into play, and I'll admit, it was kind of my way of pushing her.

I knew pushing could go either way, but I need to know that she feels it too, the all-encompassing love that's consuming me. Then Jonah's call and talking to Paige changed all of that. I wasn't going to keep my distance. Not now.

Pushing past the lump in my throat, I whisper, "Mon trésor."

At first, her expression is impassive as she flattens her mouth, but then her lips tremble as she bites her bottom lip, trying to hold back her emotions. Her eyes glass over as the unshed tears form and her façade crumbles as big, fat tears spill like a waterfall and she emits a heaving sob.

I've got her. Rushing to her, I gather her in my arms, cradling her as I lead us into the house. Alec's at my back, closing the door behind us.

"Sam, I've missed you." She sniffs into the crook of my neck. Her tears and warm breath dampen my skin, sending shivers down my spine.

"I missed you too," I whisper into her hair, her scent calming me. My arms hold her tighter, happy to have her close. I never want to let her go.

In his deep, distinguished tone, Alec quietly says, "Paige?"

Olivia peers over my shoulder at him, her gaze questioning. He plants a light kiss on her cheek and gives her a small, sincere smile.

"Where's Paige, Livvy?"

"Ah, she's upstairs, but…"

"We know," Alec interjects. "That's why we're here. I'll go up to her."

Without further explanation, he ascends the staircase, never looking back, giving us privacy and also seeking out Paige. He needs to see her to put both his heart and mind at ease. Like me, he's been worried sick. He wants nothing more than to cast his eyes on the girl who has fast become a granddaughter to him. Olivia looks on in bewilderment. Guiding her to the couch, I pull her into my lap.

"Sam, how did you know about Paige?"

"Jonah," I admit. She rears back in surprise. "Before you castrate the man, hear me out. You're right. He loves you, like a brother, and wants to see you happy. He knows I make you happy. You make me happy. He thought I should know, and he was right. You should have called me."

"But, you needed space." Her tone is small and lost.

"Livvy, no matter what's going on, I want to know—no, I need to know. Yes, we've got a lot to discuss and it may not be pleasant." I won't sugar-coat it, and a warmth spreads through me because Bas would grin at this; he was always a straight shooter. "But that aside, I'm not going anywhere. I love Paige. I want to know if she's hurt, if she needs me, if you need me."

"Jonah?" she says, as if stuck on what I said minutes before, not comprehending anything I've said.

"Yes, Jonah called me and told me about Paige being in a car accident. He told me she has a concussion and some bruised ribs. I wasn't sure about coming so I called Paige to see how she was."

Even though she'd reached out to talk, I wondered if this was the end, if she was going back to Pete. I couldn't handle that, then when Jonah called, I desperately wanted to be there for her and for Paige—but then I wondered, *what if they don't need me?* What if she was leaning on Pete? Paige was their daughter, after all, and after what had happened, I wasn't sure if she'd left her marriage or not. I called Paige to get the lay of the land before making my decision about coming or not.

"You called Paige?" she echoes, still looking confused.

Nodding, I continue, "She told me you're not talking to Pete. She's less concerned about that at the moment and more concerned that you have your big meeting with Mrs. Preston tomorrow and seem dead set on canceling it. We all know there's no room to cancel it with the hotel launch plans in full swing. I'm here to take care of Paige so you can go. I'm here to help."

Realization of what I've said dawns in her eyes as they widen, locking on me. She gasps, sucking in a jagged breath, then burrows farther into my lap. Her arms circle my neck and she kisses me with a ferocity I've never experienced before.

Heat flares within me, desire spreading throughout at her demanding kiss. Her urgency and pent-up frustration is evident in every seductive stroke and stab of her tongue, mimicking what I so desperately wish my cock was doing inside her. Tight. Warm. So, fucking sweet.

"Sam, I love you," she moans, strong and sure. Her hands cup my jaw, holding me to her lips. So damn beautiful, raw and mine.

Swallowing her words in my mouth, I growl, "I love you too."

Our lips tangle, each of us pledging our love with more than words. She is my everything. We still have a lot to discuss, but hearing her declaration renews my faith in us, in my promise to myself to find a way for us to be together.

Twenty-Eight

OLIVIA

Pulling into my driveway, the day's victory fades fast—Pete's standing at the edge of my walkway. It looks like he just got here as he's walking up the drive when he pauses and turns in the direction of my car pulling up. He's made several attempts since last week to talk to me, but I haven't wanted to. I don't want to know who he sleeps with, let alone that it's my ex-friend.

For a split second I wonder if maybe I'm wrong, if he may have tried the door. Does Sam know he's here? Sam showing up on my doorstep last night stunned and overwhelmed me with relief. We didn't get a chance to talk—he was almost reluctant to. Paige was thrilled to have our guests and there was no denying how ecstatic she was to be pampered by them both.

Preparing for my confrontation with Pete, I quickly catalogue my day, which went very well. Mrs. Preston signed off on the final designs, and all orders have been placed and set to arrive on time. All around, the past twenty-four hours have been fantastic.

I groan at the thought of having to face Pete, which will likely erase all the good of today. Walking past him toward the door, I do the immature thing and ignore him.

"Olivia," he frantically calls out while pulling on my arm.

Whirling to face him, my glacial stare prevents him from saying any more.

"Pete, stop right there. I'm going to make

this real simple. We. Are. Divorced. Who you sleep with is none of my business. Yes, if it's one of my friends, call me crazy and unreasonable"—my tone is sarcastic, unable to keep my spiel neutral—"but I do expect to be told. With that said, we're not getting back together. Ever."

"Olivia," he protests. "I broke it off with Erin. I don't want her."

Holding my hand up, I continue, "Pete, you and I being over has nothing to do with Erin. The chance to mend our marriage is long gone. The way I see it, I easily spent the last five years of our marriage telling you what was missing, what we needed to work on, what we needed to do. It was like talking to a brick wall. You remained silent and refused to talk about it or meet me halfway. I even gave you the benefit of the doubt, giving you time to digest and formulate your thoughts. No matter how much time I gave you—days, weeks, months—you never had anything to say. We can't go back Pete. We're done. I'll always care about you and love you. Yes, I love you for what we had. You're the father of my children. We made some beautiful humans and some wonderful memories. But, that's it. I want to be civil and amicable for our kids, but you and I, we don't exist anymore. There is no us."

In some weird way, it pains me to say it all again. I don't want to hurt him. Yes, he hurt me, and I guess he perhaps thinks I hurt him, but somewhere along the way, we no longer fit, no longer worked together. I tried. In my heart of hearts, I tried my hardest, fought for us, for our life together, but he didn't show up. It's the story of my life with Pete Hayes.

"Shit, Liv." His voice is heavy, pained. "I messed up. I know that now. I was a dumb fuck who thought we'd be together forever. I buried my head in the sand and thought if I ignored it, it would go away. I can't imagine my life without you. The days since our separation have been the darkest of my life. It kills me to think that there isn't a chance for us. I need you. I love you. Please give us another chance." His eyes are wide and beseeching.

His plea only confirms what I already know. At one point in time, his words would have paved the way to reconciliation. They would have given me hope and likely bought us a few more years. Now, hearing his profession of love and his regrets does nothing. I feel nothing. Empty. Hollow.

All I have is pity for him, pity that he was given so many chances and chose to do nothing. I wish him no ill will, but I'm no longer in love with him, haven't been for years.

"Pete, there are no more chances."

"Liv," he croaks, his eyes glassy.

My chest sputters; I truly don't want to hurt him. Sure, I'm disappointed in some of what's happened and definitely in the most recent events, but I want us to get along. Taking my hand, he pulls me closer. Placing my palm on his chest, I keep a small distance between us. This is goodbye, nothing else.

"You're a good guy, you just couldn't give me what I need. I think you know as much as I do where things went wrong, and I finally realized I couldn't ask you to give me something you haven't got to give." I blink back my tears. We both need this moment for very different reasons. "I've moved on. I've found someone else who I'm crazy about and love dearly. I wish you the best life and I hope you find love again—you deserve it."

As I squeeze his hand, we stare intently into each other's eyes. Even with only the pale moonlight, I can make out the distress and sadness in his features. Like myself, he's changed, and perhaps even learned and grown because of this. I wish only the best for him. I hope he learns from this and finds happiness.

"Olivia." He sighs. "I'll always love you." He pulls me in for a brief hug, kissing my hair before releasing me.

"Bye Pete."

With a nod, his voice low, he adds, "Tell Paige I love her and I'll call her tomorrow."

I smile and nod. Shifting from one foot to the other, he looks longingly at me. Awkwardly, I avert my gaze, there's nothing else to say. He needs to move on, let me go.

Twenty-Nine

SAM

Stepping out from the shadow of the house, Olivia's on the porch and she sucks in a jagged breath at the sight of me. At first, I wanted to interrupt, let them know I was there, but as she continued to explain how she felt, I couldn't bring myself to stop her. I needed to hear it.

Her words soothed my fears, eradicated any doubts. My confidence in her, in us, grew tenfold knowing that we were real, that I hadn't dreamt it all in my head. She is over her husband.

Even though she left him and demanded the divorce, the whole debacle with Erin had me second-guessing her motives. I wondered if she had wanted the divorce as a way to get Pete to change, to realize what a fool he was.

Pete's head is down as he nears. Sensing me, he abruptly lifts his head, startled at my presence and stops. He stares, bleary eyed, his pupils glistening with what I'm guessing are tears. It's in that moment that I fully realize our common bond: we love the same woman. While I'm not victorious or wish to rub it in his face, I'm fucking thankful to be the one she wants.

"Sam, take care of her." His voice is heavy and gruff, his candor and humility rolling off him in waves. His eyes hold so many emotions, from resignation to resolve to regret. "Olivia is the best person I've ever met, the most amazing woman on the face of this earth. I fucked up. Don't make my mistake."

He's beaten down, but accepting of his fate. Solemnly, facing him man to man, the weight of his words, both spoken and unspoken, bear down on me. I understand the magnitude of his confession and his warning, and not wanting to be arrogant or dismissive, I give him the respect and assurance he deserves.

"I don't intend to and I couldn't agree with you more. She is the best, something rare and precious, and I promise I'll cherish her every day."

He nods, the small, tight upturn of his lips gives away his regret before he resumes the walk to his car. Reinforcing my hold on the grocery bags, I turn in the direction of the house.

She stands, rigid, almost like she's holding her breath while watching us. Her hands are clasped in front of her, worrying her bottom lip. A small, unsure smile graces her face.

The intensity in her eyes are piercing as I climb the stairs. Stopping two steps below her, face to face, my breath stalls. Damn, she's so beautiful. It's only been a couple days since I last saw her, but having her this close, it feels like we've been apart an eternity.

Last night was bittersweet. I held her and was with her, but I wasn't *with* her. We were with Alec and Paige, and it wasn't the time or the place to have our conversation. Truth be told, a part of me chickened out. I didn't know if she'd figured things out and I didn't want to push her right out of my arms.

Now, after what she said to Pete, we don't need to talk. I know exactly where she is, and that's with me.

"You know what I realized?" My voice is low and gravelly. She shakes her head, eagerly hanging on for my next word. "When I'm not with you, everything hurts, especially my heart. It may sound cheesy, but it's true. It's the only way I can explain it."

"I know," she whispers. Her cold fingers lightly skim my lips. "Sam, I've been such an idiot. I love you so much and I should have told you long ago. I have no excuse other than that I was scared—not of you or us, but of me, of losing myself again, but I realize first and foremost, you and I are not Olivia and Pete. I love you, and every day, you make me a better person than I was the day before."

Capturing her lips, I kiss her with all my love, desire, and need for her. She clings to me, our bodies plastered together as the cold night air circles us.

"Livvy, I love you too, and I'm here to stay. You are the one for me. I was made to love you." Feeling the need to say it all, tell her my plans for us, I continue, "And we may be in different cities right now, but you know what? My career is important to me, my restaurants, but none of that means anything to me without you and your kids. If I don't have you, nothing matters. Growing up, it was instilled in me by my grandmother, Bas, and Alec just how important family is. It's the only thing that matters. That's what's most important to me, and Olivia…you are my family."

"And you're mine," she murmurs before covering my lips with hers.

She wraps her legs around my waist as I drop the groceries to the ground and items spill out of the bags. We share a laugh. *Oh well.* Grasping her divine ass, she rocks her heated core against my abs. *Fuck,* I want her now.

Having her in my arms grounds me, makes all the shit that's been going on, the loss of the best man I ever knew, more bearable. She gives me hope that I'll get through this. We'll get through this.

Speaking into her mouth, I groan, "Alec and Paige are inside waiting on me to make dinner."

Breaking apart, she rests her forehead on mine. Her long lashes flutter as her chocolatey brown eyes open, filled with love and lust for me. "When are they expecting you back?"

"Soon, but I could be another twenty minutes or so."

"How do you feel about the garage?" Her eyes slide to the door at the side of the house. "It'll be chilly, but I bet I could warm you up real quick."

My cock twitches and lengthens at her seductive grin.

"I thought you'd never ask."

Dragging me into the dark, cold space, she shuts the door behind us and lunges at me. We're all lips, teeth, tongues, arms, and legs as I pull her pants down and bend her over the workbench. Her luscious ass is up and out for me, begging to be palmed and squeezed as I ram my cock hard and deep into her.

Livvy's on the pill and I'm clean. We've already had the talk, but fuck, to be honest, I would be over the moon if I knocked her up. We haven't talked about kids and it's not a deal breaker for me, but this woman is my everything. The love of my life. My heart and soul. If I could add *mother of my children* to that list, I'd crow like a cock.

Speaking of cocks, the pale moonlight allows me to see my dick moving in and out of her sweet pussy, her beautiful ass matching my rhythm. Bending over her, I roll her taut nipple with my thumb and forefinger through the fabric of her clothes, gently tugging as my other hand mercilessly rubs her clit.

She struggles to keep her whimpers to a whisper—as much as I love to hear her come apart, keeping this on the down low is best. Having Alec or

Paige come to investigate her screams would be a serious mood killer.

As she clenches and spasms around my dick, climaxing, I too tense, every nerve ending in my body alive and firing on all cylinders. My orgasm rips through me as she wails my name before I clamp my hand over her mouth.

Before we both have had a chance to come down from that mind-bending experience, she spins around, her sensual body pressing against mine. Having her in my arms is the best. As she bestows heavy, languid kisses on me, we murmur words of love and promises of a future.

§

"Sam," Paige calls from the sofa.

"Hmm," I absently respond, my focus on the documents Bas's lawyer emailed to me.

We'd held off reading the will right away; neither Alec nor I were ready to face the reality of it all. Only last week we finally decided it was time to read through everything. To my surprise, except for their home which he left to Alec, Bas left everything to me. I was dumbfounded, though in retrospect I'm not sure why, and protested, wanting to give Alec his rightful share. Alec would hear none of it, saying he knew what Bas's wishes were and that he was successful and well off, didn't need or want anything of Bas's to remember him by.

My inheritance solved a lot of my investor problems. I hated that it came at the cost of Bas's life, but he'd have loved to hear that because of it, I kicked Thibault to the curb. This was the good news I finally told Olivia last night after Paige and Alec had gone to bed.

"I like you," Paige whispers, blushing.

Looking up from my laptop, her pretty face is scrunched into a frown. Meeting my gaze, her eyes—so dark and deep like her mother's—appear troubled. She's worried about something.

"I like you too. What's up?" Closing my laptop, I give her my undivided attention.

Casting her eyes down, she fixes her gaze on my throat. Fiddling with the frayed edge of her blanket, she goes on, "I just wanted you to know that. You make my mom happy. Really happy. Happier than I've ever seen her and…" Her voice cracks.

With one quick leap, my arms envelop her. Taking her small body into my arms, I perch precariously on the edge of the couch.

"Hey, I love hearing that. I want to make your mom happy, and you and

Drew. What's got you upset? Do you want me to make her life miserable?"

My jesting is a nod to some of the few conversations we've had about her mother where her attitude has been inappropriate and I've tried to smooth things over.

With a small laugh and a few sniffles, her eyes dance with mirth. "Nah, I do a pretty good job of that on my own." I scoff and chuckle. "I thought my dad was the one who should make her happy. I thought he did, but now I see that he didn't. Maybe he did at one time, but not anymore." Pain and confusion etch her brow and pool in her eyes.

"Hey, I'm sure he did at one point in time." Talking about Pete making Livvy happy sticks in my throat. They are over, but at some point, while I hate it, I hope it's true that he did make her happy. "Besides, he gave her you and Drew, and I know that makes her fucking happy. Shit, your mom would have my balls if she could hear me now. Let's keep the f-bomb stuff between us," I beg with mock fear.

She giggles. "Your secret is safe with me." Hugging me, she says, "Thanks Sam. I guess, I just, ah…I just didn't understand why my mom did it—left my dad," she clarifies. Her voice is small and quiet, but she's earnestly looking at me. I get the sense that she needs to say this, needs me to hear her. "I love him very much. I was afraid she'd not only move on from him, but also us, Drew and me, but…"

With her pause, she glances to the doorway, where Olivia quietly leans against the door jamb, her eyes glistening with unshed tears. Paige continues, speaking to her mother.

"I now know she won't do that. She loves us and we're part of her life, no matter what, even with meeting you." Paige glances over her shoulder at me, then back at her mom. "She brought you into our lives, didn't leave us for you."

The dam cracks and the tears fall for both Olivia and Paige. Olivia practically runs to Paige's side. Before I can get out of the way, she sits on my lap and cradles her daughter. Wrapping my arms around the both of them, my chest fills with pure adoration for these lovely ladies and joy to see them finally building a more solid bridge to each other.

Epilogue

SAM

FIVE YEARS LATER

"Bas," I yell, tearing after my three-year-old terror as he careens around the corner into the kitchen. With a frustrated chuckle, I run after him, in hot pursuit.

Entering the bustling kitchen, I prepare to see Bas creating havoc of his own, but he's nowhere in sight. My staff is busy at work preparing the lunch for Livvy's birthday. As I catch the eye of Stéphanie, my sous-chef, she smirks, likely knowing what I'm going to ask.

"Bas? He came barreling in here, have you seen him?"

Her light laughter flits through the air as she smiles at the dilemma I usually find myself in with my son.

"You mean the adorable little boy that just left with his sister?"

Nodding, I sigh. "Paige took him?"

"Yes, she's out back with him. If you have a minute, can you tell me what you think of this?" She hands me a spoon full of whatever she's working on.

I place the spoon in my mouth and savory, succulent flavors burst on my tongue. "Shit, that's fucking fantastic."

"It's the sauce for the pork tenderloin, thought I'd try something new and test it out on your guests. Hope you don't mind?"

"Damn, Stéph, that's going on our menu. You gotta let me know what you did. Seriously, it's amazing."

She blushes, a small smile gracing the curve of her lips as she shoos me away. I'm damn lucky to have her running the kitchen. Sure, the success of my Toronto restaurant, Camellia, is all mine, but I can't deny that she's certainly contributed to the reason people keep coming back.

She's a very talented chef and it's only a matter of time before she leaves to start her own restaurant. While I'll fully support her, I won't lie, I'm not looking forward to that day.

I step into the courtyard where our friends and family are scattered around the large table in the center of the outdoor space. It's decorated with balloons, streamers, and twinkling lights in the trees and along the trellis.

It's Livvy's birthday and we're celebrating with a special meal surrounded by our family and closest friends. We closed the restaurant for the occasion and while she didn't want me to, I'm glad we did.

My chest swells with happiness at my life. While a day doesn't go by that I don't wish Bas were here to see this, to be a part of it all, to meet my son, I've got a lot to be grateful for—most of all, my beautiful wife, who I adore beyond measure, and our fantastic children, Drew, Paige, and Bastien.

When I moved here years ago to be with Livvy and to open Camellia, Alec came with me. I thought the transition would be hard, especially for Alec, since he'd lived in Montreal all his life, but it was the complete opposite. He adjusted well and is thriving.

He needed the change and it's not like he walked away from his past. We both still have business in Montreal and visit often, but my heart is here with my love and my family.

At the end of the table, Olivia stares at me, a smile blooming across her face, lighting up her pretty features. Bas is running around with Paige trailing behind him, pretending to not be able to catch him. His light, playful laugh floats through the air.

Walking toward my woman, my heated gaze never wavers. She excuses herself from a conversation with Sin, Jonah, and Alec and heads in my direction. We meet in the middle, my arms wrapping around her slender waist as she leans up and lightly kisses the underside of my jaw.

"Hey you." Her voice is low and sexy.

"Hey you, happy birthday." I lightly kiss the tip of her nose as she smiles.

"Thank you. I hear this place is owned by a panty-melting celebrity chef, have you seen him?"

"What? Seriously? I haven't seen him. Will I do?"

"Hmmm." She places her finger on her lips, her smile still big and bright. "I don't know, what did you say your name was again? I think I'll have to Google you first."

We both laugh at the memory of our first meeting and our gazes soften, both of us reliving all the wonderful moments that got us to where we are today.

"You missed the appetizers. We polished them off, they were so good." She purrs, licking her lips suggestively. "I'm not sure I should eat lunch or else my pants won't fit me."

"That's where I come in." Jonah pops up beside us, grinning from ear-to-ear.

"Back off, Jonah. She's taken," I quip,

Jonah isn't a threat. He's a true friend and I've been lucky enough to watch him find happiness with the right person. Needless to say, we still carry on the usual sparring we've taken to engaging in regarding Livvy.

Quirking a smile, Olivia pipes up, "Hey, I can speak for myself, thank you very much."

Jonah chuckles. "Oh, she's taken, is she? Well we've got a date tomorrow morning," he taunts, jokingly referring to their workout. "And what say you, Liv?"

She laughs, shaking her head. Then, schooling her features, she glances from Jonah to me. She looks serious now, but I can tell it's an act, reminiscent of her joking moment before about the celebrity chef.

"I'm taken." Her tone is genuine but also suggestive, a mischievous glint sparkling in her eye.

Placing his hands on both our shoulders, he leans in closer, kisses her on the cheek, then turns to look at me, his sly grin firmly in place.

"Sorry Sam, I wish I could kiss ya. You're real pretty and all, but I don't swing that way." We chuckle as he pats me on the back before sauntering away.

Staring up at me, her eyes are heavy lidded, sultry as she whispers, "Too bad for him, but all the better for me, because I sure would like to kiss you."

She grips my hair, her tug like a detonator, and my cock hardens as she pulls me closer. Before she can make her move, my mouth crashes onto hers and I take over with an intensity that devours, addictive and furious.

Clapping, whistles, and catcalls from our guests have us reluctantly breaking apart. Her cheeks are a lovely shade of pink and I have a silly grin on my face. I scan the crowd of close friends and family, all of them smiling at us, and my heart swells. We're surrounded by love and friendship and even still, all I can see is *her*. It's been that way from the very beginning. As my smile widens at that thought, I lean in and lay another quick but no less searing kiss on *my* Olivia.

Acknowledgements

If you got this far, I hope you enjoyed Made to Love and fell in love with Sam and Olivia as much as I did! I had so much fun writing this book. These characters are so near and dear to my heart. It was bittersweet having their story end.

I couldn't have indulged and lost myself in Made To Love without the love and support of my family. My husband and daughters are my world - thank you, to the moon and back, for all you do to support me.

To **Stéphanie**, my sweet friend and loudest cheerleader when writing this book, I love you and thank you so much for all of your fangirling over this story. Girl, Sam is yours, although I wanna know that I can borrow him once in a while!

To my green indie sisters, **Kim**, **Saffron**, and **Bella**, you're amazing!! I'm so grateful for your support, encouragement and friendship. There were moments when each of you kept me sane (or as sane as possible for me). I'm beyond happy that we found each other.

To my beta readers, some of whom I've already mentioned, your feedback was invaluable. Thank you for your suggestions and support. A special call out to **Julia**! You've become a fast fan and great friend. Thank you so much for your love of my characters and stories, and your amazing teasers and videos!

And **Claudia**, my dear friend, thank you for our wild and crazy talks and your friendship. Having you in my corner and as my go-to, it means so much to me. Love you!!

To my editor, **Caitlin**, you rock! Your edits and feedback make my stories better! To my proofreader, **Melinda**, thank you for the extra pair of eyes and your wonderful suggestions. I love working with you. And **Jules**, my fabulous formatter, girl, you're work is magical. Each time I've given you one of my books, my babies, you always give it back shiny, pretty and awesome!

Najla, I love my cover. Every time I look at it, a silly grin takes over my face. You beautifully captured the sexy and sweet of Sam and Olivia and most of all, the love. Every time I look at the cover, I get a silly grin! Thank you!

To the fantastic bloggers and readers, thank you doesn't seem enough for taking a chance on me. Thank you for reading, reviewing and sharing my book. What you do means so much to me. From the bottom of my heart, THANK YOU!!

Suzanne xo

Excerpts

**Want a sneak peek of the next book, Blue,
in my standalone Love in Color Series?**

Blue (Love in Color #2) by S.M. West

Subject to Change

"Sweetness."

My tone's gruff, her name strange to my ears despite her constant presence in my mind. My throat's dry and I swallow with difficulty thanks to the bowling ball of nerves lodged in my throat. And fuck, my palms are sweaty.

Her dark hair, so dark it's almost blue-tinged, fans as she twirls to face me. After nearly three years apart, it's unfathomable how close we are, so close, I could touch her. Clenching my fists, I fight the fiercely throbbing urge to hold her, knowing she wouldn't appreciate my bold gesture. To satisfy my craving, my eyes drink her in, every inch of her. I can't help but stare. She's breathtakingly beautiful.

Surprised aquamarine eyes nail me as she sucks in a jagged breath and drops the empty tray from her hand. The loud crash and subsequent reverberating clatter has all eyes in the bar on us. We're at the family bar, The Waters, and while it's not busy with only a handful of people eating lunch, it's more than I prefer. Alone is how I want her.

Doing this here wasn't my preference, but I didn't want to wait and besides, there's never going to be a perfect time. I couldn't wait any longer. He got her a ring. A fucking engagement ring. I couldn't let him propose. *No. Fucking. Way.*

Time was of the essence. I'm in 'act now, deal with the consequences later' mode.

"Evan," her voice quivers and she sways, grabbing the bar to steady herself.

Stepping in my direction, she falters with a hint of a frown clouding her features. It's only a second, but time slows, practically stopping, as a myriad of emotions skitter across her face. I'm almost able to feel the bombardment of her memories. The times we were together, when I left her, then when she was alone. Fuck, she's gonna kick me out.

Without warning, Carys hurtles herself at me, her arms and legs hug me as she buries her face into my neck. I cling to her slender frame, one arm under her rear and the other around her back, as her muffled sobs echo within my chest. I can't tell if they are tears of joy or sorrow.

Fuck. Holding her after all these years feeds my starved soul, fills my ravaged heart. *Heaven.* Finally, I'm able to breathe with my girl in my arms.

Releasing Summer 2017

Add to your TBR: https://www.goodreads.com/book/show/34642452-blue

About the Author

SM West was born on an island paradise on the shortest day and longest night of the year, Winter Solstice. Perhaps that's why she's a night owl? She loves romance and intrigue with intensity and edge. Her stories are about characters with brave hearts who fall wildly in love. If she's not reading or writing, she's hanging with her family, planning her next adventure, enjoying a glass of wine and indulging in chocolate.

For new releases, exclusive excerpts, giveaways and more, sign up for her newsletter.

Connect with Suzanne

Facebook: https://www.facebook.com/smwestauthor/
Instagram: https://www.instagram.com/smwestwrites/
Twitter: @SMWestAuthor
BookBub: https://www.bookbub.com/authors/s-m-west
Goodreads: https://www.goodreads.com/author/show/15863987.S_M_West
Pinterest: https://www.pinterest.com/smwestwrites/

70073095R00132

Made in the USA
Columbia, SC
29 April 2017